Other Novels by Randall Beth Platt

The Likes of Me
The Cornerstone
Honor Bright
The Royalscope Fe-As-Ko
Out of a Forest Clearing
The Four Arrows Fe-As-Ko

The 1898 Base-Ball

Fe-As-Ko

by

Randall Beth Platt

CATBIRD PRESS

CATBIRD PRESS
16 Windsor Road, North Haven, CT 06473
800-360-2391; catbird@pipeline.com
www.catbirdpress.com

Our books are distributed to the trade
by Independent Publishers Group

This book is a work of fiction, and the characters and events in it are fictitious. Any similarity to real persons, living or dead, is coincidental and not intended by the author.

Library of Congress Cataloging-in-Publication

Platt, Randall Beth, 1948-
The 1898 base-ball fe-as-ko / by Randall Beth Platt.--1st ed.
ISBN 0-945774-47-8 (alk. paper)
1. Baseball teams--Oregon--Fiction. 2. Ranch life--Oregon--Fiction.
I. Title: 1898 baseball fe-as-ko. II. Title.

PS3566.L293 A615 2000
813'.54--dc21

99-053066

For the one,
the only,
Elsa

you again?

Hello? … Who? … Speak up, son! … Well, I'll be a hogtied rattlesnake! You again…? You mean to tell me you ain't got your filla me yet?… Uh huh … yep … Ol' F.D.R. hisself, eh? … Why sure! It's the middle of the damn Depression, you bet your Royal typewriting machine I got a few things to tell him! … 'Course, I'm patriotic … I know you need the work, son, but … Yeah but, that don't mean you can cull my brains clean, that's what I got bankers and lawyers and family for … Why don't you go pick on ol' Will Rogers? He knows almost as much as me, but I sure as hell can outride him … Oh, he is, huh? … Well, Alaska ain't no place for a Oklahoma farm boy, and when he gets back you can tell him I told you so … Hell, don't sound so … Well, sure we had fun last time, but … 'Course I like you … like most writers you're a little cluttered with thoughts, but I like you … You do? … Well, can't argue with you there. Oh, all right, damn it, come on over … But son? You gotta promise me one thing: If Franklin Delano Roosevelt gets a hoot outa all the fe-as-kos I get myself in and outa, then he can dang well set back some day and hear how I think we're gonna get ourselfs outa The Big Trouble we're in, and it ain't got nothing to do with war. All right … I'll be here … Oh, and son? This time, bring a bottle of the good stuff.

*

So, what kept you? Thought you was so all-fired-up to pick more yarns outa my brainpan. All right, come on in and inquisitate.

Turna the century? Ain't you rushing things just a tad? Hell, lots went on betwixt '93 and home base. You know, home base, turna the century … I always think of a century like a baseball season. You start out at home plate and then move on to first, second, and third base — you know, with runs and strikes and outs and, hell, players and spectators. So don't go rushing the century till all the runners is in.

Base-ball. Takes me back to 1897. Now there was a year. Yep, 1897 was the year I got base-ball. Or maybe I oughta say, 1897 is the year base-ball got me.

Now, the reason I say 'I got base-ball' is to akin it to religion, which in a way it sorta is. Sorta like booze or tobacco or cards or women — addictions they call 'em. And like most addictions, it started out small — first just a little outa necessity, then a hair of the dog, then a full out'n'out wonderful disease for which there ain't no cure. Watch my face. Don't my voice sound sorta like slow running pine tar when I say 'base-ball?' Listen: base-ball. Baaase-ball. Base-balllllll. Hear the affection and affliction in that word? And hell, 1897 was … what, dang near 40 years ago? I shoulda oughta out-smarted that addiction by now. I guess I shoulda out-smarted alota things by now. But hell, I'm only 70 and some change. Lotsa things is still fresh in me. Like the memory of that year, 1897, and, in particular, the fall of '98 …

Remember the story of Jack and the Beanstalk? That one about the boy sent to town by his poor'n'sick'n'tired mama to sell a cow which was all they had in the way of barterable goods? Poor ol' raggity woman, got nothing to eat and no teeth to use on it. All she had was this scrawny ol' cow who she thought too mucha to slice and fry. So this poor ol' woman in desperation sends her son to town to sell the cow and bring home the money so's bills could be paid and food be bought for the winter stores. Remember how this boy, green and ripesuck as allgetout, bumps into this nefarious huckster? This shyster — probably a outa work lawyer — takes this poor kid and shears him a good one. Takes the cow — who was probably mooing a warning at the kid — in exchange for a handful of beans. Beans! Not even eatable beans! These, touts the salesman, is special, magical beans. The holder of this bag-o-beans will be forever taken care of. Well, the kid was taken, all right. So, there goes the cow, who was probably mooing something on the line of 'good riddance!' by then.

So insteada saving the farm, the widder's son comes back with nothing more'n a face fulla grins, a pocket fulla beans, and a heart fulla dreams. Beans'n'dreams all to the tune of his momma's screams. Reckon she liked to have killed him.

Now, you might wonder what a toothless ol' widder women, a broke-down cow, and a hand fulla so-called magical beans has got to do with Royal Leckner and base-ball and the famous Four Arrows Ranch. It's what you scribing types call a meddy-four. So, you just keep that fairy tale in the backa your mind whilst I recalculate the events of 1897.

Now, as you will recall, in 1897 I'd been foreman of the Four Arrows Ranch in that cozy corner of Northeastern Oregon for close to 13 years. Like I mighta mentioned onct before, I'd always planned on moving on and finding me my own spread, but when Leviticus and his crew came on board in '92, well one thing led to another, and before you know it I was hitched to ol' E.M. Gallucci, of whom you have heard tell and are therefore given fair warning.

Okay, okay, I recognize the face of 'whoa' when it's staring at me. I ain't seen you for some time and I reckon you need something in the way of a refresher. First, what say we refresh our souls with that rye you brung, then I'll refresh both our memories. Rye always brings back things just the way they happened, with only a minimal of grandstanding and leather stretching.

'Course, anytime you mix base-ball with horses and cows and opinions and women, you're bound to get a grand stand nowanthen.

PART 1

one

So there we was, late summer of 1897, me and my bride and all my charges. My charges, may I remind you, was alla the Four Arrows Ranch, including alla its critters, working men, affiliates, and more sleepless nights than a young man of 29 oughta have. Sleepless onaccounta there was always something for me to worry about. We'd had some hardscrabble years following the Panic of '93, which was not so-named as a tribute to my wedding. Cattle prices was just about at low tide, forcing me to cut the herds back and take more serious the feed markets. 'Course, wheat, oats, and alfalfa was looking real good to me by '95. Other outfits from Pendleton to the Palouse was making out right equitable with feed crops. Problem was, my boss, the owner, Leviticus Perrault, was a animal lover and he fought me tooth'nail'n'hide the notion of selling off more beeves to make way for wheat fields.

You see, he didn't think too much about the money part. 'Course, he didn't like selling the critters off just to become steaks either, but at our annual sell-offs we'd distract him enough to get the cows to market. Onct he'd started working the herds like one of the regular hands and started seeing how worrisome and downright stupid a cow can be, well he dropped his notion of naming each one, and by '95 he even worked up the grit to scorch a brand all by hisself. Bawled louder'n the calf did, but he did it.

By '95 we'd pretty much settled down to normal life on the Four Arrows. 'Course, what's normal to most ranches and what was normal to us is two entirely different things, as you are quickly being reminded. Normal is one of them words that really ain't got a standard of its own. I mean, my normal and your normal is pretty much just opinions, and there's just no way many people could pin the word 'normal' on Leviticus or his wife Lou(ella).

They'd come to be on the ranch by that peculiar set of circumstances which is still referred to as the Four Arrows Fe-As-Ko. Well, to refresh your memory, Leviticus and Lou(ella) was … to say it kind-like, they was … well, mentally outa sorts. Which ain't saying they wasn't the nicest, politest human beings ever set down on earth. 'Member? They was sorta short-sheeted in the intellectual department. Lou(ella) had her a real anxious fascination with numbers — she could work numbers inside, outside, upside down and inside out, and she was never happier'n when she was doing just that. She was just a itty-bitty hop-o-my-thumb — about as tiny as a fully growed woman can be and not be a midget. Sweartagod, she was so short she'd have to stand on a box just to spit, but she didn't care, especially when she gave her height in millimeters, which any way you calculated it made her still only four-and-a-half feet soaking wet. Lou(ella) is spelt that way onaccounta when we first met her we all thought she was of a masculine gender and thusly called her Lou. We added the (ella) onct it come to our attentions she was a fully-growed lady and not a raggity rough-scuff boy.

And Leviticus? 'Member him? He looked normal enough — even handsome to some, tall and straight and strong. Taller'n when you first come to know about him, onaccounta onct he became rightful heir to Four Arrows we all swore he grew a few more inches, like well-fed and happy young men can. The boy was mild as sweet milk. He was about as comeatable as a feller gets, and if you ever hear me refer to him as short a hat size, it's — well, it's because he was, and he'd be the first one to bring it to your attention. But I have learnt to not judge the frog by the size of his legs, so you will also hear me refer to Leviticus as one helluva nice yap and about as blowed-in-the-glass honest as they come, and that right there made him quite a commodity. And I don't know about you, but I'll take nice and honest over smart and fox-like any day. But, I am sad to report, him being honest and nice also made him quite a bulls-eye on the target of foul play.

So Levi and Lou was owner and wife, and my legal employers and my charges all in one. Well, I always speculated as how if they was each working independently, they wasn't totally present in the here'n'now. But put 'em together and get 'em working on one thing at onct, and you had yourself a right savvy coyote.

We had us all the regular hands we needed, depending on the season. Had me Jay Smyth, one of our top hands. Best natural horse wrangler I ever knew. Good kid, a little jumpy. Snorty and impatient, like all kids. 'Course he wasn't no kid no more — he musta been all over 20 — but he acted like a yearling, and so like a yearling we treated him. Then I had me ol' Zeb Hardy. Wise and calm and slower'n a glacier. 'Course, he was getting on — not sure of his exact vintage, but he musta been 45 by then — and even though he complained more'n he shoulda, he was also there to ease me down when I needed it, and I spent alota my foreman time diplomating, of that you can be sure. Well, that was just one plight in this poor ol' cow waddie's life and, when I look back on it, settling hashes and standing up for those who can't quite stand on their own was right pleasurable work. 'Course, ain't all work pleasurable with a backward glance?

Oh, we'd have us a hullabaloo nowanthen — like keeping their minds on ranch work and such. Fact is, as I recall it, I worked real hard keeping the men's minds on things cattleish. Especially come spring, when a man's mind, or a man's half-mind, turns to things more naturish. Like sunny afternoons, warm breezes, fermented hops, roasted peanuts, and all in the accompaniment of a fascination new to us in the town and outshirts of Idlehour, Oregon. Base-ball.

Yep, things would go alongst fine till we'd hit us one of them fe-as-kos which my wife would foretell with the conviction and passion of a traveling preacher low on conversions.

Good ol' E.M. — my wife, my keeper, my fortune maker and breaker and teller all rolt into one. Remember, she was a accountant back in the days when women wasn't allowed to count past their fingers, and if they did, there damn well better be a few 'ummmmms' involved. 'Course, now that I think about it, early on E.M. did utilize them fingers more'n onct to calculate a sum. I recall her onct telling me she hated numbers and the feeling was reciprocal. Some accountant, I remember thinking. Then, when Lou(ella) comes into our lifes, well, all need for fingers, toes, or abacuses flew out the window, for Lou(ella) was a walking, chattering, computating wonder. With E.M.'s nose for profit and trouble, both of which she could sniff out in a hurricane, and with Lou(ella)'s number fascination, I have no doubt they coulda cornered any market for any commodity up to and including the cattle market, if I'd been smart enough to encourage it. Fact is, it was E.M. and Lou(ella) who ran those cattle versus wheat figures under my nose.

'Course, being tied to the snortin' post with E.M., I was treading light, of that you can be damned sure. And Leviticus, onct he married Lou, we knew all hope of control was out the window. He had such a full barrel of love for her I don't recollect even onct he told her no. That didn't get me very far as foreman and overseer of things, but I did the best I could. And E.M. was only sometimes on my side of the fence. That sure made matters worse, and our marriage from the get-go was a rocky ride.

Like I told you, it was 1897 when all this started. None of us could make no holler about the real soft winter and, being as our corner of Oregon could be damn troubling sometimes, we alla us at the Four Arrows counted our blessings with the bawl of every calf and the swish of every foal's tail and the blossom of every bud. Our second crop of winter wheat came in strong and fine and none the worse for wear, the momma cows had wintered fat, and we even had us a barn-and-a-half of hay left over, which Leviticus decided to send, free of charge, to some friends of ours up at the Spokane Indian Reservation, onaccounta he'd heard they'd had a barn fire and was low on chewables for their stock. Now, this here is basically a good trait — sharing leftovers. In fact, Leviticus got the idea from me. I was always saying that having alota money or extra hay or too mucha God's plenty is sorta like a pile of horse apples — don't do much good unless you spread it around.

Then ol' E.M. calculated that if we was to sell off three fourths of the herd, let the pastures winter over, till 'em next year, then drill oats'n'wheat (maybe peas), we could show a better profit within three years. Course, first I put up a fuss. Me? A gully-jumping, dust-raising granger? Me? Farm? Then she allowed we shouldn't hang everything on one nail. But I put my foot down on the pea-idea, telling her I'd be damned if I'd be a farmer of peas, for cryinoutloud. Well, shortly thereafter E.M. was setting in Idlehour when it was pea harvest time, and when she got a noseful of what them sunned-out pea shucks smelt like, well, profits be damned, says she. That smell changed her mind about farming peas, fast'n'forever.

Well, then Leviticus had wanted me to start up some sheeping, which, being a good cowman and something in the way of a traditionalist, I fought hoof'n'tooth. Sheeps is nothing but hooved locust, real hard on land. But he was boss and showing initiative, so I caved in and bought him a small herd of starters. I still smile when I see Leviticus riding herd on the bunch that first day, singing 'Bringing in the Sheeps' loud and clear, the sheeps a-scattering all directions at onct, and bringing all the other hands to their knees in laughter, even spooking a few novie cow ponies. Cute little critters, sheeps is, but dumber'n barnacles and just about as easy to organize. And then sheeps leads to dogs, of course, to unionize them.

Now, I had me a fascination of my own: quarter horses. Racing quarter horses. I'd bought me a coupla brood mares and a stud, and even though a quarter horse looks perfectly natural on a spread like ours, I knew I was a helluva lot more interested in cutting quarter-mile times than I was in cutting a calf from a crowd.

So, with such a grand-looking tally on our books that year, I bought three more mares and another daddy with great running potential and thought, hell, if you could make money racing horses, why follow herds or cut wheat? So, I had a sizable investment in those horses — including the making of a quarter- mile track and plans for a training barn the likes of which no one in those parts had even seen.

So, betwixt Levi's dreams and my dreams, Four Arrows was getting to be a regular zoological society. I was bemoaning my zoo keeper status to E.M. one day towards The Fall. Now, you may think I'm referring to 'the fall' as in autumnal harvest, apple cider, and the colors gold, amber, and brown. But the fall of which I refer I have come to think of as 'The Fall' — as in Roman Empire, from grace, House of Usher — and all in the accompaniment of the colors of black and blue and deficit red.

So, how could a year which began blessed with so easy a winter, a healthy herd count, a good three-year plan for the ranch, work for everybody, giveaway calfs and hay, and even sheep for cryinoutloud, take such a tragic turn towards disaster in just a few days' time?

I can tell you in one simple sentence:

Jack was a sucker for dreams.

Don't look so damned confused. I got me a whole book to explain it in, don't I?

two

Now, I know you been to writer's school and have your own way of putting together a story. But I'll help you some and offer you this in the way of a plot-thickener:

"What you mean you wanna go to Portland?" I asked my wife, Elijah Marie, but known as E.M. to everyone wanting to keep their heads attached. "You mean to see your daddy?"

"You know perfectly well Daddy's in Salem," she said, combing out her long, black I-talian hair.

I caught her reflection in the vanity mirror. She stopped her brush, mid-stress, and looked at me. Even though we'd been married four years, I still worried that suddenly I would be walking blind-like upon terra incognita and brushes would go flying. We both knew her daddy'd been sent to the Oregon State Prison for extortion, but E.M. always dared me to make any flash of wit about it. *She* could, but heaven help poor Royal if *he* did.

"Well, ain't your momma still working the Mississippi?" That also was a risky subject for Royal, speaking of her momma taking up a gambling career so late in life.

She set the brush down, so I relaxed some. She turned around and said, "Now, Roy, I don't want you to get all in a pucker about this. I know you're going with Leviticus and Lou(ella), but you know how you hate contracts and I thought …"

"E.M., this here's just a cattle sale, not some highfalutin' big-city corporation contract. Leviticus and Lou need to know how these things is done. So alls I'm gonna do is stand over their shoulders and make sure they do it right."

"Well, I just have this *feeling*…"

"Now, things is all arranged in Portland. My agent's got range delivery all lined up. I'm just gonna walk 'em through the whole sell-off process. Easy as dammit. Ain't no need for you to come, E.M." She turns and looks at me, and I'm getting edgy so I add, "E.M., if you and me are ever gonna get off Four Arrows and get on with our lifes, then…"

She then looks a little mother-henish and says, "But Portland's such a big city. What if they get lost?"

I set down, onaccounta her 'what ifs' was like gum drops — one just naturally led right on to another. "I won't let 'em outa my sight," I said.

"What if Leviticus eats too much candy?"

"He'll air his paunch like he always does."

"What if Lou starts counting something like telephone poles and wanders off like she did in Spokane that time?"

"Tell you what, E.M. I'll have Jay do nothing but follow Lou, and I'll have Hardy do nothing but follow Levi."

"Jay? Ha! He's just as much a worry. What if he finds some rantankerous female?" She turned and looked about as pretty as she ever did — hair all undone, mouth sorta pouty, and all in all looking real motherish. "Seriously, Royal, I'm worried. They're just like children. Even Jay."

"What you gotta remember, E.M., is they gotta learn how to handle things on their own. If we're priming Jay to be top hand someday, then he…"

"Yes, but why Portland the first time? I *know* Portland. Dens of iniquities, chippies, swindlers!"

"I'll tell 'em to stay clear of law offices," I said.

"Why not Pendleton or even Spokane? At least they've been to those places."

"E.M., I'm gonna be shadowing 'em every step of the way. What could go wrong?" I started brushing her hair for her and added, "Now, E.M., it was you convinced me to sell off so many head. Portland's got the best price."

"But if I don't go, I just *know* something will go wrong."

"How do you know?"

I stopped brushing and looked at her in the mirror. Think my heart thunked a few unscheduled beats. She wanted the brush back but I held it higher and re-asked my question. "E.M., what makes you *know* something's gonna go wrong?"

"Well…" she attempted, her eyes a-settling on her top dresser drawer.

I knew what she thought she was hiding. I pulled the drawer open and, sure enough, there it was — her Weee Geee board.

"Didn't I tell you to get ridda…?" I said, pulling it out.

"I did. It'd gone stale anyway."

"Then what's this?"

"My new one," she replied logic-like.

"You went out and bought a new one when I expressly told you to get ridda that last one?" (Oh, what I had yet to learn about women!) "All this is hogwash, E.M.! All this stupor-natural cocky pock!"

"That's *super*natural, Royal."

"Not when you believe in it, it ain't," I said.

"Well, it may interest you to know, Royal dear, that I consulted Ouija when you proposed!"

"You mean to tell me you planned out a whole life together based on a parlor game?" How come, I was thinking, I'd come in to talk to my wife about who-the-hell-remembered-what and now I was hollering about her marrying me onaccounta some Weee Geee board told her she might as well!

She just continued to brush her hair, looking fondly at herself in the mirror, and said, "Yes."

"Well, it's a damn good thing for you I wasn't no villain or murderer or worse, E.M.! Or, oh, I suppose Miss Weee Geee there woulda mentioned that in passing!"

"Fine. If you don't believe me when I tell you there is trouble in Portland, then check for yourself." She plopped the navigator thing on top of the board.

"Here, I'll even warm it up for you."

So she puts her fingertips on this pointer on pegs, closes her eyes, and says real high-pitched, "weee-geee-weee-geee-weee-geee-weeeeeeeeeeeee-gee!" No kidding, sounded like she was defending her pig-calling title at the Umatilla County Fair.

She musta got her connection, because her calling stopped and her fingers sorta got real light on the communicator thing. "Will there be trouble if I don't go to Portland?"

I watched her eyes and it looked like they was keeping closed tight. "Watch what it says," she whispered outa the side of her mouth to me like she didn't want to break her spiritual connection. I looked down at the board and her hands traveled fast-like to the big "YES" printed in the upper-left corner.

"There, you see?" E.M. concludes.

"You did that, E.M!" I said.

"I did not!"

"That's nothing but a toy!"

"Is not!"

"Is too! And you're too old to play with toys, E.M.," I finalized.

That was a risky one and we both knew it. She glared at me and growled, "I'll take *that* under advisement!"

"Well, for sure you ain't going to Portland now, E.M.! You mighta talked me into it for a million reasons, but ain't one of 'em onaccounta that stupid Weee Geee says so!"

She shot me a mean one, got up, said what I'd heard her say on many a occasion: "Mark my words!" and left the room with a right sturdy slam of the door. I hated when she prophecized me that one. It had come at the turning point of many a fight betwixt us. I didn't see as all this foofaraw called for marking her words or slamming doors and such. So I set on the bed, wondering what the hell I should do. I locked the door and set the weee-geee board on the bed. I got my long fingers on the traveler thing'ma'jig and whispered weee-geee-weee-geee-weee-geee sorta like E.M. did, only without alerting every pig in the state.

My fingers began to move and I asked out loud: "Should I let E.M. go to Portland?"

Three times I asked, changing my voice each time. I got yes, yes, and yes. Well, I didn't care what it said, I was gonna stick to my guns on this one. And I did. Stuck to 'em right up to bedtime that very same night.

E.M. and her damn mystics, I remember thinking when she informs me she had verified her findings with her horoscope in some ladies' magazine she got. Well, the lights was low and Lord how her hair did shine so blue-black and oh the flash of her big brown eyes…

So, before falling asleep I informed E.M. she could go to Portland (which she already knew) but just to shop and maybe see old friends. She wasn't gonna get no say in any matters cattlish — that was all up to Leviticus, owner of the cattle, and Lou(ella), wife to the owner of the cattle. And with me overlooking the details, things was all gonna turn out just fine, and 'don't you worry your pretty smart head about anything, E.M.'

Apparently she didn't.

three

So there I was next day in my study, going over the details of the upcoming cattle sale with Leviticus and Lou(ella). Now, unless you've known folks with these peculiar natures yourownself, you may not appreciate patience being a grace. 'Course, I'd known Leviticus for five years by then, and I was almost used to him and his ways. Lou(ella) was another situation entirely. Hard to get used to her ways.

Now, you gotta remember folks like these — folks who don't exactly see the world like average folks do — well, they can be a real challenge. Take Leviticus firinstance. He could latch onto something with gator-grit — you know, onct a notion is in his mouth, he just don't let go till he's ready. And onct this notion was in his maw, he'd mangled it some, so you wasn't sure what he was saying. At first we thought he was harda hearing. So E.M. did the horehound candy test. Now I myownself don't much care for horehound candy — maybe it's just them two words stuck together. But Leviticus, who was the victim of a deprived childhood, you just try keeping horehound candy away from him! So, E.M. stands four rooms away and carefully unscrews the lid to the horehound jar. Since Leviticus was there faster'n you can spit and holler howdy, before she'd even gotten the dang lid off, we knew he had the ears of the village gossip.

So, it wasn't what he heard, it was the *way* he heard things that always kept us on our toes. We was always real careful about what we said or did around Leviticus. Like one summer when E.M. came home from a Hens' Rights Rally down to Pendleton and she was spouting Women's Suffrage! Women's Suffrage! and before you knew it, Leviticus was likewise spouting his own version, "Women! Suffer Your Age!" Which of course I liked better, but only when E.M. wasn't around. Then, pretty soon it catches on, and before too long we was alla us spouting it. So, if you ever met up with Leviticus, which you just might someday, watch what you say or else he might say it better.

The tough part was getting everyone ready for the train trip to Portland. The cattle was the easy part. We had us a shortline put in that could run cattle and hay and such from the ranch into Idlehour and then on to Portland via Milton and Points West. Lou(ella) had calculated for us the distance betwixt us and town and figured in the average weight loss a cow suffers walking that distance, figures it in with the pay my hands get escorting all them cattle, and then she announces we could save this much money building us our own railhead. Hardy, me, and Jay laughed till E.M. brings to our attentions shipping costs and delivery charges over a ten-year period, and we stopped laughing and hired us a bed crew.

'Course, whether or not she factored in the time element, I do not know. Problem was, our little spur of railroad was damn slow, when all five cars was loaded. Sweartagod, I coulda caught malaria on our loading dock and been cured of it by the time we reached Idlehour, some four miles away.

'Course, we had us enough railroad barons back then, and I didn't much approve the idea of competing with 'em. But it was Four Arrows land and we didn't need no right-o-ways, and having us our own train depot in Idlehour got the town folks all proud, moving 'em up a notch from Podunk status. And it did put lots to work, and since E.M. got her own papa to get some of his hunk-o-tin, high-sportin' friends to slap in another short line betwixt Idlehour and Milton, well, then it seemed like the way to go. So, that's how the L & L Shortline come to be ... complete with a little puffer-belly steam engine — ol' Bess we called her — we brought down from our leased timber tracks. So Lou(ella) was pretty dang smart, considering she also had a neglected youth and no education that she recalled. And long as we let Leviticus steer the engine every so often, it was all fine'n'dandy with him how his money got spent.

But we had to start two days early to steam our cattle over to Idlehour, where they'd be held and fed a good fattening grain. Took our five cattle cars, twelve hands, and 48 straight hours of back'n'forth, but all 1200 head was setting pretty by the time my five humans was ready to leave.

Now, compared to humans, cows is easy travelers. The tough part about any here-to-there operation was getting E.M., Lou, and Leviticus organized all at the same time. Levi had to tell everyone goodbye, including his sheeps; Lou had to count the cattle for one last time and make sure her tally numbers was right; and E.M. had to keep running back into the house to make sure she'd packed this, locked that, consulted her Miss Weee Geee friend, and changed her hat about sixty-three times.

'Course, the one she finally settled on looked like some poor pheasant had been run over by a race horse and they had erected the leftovers on a hat to commemorate the event. But when E.M. asked me about how I liked it, I wise-like recalled that flattery sets in the parlor and honesty gets booted offa the porch, so I just said it looked right pleasant.

Well, we didn't have us anything so luxurious as a Pullman car to take us down our own railhead to Idlehour, and my wife said we humans wasn't fit for cattle cars. (Or was it the other way around? I wondered.) Anyhow, we had a flatbed for shipping machinery and lumber and such, and so we just outfitted that with some nice chairs, a table, a crock of lemonade, and a big umbrella, and I'll have to say, E.M. looked like ol' Cleopatera with her entourage — Hardy, Jay, Leviticus, and Lou(ella) — all barged up, plunder and portmanteaus around 'em, awaiting the flooding of the Nile. 'Course, I never heard the end of it that I'd had Cleo's barge-car lined up after the five cattle cars and oh, after two days of toting cattle, the smell was damn ripe, not to mention all them flies standing in line to try the lemonade. Anyway, that's how we alla us got to the train depot in Idlehour. 'Course since cattle smells never onct bothered me, I slept mosta the way — flat on my back, the train slowly pulling us along and the September sun on my face.

So, by the time we got there all we had to do was tally the last five cars, pay off my hands, and sign on some new men for our winter season. By noon, I finally had everyone loaded on the train to Milton.

Now, they got this thing, you literaturish types know it, it's casting a shadow on the future. What's it called? Right, foreshadowing. Anyhow, I got foreshadowed standing right there as we was loading on the train. Come complete with a cloud darkning the sun and even a chilly little breeze, as I recall.

I had just witnessed all five of my folks walk up and get safely onto the train. The train started to move, and I was just commencing to climb aboard. Then outa a window comes E.M.'s head, feathers catching in the window till her warbonnet falls off, and she hollers. "Stop the train!" And dang if the train didn't do just that and with quite a jerk, I will tell you. I dang near fell off.

"Leviticus!" E.M. screams at *me*, like wasn't I stupid for not knowing he'd walked on the train, down the aisle, and then got hisself right back off at the end of the car!

She pointed acrost the train yard. I ran around the last car. There in the train yard I saw the big distraction. A stampede? Nope. A showdown? Nope. What I saw was just two young boys playing in the train yard. Each had a puffy leathery glove on, and they had this whitish ball which they was throwing back and forth. 'Course, I knew it was a base-ball and I knew they was just playing catch like all boys do. I hadn't been living under a rock. Them gloves was a new one for me though, but that ain't the point. The point is, they was throwing this ball and right smack dab in the middle was Leviticus, about as transfixed on a object as I have ever seen him. His face went back and forth, eyes on the ball, mouth sorta opened. I gotta tell you, I thought maybe he was gonna get hisself hypnotized the way he watched them boys throw the ball.

Now, here's a good spot to remind you of something about ol' Leviticus. He spent his boy-years pretty much under lock'n'-key. Didn't have him mucha anything in the way of toys. Maybe it was for that reason that he had become a rock-thrower. Now, all kids'll pick up bad habits — like biting or lying or forgetting where the outhouse is. But ol' Levi wasn't like other kids whatsomever. So by the time he come to us at Four Arrows, his rock-throwing was a habit I couldn't ever break him of, but to tell you the truth, it was a habit that came in right handy from time to time, onaccounta all his rock-throwing had built him a fine strong arm. He could hit a crow atopt a corn stalk, plug a rabbit outa E.M.'s garden, and even onct stopped a chicken thief right in his tracks. Made a believer outa alla us, especially the chicken thief. 'Course, I had me a time teaching him the difference betwixt just plain annoying critters and using his God-given talents for what they was intended.

So, anytime Levi saw anyone hurl anything, I knew he'd be all for it.

Now, before I could get his attention to get him back on the train, one kid missed the ball and it tipped over towards Leviticus. Levi bent over and picked it up. He smiled over at me, then back down at the ball, looking at it like it was a ace-high straight and a cocker spaniel puppy all peeking outa the Holy Grail.

One of the boys called out, "Hey, mister! Toss it back!"

Well, 'toss it back' just wasn't in Levi's repertoire. Not putting that ball to good use was just a plain damn waste. So instead, Levi picks him out a target. I called to him he better hadn't oughta. We'd learnt about windows the hard way long ago. He grins back at me, then changes his sight from the row of warehouse windows to the water storage tank above the tracks.

Well, he just loved to watch me watch him site a target. Before I could advise him otherwise and before the two boys could get to him, he'd given the ball all he had and damn if he didn't hit the pulley that held up the water spout, and damn if that water spout didn't come swinging down, and damn if that water didn't start spouting out like Multnomah Falls, and damn if we didn't alla us go running!

Well, Leviticus woulda gone running back after that dang base-ball if Lou(ella) hadn't climbed down off the train and started yanking him away by the belt and announcing the current time, "Twelve-oh-two … twelve-oh-three!"

"Ah, Lou, you take the cows. I wanna stay…" he said, whirling around and swinging her around with him. "Lou?" He did it again.

Then Jay, now sticking his head out the window, hollered, "Leviticus! Get your … back here!" sounding more like he was warning his kid brother than his boss.

"Royal, can I get a ball like them two have?" Levi asked me, his blue eyes bright, his handsome face grinsa hope.

"For your birthday, but we all gotta get on that train *now,* son!" says me, watching the train station man coming around to inspect the flood.

"I want one now. Can I have one now?"

"Lou(ella) will buy you a whole box fulla balls onct we get to Portland, won't you, Lou?" It was one of them rhetorical questions which was sorta pointless to ask Lou. She stopped, put her head down, and was calculating Godknowswhat.

Then E.M. stands on the platform of the last train car and calls out, lyric-like, "Levi? Lou? Lemonade!" She holds up her travel jug and waves it in the air.

Well, much as I hate to admit it, that did the trick, and I knew I was gonna hear a big 'I told you you'd need me!' from E.M.

Well, we all got back on board. The cattle was looing, the whistle was tootning, and the conductor was swearing and probably wondering why he'd got stuck with such a crew on what was otherwise a beautiful day. E.M. was plucking off the broke feathers on her hat and tossing 'em outa the window, and Royal was holding up the rear, standing on the back car platform, watching Idlehour slowly disappear behind him. And with it, the nice, easy-like lifestyle to which he had become accustomed.

four

So, the trip started out a little chilly betwixt E.M. and me, but by the time we was approaching Portland some twelve coolish hours later, things was pretty much back to normal. She and me never grudged much back in those earlier days, but I gotta admit we was surely going through a 'spittin' period' just then. You know, little things mostly setting each other off. And I knew at least twelve times a year E.M. was gonna get edgy, so I automatical gave her some free range.

Well, it downright amazed me how much Portland had changed in the eight or so months it'd been since I had been there last. It was coming along real good. Lotsa commerce and building and improvements. We was surely moving into a whole new age what with the turna the century approaching us. Even though we thought we was real modern back at Idlehour, with our indoor plumbing, hot water, electricity, telephones and all, it was nothing compared to that Portland town. Most interesting to me was a few of them new motor cars a-rattling proud'n'-pretty as you please right down the middle of the streets like they owned 'em, turning heads and spooking horses.

Well, you know things in my life don't usually go the way they're planned. And you know there's been days in my life when one mistake just follows another. Sometimes I wondered why I ever bothered to plan things out as much as I did. Here's an example. Upon arriving in Portland, I took Leviticus to introduce him to our cattle agent, only to find a note pinned to his door saying he'd been called away on unexpected business. I said to Leviticus, "Looks like we have to come back later."

"Don't he want to buy my cows, Roy?" he asked, looking a might chop-fallen.

"Sure he does. Just means he ain't here now."

Then Leviticus pulls out the cattle sale contract from his inside coat pocket and assures me, "Still got the papers, Roy. Ain't lost 'em."

"Good on you, Levi. You just put 'em back now, safe'n'-sound. We'll come back later and you can do what?" I asked him, hoping he'd remembered how we'd gone over this part of the cattle sale.

"Sign on the dotted line!" he answered, all fulla grins.

"That's right, Levi. Remember, nothing's official till you've done that. You been working on your signature like I said?"

"Got it down real official, Roy," he said. "Leviticus Perrault! L-E-V-I…" Well, since I knew how to spell it and didn't need no run down, I hushed him and took us back acrost the train yard to meet up with the rest.

I informed my charges and E.M. that we had us a whole day now to see the sights. Whereas I thought E.M. might be all for that, she stops and, sweartagod, she dang near looked like she was sniffin' the air for signs of trouble.

"What do you mean your agent's been called away on business?" she asked. Then she points to our cattle being loaded outa the cars. "What's all that? A hobby?"

"No, E.M., there's just a note saying he'll be back late this afternoon, that's all…"

She looks at me and then puts her hands on her hips. She says, "I don't like it."

"Like what?"

"You know what I don't like, Royal. Everything's askewy."

"Askewy?"

"Awry."

"You speakin' English, E.M.? Or that some secret Sam Script you learnt from Miss Weee Geee?" teases me.

"Don't you make fun of me, Royal Leckner!" she snapped.

Well, that line was just gonna turn things sour onct again, so I made a dangerous suggestion to get E.M.'s smile back. "Look, E.M., you been sportin' for some new hats for some time now. Why don't you go to Meier and Frank's and see what's new this season. Maybe Lou'd like to go with you."

"Unt uh. Gotta find Levi a base-ball. Promised him a base-ball, Roy," Lou says.

Well, I don't know how I coulda forgotten that, onaccounta that's about all them two talked about the whole damn train ride to Portland.

So we agreed. E.M. said she'd do some shopping, then maybe take herself over to the offices of Howell, Powell and Gallucci, her daddy's accounting firm, and say hi-howdy to the clerks there she onct worked with.

So Hardy, Jay, me, Lou, and Levi boarded us a street car and went this way, whilst E.M. found her a cab to take her into town that way. We agreed to meet at the Willamette Hotel at seven.

We found us a big, grand general mercantile and we alla us found something in that store to occupy our tastes. Jay found the men's hats, Hardy said he needed some Bag Balm for his scratchy knuckles, Lou and Levi headed for the sporting goods, and me, well, I found me the fishing section.

I knew E.M. wasn't gonna in any way keep her hat buying to just a few, so I reckoned I had me a toy coming too. I went ahead and bought me the best trouting rod'n'reel in the joint. Hinckley Special. I'd been drooling over one for months. I picked it off the wall, and the salesman allowed maybe I oughta try a few casts first, which I did out back in the alley. I spied me someone's longjohns swaying in the breeze — looking almost human, almost like a prizefighter doing his dance and a-taunting 'Come on. Right here. Hit me right here!' I first looked right, I then looked left, and then I cast out my line, listening to the fine wheeeeennnnng-ity click of the reel. Dang if I didn't catch them longjohns right in the outhouse accommodations. Sweartagod, sunk my sinker right into the back hatch. But they was gonna put up a fight, wasn't gonna come easy, nor was my wrist action good enough to unsink me from 'em.

Just then a woman comes dang near outa a window yelling at me to let-go her husband's longjohns, and I was obliged to suffer the indignity of undoing my sinker from that delicate placement and all in the accompaniment of that city woman's right colorful bellicosity.

Well, I knew that was the right rod'n'reel for me, and after I'd made it an accessory to a laundry line crime, it was only fitting it and me should be forever paired. That's it, there, hanging over the fireplace. Ain't she a beauty? Best willow rod you'll find anywheres.

Anyway, I arranged to have it delivered to the train depot along with all the various and sundries the rest had rung up. 'Cept the base-ball, which Levi was maybe thinking of having surgically attached to his palm.

"Say, you folks might want to take in a ball game while you're in town," says the store clerk. Then he pulls five tickets outa his cash register and says since the game is just about to start and we might miss a inning or two, that he'd give us these five Annie Oakleys — those're free tickets, case you didn't know — and we could alla us spend a afternoon watching a exhibition game of base-ball.

Well, if all those stars and mystics and Weee Geee spirits was worth even half the import ol' E.M. attached to 'em, then

I reckon I woulda said no thanks, we're heading to the zoological gardens.

But I didn't hear nothing but "Say, Royal, that's a good idea," and "Can we, Roy?" and from Hardy, who shoulda known better, "Come on, Roy. Can't hurt seeing us a ballgame."

So we did.

My next mistake that day was calling the offices of Howell, Powell and Gallucci and leaving a message for my wife indicating I'd run into a opportunity and onaccounta it we was seeing us a base-ball game.

One look at the base-ball park and I knew why those tickets was free. Mighta been the only way to get folks to pass through the turnstile, outsida paying 'em to.

But the sun was nice that day and it was a pretty setting and, here's a confession: it was my first ever base-ball game. No foolin'. Jay and Hardy had seen 'em some playing in the small towns, but I never held much with setting for a coupla hours watching fully growed men play a kids' game.

Levi and Lou, of course, was having the time of their lifes what with all the popcorn and peanuts and such. E.M. would skin me Royal if I let 'em eat till they got sick, so I had my hands full. Every time I settled 'em down into our seats, they was going off in another direction. Jay of course was too busy making eyes at some — well, maybe they wasn't chippies, I don't know onaccounta I'm still not sure what a chippie is exactly. Anyway, they was all casting glances back'n'forth, and Hardy, he was deep asleep.

Well, even though I'd spent many a day watching baby cows wander in all directions at onct, I have to admit I was losing sight of Lou and Levi at that ball game. They'd both gone down to find the privies, and normally that's no problem.

Well, I gotta admit, the action on the base-ball field was — well, maybe action ain't the right word. Fact is, it was pretty damn dull. The teams playing was some boys from back east called the Bowery Bulldogs, and they was up against this other traveling team from Kansas City. Now, why they all come together to play at Portland, I had no idea. They was just being exhibitionists, I reckon, like it touted on the tickets.

Just as I was wondering if I should go find Levi and Lou, the crowd all stands to their feets and starts laughing. Maybe base-ball was funner than I thought. I stood up and looked around to see what was so damn funny, onaccounta I coulda used a good laugh about then.

Ever gasp so loud you think you might pull in your toenails? Well, there Levi was, standing down on the base-ball sidelines. Now, the base-ball man who was just then battning the ball hit him a big one, and it went clear over the pitcher man's head. But Levi, being one quick study on what to throw to who, took his own new base-ball and tossed it to the first base man. Knocked him clear off his feet and the crowd went wilder.

The official men who was keeping order on the field was falling down on their jobs and all confused and scratching their heads when they come up with two balls for one game and a first base man out for the count. 'Course, Levi goes running to get his base-ball back, and pretty soon it's folks and opinions everywhere out on that field.

Now, that was bad enough, but that ain't the baddest part. The baddest part was me, having to go out there and extricate my charge, and in so doing that extricating becoming the center of the situation. And I reckon that's how she spotted me.

Who? Augusta Gallucci Chumsky Wainwright Carter, that's who.

E.M.'s half-sister, part-time nemesis, and full-time trouble.

And Royal's downfall.

five

The mere mention of that name was enough to make my blood stop cold and commence to flow in the opposite direction. Now, alota of my fear of this woman had come from years of E.M.'s horror stories. I hadn't had me too much first-hand experience with this woman, but like you mighta determined by the length of her name, I was maybe the only man in the state of Oregon who hadn't.

Good looking? We got us an expression these days. Reckon we got the flickers to thank for it, but it's called "S.A." — the "S" standing for Sex and the "A" standing for Appeal or, in this case, Augusta. None of us knew much about sex-appeal back in '97, but that don't mean certain women — Augusta most especially — wasn't covered head to toes with it.

So when I hear this voice fulla heaven call lyric-like outa the chaos, "Royal? Royal Leckner, is that *you*?" I turned around and stopped dead in my tracks. Before I could think and maybe deny it was me, she had me by the arm and was sweeping me away. I did have the presence of mind to go back for Levi and Lou, but as if I was snagged on Augusta's fishing line, she quick-like reeled me back in and off the field.

"Why, it *is* you! How wonderful! How long has it been? Oh, but let's not talk here. Let's go up to the clubhouse where we can be alone. Bring your two little friends with you."

Reckon I looked pretty damn confused as she leads us up to a room with a sign on the door that said,

Private Clubhouse
Owners, Managers and Their Guests Only

'Course, what it shoulda said was,

Private Den
Lions and Their Meals Only

I took me a pause at the door. Augusta turned, gave me a pearly smile, and said, "It's all right. You're my guest."

And I, Daniel-like, followed the smiling lioness right on in. What's worse is I made Levi and Lou come with me.

After some introductions to some fellows playing cards in there, I was quick to learn that my sister-half-in-law was none other'n the owner of the Bowery Bulldogs.

"Do tell?" was all I could muster.

"Well, the divorce was *so* nasty and *so* public that I just thought, 'what the heck, just take the team if that's all the bum has left, and do with them what you can,'" Augusta tells me, going to a nice bar in the corner. "As I recall, you drink rye, but I just happen to keep on hand this lovely champagne. Some for your friends, do you think?"

"Ah, just sodas for Levi and Lou."

I shoulda never let it get so cordial. I shoulda remembered the battle that them two Gallucci women had waged since they became sisters through their common daddy.

Fact is, I was sorta mesmerized. That's the sorta woman Augusta was. Butter don't melt in her mouth, but you oughta see how everything else in her presence does! So we have us a champagne drink, and talk gets more relaxed, and pretty soon I let on why we're in Portland and yes, wouldn't it be nice to have her visit us some day and E.M.'s doing fine and won't she get a kick outa us running into each other and all that sorta talk. I shoulda known no lion ever chit-chatted incept before the kill. But betwixt the French perfume and French champagne and well, hell, she *was* kin…

"Cattle sale, hmmm?" she says, totally skipping over the family talk and stalking toward Levi. As unworldly-like about these things as little Lou was, I gotta tell you, she was setting up a little straighter whilst Augusta applied her charm to Levi.

And you shoulda seen Levi gush back when Augusta said, "My, my, *my.* The last time I saw you, Leviticus — that was your wedding, wasn't it, Roy? Well, you were just a boy. Look at you now, Leviticus. Here in the big city, negotiating a great big cattle sale and everything! Another soda?"

"Just gotta sign me on the dotted line!" Levi said, taking another soda from her and bringing out the sale papers from his pocket.

"Come on, Levi," Lou said, pulling him. "Let's go get you another base-ball."

"Oh, so you like base-ball, do you?" Augusta asked Leviticus.

"Uhhh huhhhh!" he said, grinning big at her. "I *love* base-ball!"

"Levi," Lou continued, now pulling him by his belt toward the door, "let's go look for base-balls!"

Well, Augusta coulda been the most beautiful thing he'd ever set eyes on, but getting him his base-ball back struck him as the thing to do, onct Lou got his attention. I have to admit, I wanted to go with 'em and was starting to say so when Augusta says, "I know! Why don't John and Jackie here take you both down to the field and let you watch the game with the players. You can even have one of their very own base-balls! Would you like that?"

Stupid question.

But bright idea onaccounta that made us now alone in the clubhouse. So here's as good a spot as any to tell you, I reckon ol' Augusta woulda set her eyes on me if she wasn't so scardt of her sister and maybe if I was a tad richer. Men just know these things. Can see it in a woman's eye clear acrost the room.

So the four start to leave and Augusta says to one of her men, "Oh, and Jackie?"

"Ma'am?"

"Make sure they get everything they want. Make it a real treat for them, hmmmm?" He nods and they leave.

Augusta and me was setting, looking out the window on the base-ball game. I looked at the clock on the wall. I knew that downing my champagne real fast would look rude and like I wanted outa her clutches fast, but that's what I wanted.

"Don't worry," she said, indicating my charges being led by her charges. "They're in good hands."

'Course, it wasn't them I was most worried about. It was that all-too-familiar-looking hat which I saw a-bobbing its way toward the Bulldog's line-up.

I watched E.M. find Levi, and I watched Levi point up our direction, and I watched Augusta's face as she watched E.M. start a-drudging up the steps.

I stood up, and you know that feeling when you know you got exactly three seconds to either disappear or arrange your story or dive under the rug? You sorta just pace a few steps and then you grin when the door comes flying open and your wife says,

"Well, Royal, you might have invited me to your little party. You know how much I like..." She picked up my empty glass, gave it a sniff, and then added, evil-like, "Champagne!"

"Elijah Marie! What a lovely surprise!" says Augusta.

E.M. turned on her sister and said something alongst the line of, I shoulda known!

Unruffled, Augusta just asked, pouring her sister a glass of champagne, "Well, how is it you *did* know?"

E.M. took the glass, downed it faster'n jack, and replied, "Well, when I walked into Daddy's offices, Mr. Powell hands me a note saying Royal's here at this base-ball game. 'Oh really?' Powell says. 'How interesting.' 'Why?' I asked. 'Because that's where your sister is, too,' he says." Then she looks at me and de-codes from my message, "That's some opportunity you ran into!"

"E.M., you don't think for a minute…" I start.

"Seems to me this isn't the first time I've caught you two sipping champagne in private!"

"Well!" Augusta says. "For the millionth time, we were *locked* in that ice house! What would you have had us do, freeze to death?"

But E.M. wasn't gonna go treading in our pasts together. Not when there was all this present to be wading through. She pours herself another glass, and from there it was all downhill. We began a threesome of accusations, finger points, HAs! and whistle-wettning with champagne betwixt it all.

I finally pulled on my hat, looked at my wife, and tried to leave her with this one: "So much for trust, E.M.! So much for every damn thing!"

"Royal, where do you think you're going?" E.M. demanded, sounding like she wasn't done with me and I wasn't excused just yet.

I was more'n roiled. I was about as heated up as I think I'd ever been at her. Her thinking I woulda had anything to do this ways with her sister was more'n I was willing to listen to.

"I'm going back home, E.M.!"

"To Four Arrows?"

"Yes, to Four Arrows!"

I had my hand on the door.

"But what about the cattle sale?"

"You handle the cattle sale! You and your damn Weee Geee was so damn sure something was gonna go wrong if you wasn't here, then fine! You make sure it all goes right! I'm going home where you shoulda stayed in the first place!"

"Fine!"

"Fine!"

Then Augusta waved a sweet little nice-seeing-you, and I stomped outa that room, outa that base-ball park, and back to the train station, where I picked up my Hinckley Special and set with it betwixt my legs, waiting for the next train back eastwards.

Christ, I was thinking, gonna accuse me of stealing a cow, I sure as hell mighta got a damn kiss outa it! Like I said, E.M. and I was in a 'spittin' period.'

But by the time I was halfway to home, picking out the stream I was gonna go fish in, I was settling down some. Fact is, I think I even commenced to laugh about the whole damn thing. Me and Augusta! Cripes. Just onaccounta E.M. had had no less than six beaux stolen from her by her glorious, notorious sister. Jees. Maybe that wasn't so funny to E.M., after all. And it *did* look bad Gus'n me being hauled, half froze and drunker'n lords, outa that ice house.

Maybe I did decide to forgive her when she got home, and things for us could onct again commence to normal. Oh, there's that damn word again! Normal.

six

By the time I set foot on Four Arrows land, I was my own ol' self onct again. Had me my new Hinckley Special and had me a day or two without my worry-crew or my wife, so hell, thinks me … fishin' time. I'm overdue.

Normally, Hardy was my fishing partner. I coulda gone alone, but sometimes it's nice to have another angler setting acrost the fire at night to swap drinks, stories, and wisdom.

So then I think, what about ol' Sully McGinty? Sully was our train engineer and our blacksmith out at Four Arrows. He came with the engine when we pulled it offa the logging operations, and since we only used the train occasional, I had to find other work for him. Although Leviticus woulda been happy to have him work the train back and forth to Idlehour 24 hours a day just so's he could play railroad whenever he wanted.

Sully McGinty. Actual, it was Sullivan, but hardly no one ever got called their whole name onct they was parta the Four Arrows crew. You might think betwixt his name and his two jobs of train engineer and blacksmith, he was a big man, but he wasn't. Sully was just a medium sort — maybe 5 foot 8. Well built, but not thick like you want to think blacksmiths are. Reckon Sully was about 35, maybe 40, hard to say. Past his bloom, at any rate. 'Course, the older I get, I make note a man's bloom gets older and older too, but back then I thought 40 was older'n dirt. Anyway, he'd been with us since 1895. He was a nice-looking feller, and E.M. was always wondering why it was Sully wasn't hitched. You know women, they can't stand a man being content and unlady-broke at the same time. So she'd try to fix him up with some spinster or widder, but things never worked out.

Sully was a real different sort, which is why, of course, he fit in just fine at Four Arrows. He was kinda quiet, not so much shy but closed-mouthed, and sometimes it's nice to have a quiet man around. And like all different sorts, he had him his peculiarities. He hummed. Sweartagod, he'd hum whilst horseshoeing, he'd hum whilst hammering out a wheel, he'd hum whilst chopping wood. Odd thing is, the tenser the situation, the faster he hummed. He had him a nice hum, though. And I always planned on asking him if he knew any words.

Anyhow, I found Sully a-hummin' and a-hammerin' in the smithy shed. "Hey, Sully," I said.

He said, "Woulda fired up Bess if I knew..."

"No, I came back alone. It's a waste a' wood and your time just to chug *me* back home."

He nodded and went back to his smithing.

I watched him hammer some more. Sully was right good at that. Hit his mark every damn time. Then he stops, looks at me looking at him.

"Look what I got," I said, holding up my new Hinckley Special, probably looking about six years old.

He looked back at me, slipped the red-hot horseshoe into the water barrel, and gave me a small smile. "Hinckley Special."

I looked at him, my mouth wide open. How the hell'd he know that? So I asked him.

He went to a corner and pulled out his own canvas-wrapped rod'n'reel.

"You got one too?" I asked him.

"Arrived yesterday."

"Know a good stream?" I asked, thinking I was about to find myself a new fishing partner.

"You know the Little Minnie?"

"Up off the Baby Blue?"

I could tell by his glance at me that he'd found hisself a fishing partner too.

This is how our fishing trip went: We packed our horses in silence, rode up the Baby Blue Creek in silence. Sully took the north side, I took the south side, and the only sound we shared all day was the water swishing gently betwixt us, the sound of our casting rods, and then at dark the sound of fresh trout sizzling in the cast iron skillet, gently mixed with Sully's humming of a opera tune.

It wasn't until I pulled out a bottle of anti-fogmatic after dinner and offered to buy his thirst, and that bottle'd gone back'n'forth a few times, that Sully stopped humming and started talking.

I'd learnt a few things I hadn't heretofore known about Sully. I come to find out that he had him a education — come from one of them fancy back-east schools. I asked him how he gets from a comfy East Coast brainery and the opportunities that musta brung to the operation of a steam engine 'way out west. He just took a swig of rye, smiled into the fire betwixt us, and replied, "Well, my degree *was* in engineering."

"Maybe you're just the western type. Somehow, I never figured you for a easterner. Maybe you just started walking west and didn't never stop." Yep, I was digging. Probably too distinguished with rye to consider my manners.

"Oh, I ran into some trouble. You know how it is when you're young, eager, think you know everything."

"No fool like a educated fool?" I asked, making note I just learnt more about Sully than in the whole two years I'd known him. But it was the way he held up the flask of rye when he said it that I think I got the flavor of his words.

"Drink brings lotsa good men to bad things," I said.

"So do women," he added. He capped the flask, handed it back, and turned in.

Sully and I fisht for two days, mostly in the silence that a married man can usually only dream about. We didn't talk any more about falling from grace at the behest of liquor or women, nor did we discuss college matriculations and east versus west. Nor did we talk of engineering anything more important than flies on lines, trouts in pans, or new Hinckley Specials being cast out over the water.

Sturdy fondships can come outa times like that.

'Course, I was expecting E.M. and my troops to be home waiting for me when I returned. E.M. all fulla humbleness for her suspicions, my crew ready for fence patrol, and my life pretty much ready to begin its casual, easy-going pace.

Shoulda known better. Insteada finding anything resembling a goodly portion of Humble'n'Peace Pie, alls I found was a piece of paper tacked to my front door.

It was a telegram. Shortest one I ever got in my whole entire life. It said:

> Dear Royal stop I forgive you stop your loving wife.

You know, every time I recall that telegram I am struck by those last four words, 'stop your loving wife.' Like as though I could. Like as though *she* forgave *me*!

So I did what any normal agitated husband would do: Went inside, poured hisself a drink, made a toast to his wife's portrait, set around counting my thumbs and trying to square the circle which was my wife, and awaited her next move.

It came around noon the next day. I was on the front porch, called there by the warning of dust on the horizon. I took a step closer, using my binoculars, which I always kept close at hand in case of intruders, robbers, telegram deliveries, and such.

I could make out two wagons. The first was E.M. in a long cargo wagon, setting betwixt Jay and Hardy, who was handling the ribbons. I narrowed my gaze to her face. She was not smiling. Then I looked at Jay. He was grinning big as life. I looked at Hardy. He looked like he'd been drinking. In the wagon was stacks of God-knows-what all covered up with tarps.

I took my gaze to the wagon following. It was overloaded with men. Thinking maybe E.M. had run into our ranch hands all drunk and disorderly in Idlehour or Milton or maybe even helling around Portland, I didn't get too worried when I heard some drinkative singing.

I didn't get too worried when I saw some yap fall offa the wagon.

I didn't get too worried when no one even noticed.

Nope, what upset me was outsida my own five returning sheeps, I didn't recognize one of them men in the wagon.

I know I had my hands on my hips as I stood on the porch and waited for the two wagons to pull up to the ranch house. E.M. and Jay and Hardy and Lou(ella) and Leviticus nearly all ran over each other falling outa their wagon, coming through the gate, and scrambling down the garden path and up the porch steps.

They was all talking at onct and all talking at me. Five big sails a-blowing and hardly any ballast to hold 'em on course. So all I got was a glimpse of what each one said:

Lou(ella): Ten-thousand-six-hundred-fifty-three!

Leviticus: Lou got me my base-ball, Royal!

Hardy: Now, Royal, I know this *looks* bad…

Jay: Hot Cha! Wait'll those high-falutin' Pendleton boys see this!

And of course, the corker:

E.M.: Now, Royal, I can explain …

seven

I reckon I just stood there scratching my head and looking pretty dang dumb. E.M. scampers up the porch steps, hiked skirts and all, and believe me, a woman the likes of E.M. just don't scamper real often. I mean, she might run, she might definitely stomp, but scamper — only in her most croquettish moment would E.M. scamper. But I stopped the croquette halfway up the steps with, "Stop right there, madam." (Me calling my buncha calico 'madam' always made her stop, sometimes even throw something.)

She stopped just in time for alla us to be treated to the wagon load of whatevers coming together in a off-key harmony:

> Oh, take her back, Mother, for she's no good,
> Oh take her back, Father, she's cold as wood.
> Oh take her back, preacher, she's slipped her hitch,
> Oh take her back, take her back, you son uvvvv a bitch!

That was the chorus from 'Havre Can Have Her' — I knew it by heart, but had never heard it bulldozed so dedicated, nor so painful, nor this far west of Montana, nor as a overture to me hollering at my wife.

The men ended their song, passed around some bottles, whooped, hollered, lost a few more offa the end of the wagon, and all'n'all had no idea where they was or who they was.

E.M. saw my face, grabbed my arm, and pulled me into the house. Onct inside, I shook off her arm and did my famous stance — arms acrost my chest, legs apart — hell, if I was packing iron I suppose I woulda placed my jacket back behind my gun, as a prelude to a duel. As it was, my trigger finger *was* a tad itchy.

"Start talkin', E.M., and don't start your pitch too high, else you might not make the whole hymn," I warned.

"Really, this is nothing more than a singed cat..."

"I haven't even *seen* your cats, let alone..."

"No, no, I mean this isn't as bad as it seems..."

She looked like she was ready to enlighten me, but stopped whilst she waited for Leviticus and Lou(ella) to run through the room.

"Where you two going?" I demanded.

"My boys is thirsty," Levi announced, his face lit up like the Fourth of July, and then he made a bee-line for my liquor cabinet.

"The hell they are! You tell your boys..." I began. "*Your* boys? What'd you mean *your* boys?"

"Now, Royal, why don't you set down," E.M. says. Then to Levi she says, "Take them all to the bunkhouse. Lou, you tell Anita there'll be a few extra for dinner."

"Twelve!" Lou(ella) sparks out.

Levi ran that way and Lou ran the other, slamming doors and all kid-like.

I set down in my favorite chair, the one made outa the horns, hoofs, hide'n'holler of one of our most notorious and, I might add, deceitful cows. It always made a sorta groan whenever I set in it, like it was always getting the last word on things. It damn near bawled as I plopped my weight into it now.

"Royal, I *warned* you I had bad prognostications about Portland."

"They wasn't *your* bad prognota-what-you-said, they was Miss Weee Geee's, and looks like me leaving you to your own devices in Portland was a big mistake, E.M. Who the hell are them men and why are they here?"

"Will you stop interrupting! I'm about to tell you, Roy."

"Make it wide, not tall, E.M."

Then she starts onct again to tell me, but I could tell she was a bit baffled.

"Maybe I better set down, too," she said, taking out her hankie and fanning herself with it. "Whoa. It's hot in here."

"Fainting ain't gonna get you outa this, E.M., so get on with the funeral!"

She scorched me a good one and said, "I have never stooped so low as fainting to get out of anything in my life! It's just I don't know where to begin."

"Then let me help you out some. Here, finish this sentence: I hired a buncha lushington hands knowin' full well we got more lushes, I mean hands, than we can use, because...?

E.M. looked at me and smiled a little crooked-like. "Oh, no *wonder* you're upset, Royal. Those aren't *ranch* hands." Her smile got bigger and she soft-soaps me with, "Why, I know better than to hire ranch hands when you're the best judge of hands west of the Mississippi."

"Damn rights I am," I said, thinking for a brief innocent second that that was that. Then I got to thinking, "Well, if they ain't hands, what are they?"

She asked, "Don't you recognize them?"

I took a long look, and I reckoned halfa their mommas wouldn'ta recognized 'em, or owned up to it even if they did.

"No!" says me.

"Well, you should, Roy," E.M. said. Now here I detected a change in her voice. "Or perhaps you were too *distracted* to notice."

"Notice what?" I asked.

"The Bowery Bulldogs," she announced, superior-like.

"The Bowery Bulldogs?!" I echo. "What in name of the Seven Vestal Virgins of Cologne are the Bowery Bulldogs doing following you home from Portland?"

So then she dissolves back into her chair, hands to her face, slumps over, and commences to cry.

We'd only been married four years, remember, and I still wasn't used to E.M. crying. Fact is, she hardly ever cried. I wasn't sure if I should put my arm around her or tell her to snap outa it, so I did neither and yelled instead.

"E.M., you stop your blubbering and..."

It was then I saw she wasn't crying at all. She was trying to hide her snickering. I thought she was pulling the long bow on me and she was saving up for the moral, so I started to laugh with her and asked, "Okay, E.M., what's going on? This a joke? You getting even for me calling Meier and Frank's and tapping your shopping credit?"

Like I said, I was still learning things about women. She skins me with a wicked eye like I was really gonna pay big for that one. But she just said, "Maybe you better be talking to Leviticus."

"Why? How many hats did *he* buy?"

"Twelve, to be exact."

Now I was really flusticated. I looked out the window to see the twelve Bowery Bulldogs a-wandering around the bunkhouse. "E.M., do I gotta remind you this here's a cattle ranch, not no silo circus?"

"Oh yeah? Since when?"

So I turned around and said, like I was to say so many, many times again in our lifes together, "E.M., you quit trottin' away from the pole and tell me plain and simple: what the hell you up to? And don't bother lookin' for the soft spots!"

She straightened up and snapped, as she was to snap so many, many times again in our lifes together, "What the hell am *I* up to?" Then she starts circling me and pointing a finger, and I'm trying not to slump, and she continues. "*I* didn't buy that team! *I* didn't tell Leviticus to go buy a base-ball and the whole damn team that comes with it! *I* didn't take him to a base-ball game and *I* didn't walk smack dab into a mare's nest and *I* didn't swill French champagne and get all ooo-lah-lahed by my sister's spellbinding, goey-eyed talk, and *I* sure as hell didn't teach Leviticus how to sign on the dotted line!"

It was quite a speech and one that had probably been under rehearsal all the way back home. But I held tight and stayed on track.

"Now you hold on, E.M.! Maybe you didn't do any of those things, but *I* ain't the one with a dozen Bulldogs followin' me home!"

We stalemated for a few seconds, catching our breaths and thinking eacha us about our next tacks.

"Look, Royal, it's pointless for you and me to argue like this. What's done is done. Four Arrows now has, as one of its assets, a base-ball team! A bottom of the barrel, Z-League, can't hit a note, can't catch a cold, can't toss a coin base-ball team."

E.M. was, amongst other things, a good describer.

But of all her descriptions, the one that stuck with me was 'assets.'

"Assets, E.M.? How can they be our assets when them Bulldogs belong to…" It was then that all the chickens was startin' home to roost.

And together we said, "Augusta."

E.M. turns and gives me her famous dry grin — that mocking, sly, and-it's-all-*your*-fault grin of hers. "Yes, I imagine Levi had signed on that damn dotted line of yours just about the time you walked out of the ball park," she informs me.

"You gonna get to the improvement, E.M.? When I left him he was just watching a damn base-ball game!"

"Oh, Suffer Your Age, Royal! You know how stubborn Levi is! He may only have half a mind, but the half he does have is damn hard to unset! And that day his mind was set on baseball!"

"E.M., just tell me, without the taffy and the flapdoodle, what the hell happened to all our cattle!"

"Correction: *Augusta's* cattle."

"You mean he traded 'em?"

"Straight across the board."

"All 1200 head?"

"Yep. Every damn one of them. Actually, it was Lou(ella) who said it best. She said that came down to four-thousand, eight-hundred cow-feet in exchange for twenty-three ball-feet."

"Twenty-three?"

"One of the players has a bum ankle," E.M. allowed, pouring us both a drink.

Just then I felt like all four-thousand, eight-hundred of them cow-feet had toe-tapped 'Tally One for Me' right acrost our futures.

"But E.M., when you found out…"

"I tried, Royal, believe me, I tried. But you know that slum-guzzling, no-good, double-crossing sister of mine! By the time I'd figured out what happened, she was gone."

I looked at E.M.'s eyes, which was about as get-evenish as I had ever seen 'em. "You think she did this to you on purpose?"

"Of course she did!"

"Think maybe she was trying to get at you? Or at me?" I asked, careful-like.

"Oh wake up, Royal! She's still mad at me about chiseling her out of the silver mine deal!"

Then she looks at me and points a finger and says, "But

that doesn't mean for one minute I'm letting you off the hook about that little scene!"

"Your telegram said you forgave me," I countered before I could rightly recall it was *me* still mad at *her.*

But she had me good. All she said was, sorta resigned-like, "It doesn't matter who caught the Tartar this time, Roy. Fact is, we did. Twelve of 'em."

I know I shoulda been thinking what Tartars meant to Four Arrows and what it meant for Levi and Lou and alla our hands. I shoulda been thinking about twelve more mouths to feed, wheat and cattle and such, but alls I could think was so much for me and E.M. ever getting off Four Arrows, so much for us getting on with our lifes, and so much for Weee Geee future tellers.

Weee Geee! thinks me. It all started with that damn Weee Geee! I stood up, fetched Mr. Smith and Mr. Wesson from my holster hanging on the coat rack, walked into our bedroom, and fixed my eyes on the top drawer of E.M.'s dresser.

I opened the drawer and there she was — Weee Geee — her Yes and her No looking up at me. Mighta even heard a far-off laugh. So I blasted the dang thing with all six chambers. 'Course all sortsa pieces of E.M.'s undergarment fineries goes fluffing up and about the room, and I reckoned I'd be signing on the dotted line for the delivery of a brand new armoire, but at least I felt better about the whole thing.

That brought my crew all into the house, and they knew by my face, my smoking gun, and the French lace hanging offa my hair that I was looking for explanations and maybe even some more revenge.

Well, Leviticus and Lou(ella) and Jay and Hardy, alla 'em looked at me more sheepish than all of our 225 head put together, including the sheepdog. Each was holding one of them big, puffy base-ball gloves.

Hardy comes to me and says, "Say, Roy, where were you when things all went haywire?"

Then Jay comes up with, "Hey, I think for onct ol' Levi made out all right for hisself! Hot Cha! Now maybe we can have us some fun around here!"

Then Leviticus comes over to me, sorta bounces a little like he does when he's extra glad, and announces, "Got us a base-ball team, Roy!"

Well, if you could see the grinagog on his face, see the spark in his eyes, and hear the kid in his voice, I suppose you'da asked the same damn thing: "You reckon any of 'em can fork a horse?"

eight

'Course, first order of things was to sort alla this out and see who was on what base. I went out on the porch, agitated the communicator, and I don't care if you've been raised in a big city, on a ocean, on a ranch, in the lumber hills, or in downtown Hell, a dinner bell is a dinner bell, and when I clanged ours you shoulda seen them men come running.

Before I could count the years I'd been hitched — 1,2,3, seemed like 40 — I had me quite a mob assembled before me. The regulars come in from their chores, and though they was small in numbers, they was big on curiosity. It was the same with the new buncha Bulldogs. They all looked at each other like, wasn't this gonna be a show! Like maybe each man knew there wasn't near enough work to justify the numbers, and so who the hell are you and what the hell are you wearing and don't you come any closer to my horse and just what the hell you staring at?

Even the horses was curious about this new wagon load of encumbrances. Hell, horses can smell a badger hole and avoid stepping into it, which was a dang sight better'n my five humans did in Portland, so I was carefully watching the horses, who was carefully watching the new crew.

E.M. and Lou(ella) and Anita was setting on the front porch. E.M. because she was gonna do some of the explaining, Lou(ella) because she was plastered next to Leviticus, and Anita the biscuit roller because she was damn mad about the twelve extra mouths to feed and I guess she wanted to see if any of them wasn't worthy of her labor.

"I suppose you're all wondering why I've called you here," I finally announced after clearing some dust outa my throat. I knew I had to keep that famous creak outa my voice that first meeting and say things honest and simple and like they was, of which I didn't have a clue. But men can mutiny in a fartbeat, and so I put on my best foreman face.

"Seems like we got us some guests here to Four Arrows," I began. Sweartagod, it was like a union meeting, with the yeas on one sida the yard and the nays on t'other. The cowpokes looked over at the ball players and visa versa.

"Now, as I understand it, you fellers there is the Bowery Bulldogs," I said.

One come forward. Had him the longest handlebar mustache I think I'd ever seen, and he says, "Damn right we are! Best ball club east of da Hudson!"

Well, I didn't think that took up too much territory. Now, had he said Mississippi or Missouri, then I suppose he mighta gotten some ooohs and aaaahs outa my hands. As it was, there was nothing but silence.

So I continued, "So why don't you all introduce yourselfs to the others. Meanwhilst, is there a bellwether-man who can come up and talk to me in private?"

The Bulldogs just looked at me. "You know, a ranahan?" Nothing. "A straw boss? A top man?"

"Well, Corky's the tallest," one yap indicated, pointing to the six footer with the handlebar and a real mean eye.

"Who the hell's in charga this team?" I finally bark.

They looked around to each other, milled some, grumbled some, and then pushes one man out infronta the rest. Now, if you had asked me to pick outa that line up of rowdies which one was the ring leader, I'm here to tell you it wasn't gonna be that one. He was the smallest of the crew, wore specs, was skinny as a undernourished hat rack and even a little shaky. He was also, I made note, the only Bulldog who was able to navigate.

"Oh yes, Royal," E.M. says, going down the steps and escorting this little feller back up. "This is Billy Rohrs, the team manager."

Well, my opinion of managers everywhere needed some examination, I thought, watching my wife nearly help this Billy Rohrs up the steps. I also had to onct again wonder how it is some folks get stuck with names they know they can never live up to.

"Billy, this is my husband, Royal Leckner."

Well, the way he sorta shrunk from my handshake made me realize E.M.'d been talking me up some.

"How do you do, Mr. Leckner. I've heard a lot about you," he confirms. His handshake was mushy as milk toast, which right there made me wonder how he could manage a flower cart, let alone a base-ball team.

"Here, come set in the shade, Billy, and we'll start working this out," E.M. said. Then the most peculiar thing happened. When Billy comes forward, Leviticus pops up and starts pumping his hand until little Billy's arm like to have come unscrewed.

"Hi ya, Billy. Billy's my friend, Royal, he's nice," Levi says to me. Well, I gotta tell you, I think I was a little bit jealous onaccounta I don't think I'd ever seen Leviticus grin so big at anyone else but me.

And what was even stranger was, Billy didn't have one ounce of fear or dread or suspicion or even impatience in his face whilst he said howdy to Levi and let him work his arm up'n'down so. That just hardly never happens. He smiled up kind-like at Levi and took his hat off and stored it under his arm when he gave his regards to Lou(ella). "Mrs. Perrault," he said.

'Course, I don't think I'd ever heard Lou(ella) referred to as Mrs. Anything before, and for a minute I had to look around and see who he was doffing his cap to.

So I then add, "This here's our cook, Anita," showing him Anita, since this was apparently becoming a porch social and not a what-the-hell-we-gonna-do business meeting.

Anita, who I don't recollect ever having seen without some sorta kitchen dofunny in her hands, gives his hand a hearty shake. She said (remember now, Anita was Mexican, and when she come to us she was pretty set in her so-called English, plus she had her a real contagious lisp), "How do ju do, and eeeef ju think I cook for alla ju then 'ust too dam bad!" (Remember too, what English Anita did come with was learnt to her by cowpokes and timberbeasts.)

And you know what? In perfecto Spanish, Billy said what I heard to be, "Oh please, Miss, we wouldn't dream of imposing on you. And we will be honored if you share a meal with us now and then from our humble cook stove, which we never travel without."

Butter melts in hell slower'n Anita's face did. Imagine, someone not only speaking her language so good and so far north, but him also inviting *her* to a home cook meal for onct.

She therefore insisted that we set out the tables and benches in the backyard and alla us have a good welcome home picnic, bar be que, hand-cranked ice cream, cold beer from the ice shed and all. Anita flashed him a bit of a smile and yes, I think she was flirting with the little feller. Then she left, inviting him to borrow any ingredients they might need from her kitchen, which was a sure invitation for a case of Cupid's Cramps as any I'd heard.

So I set the others down and looked at the two factions out front. They was done with their introductions, milling around, and I noticed they was all now what-if'n each other some.

So I told 'em all about the picnic out back for later that afternoon, told my boys to set the Bulldogs up in the extra-hand bunkhouse and to make sure they was all comfy after their trip. I made note that several of the Bulldogs musta been feeling the effects of too much booze'n'travel and suggested they get some rest.

You shoulda seen the looks my regular homeguards shot me when I said that. One of the boys grumbled up at me, "Want us to tuck 'em in and hear their prayers, too, Roy?"

That brought some laughs from the hands, some sneers from the Bulldogs. 'Course, I think a little nap was what we alla us needed.

I pulled up my chair to join the rest of the so-called managers — my camarilla of advisors — me, Leviticus, Lou(ella), E.M., Jay, Hardy, and Billy Rohrs. Providing we gave the two women a vote — and heaven help us if we didn't — there was seven of us there so gathered, and at least that left room for a tie breaker vote.

Well, maybe vote ain't the right word. Can't vote if there's no choice. And we, after E.M. showed us the signed, sealed, and delivered trade papers for the World Famous Bowery Bulldogs, we was apparently stuck. There wasn't no going back to Portland to track down Augusta Gallucci Chumsky Wainwright Carter, who swapped Jack, I mean Leviticus, the whole bag-o-beaners.

But all was not lost, onaccounta that get-even smile was back on E.M.'s face. She catches me like she can read my mind and says outa nowhere, "Don't look at me that way, Royal. You *knew* my family had a sordid past."

"I don't care how assorted it is, I ..." I stopped, wondering if we wanted all them ears filling up on her dirty laundry, so I said, "E.M., you reckon they all need to know this?"

"Oh, I told them everything on the train back here."

"Everything?"

"That's right, Roy," Hardy says. "The missus made a real clean bres…" he caught E.M.'s face and then finished, "brisket of it."

'Course, talk of clean briskets made Levi and Lou snicker some, and I heard Levi whisper to Lou, "E.M. caught Roy in the hen house!"

"Just what did you tell 'em, E.M.?"

"The truth."

"Which is?"

"Which is my sister tried to get her claws into you. Onct again."

"Yeah, but I hear she's real smick-smack, Roy," Jay says, like I was to be excused no matter what happened in that hen's house. I knew I was dead no matter what I said, what with everyone looking at me.

It was Anita who come to my rescue as she came in totin' refreshments. "A-gooos-ta? Who is A-gooos-ta?"

E.M. sighs heavy and then she starts reeling off words fast and like they was memorized. "Augusta is my older half-sister from my father's first marriage to a woman from back east of questionable background but of certain wealth, and she and I have been enemies ever since."

"Ever seeeence what?" Anita asked, setting herself down and leaving me to pour my own coffee.

Then Jay pops up and answers, like it was quiz night in the bunkhouse, "Ever since she did her out of the oil rights!"

"No, set down, Jay," Hardy says. "That came later."

Jay looked a little disappointed, but he set back down.

Hardy then adds, "You're way off, kid. Remember when they was in boarding school in 'Frisco, that's when…"

E.M. gave a sweet little 'ahem' and they all came back to her attention. I made note to practice that ahem, onaccounta it usually took me five or six downright coughs to get attention.

"Augusta and I weren't raised together, of course," E.M. goes on to Anita like she was catching her up on the local gossip, which, I guess, in a way it was. "But my father always tried to get us together. Well, you can imagine how mother felt about that. Anyway, we did go to boarding school together, and talk about natural born enemies…"

"Ah," Anita said, giving E.M.'s hand a pat of simpatico.

"Anita, do you think we could get some cream?" I asked.

She gives me a dirty look and disappears into the kitchen.

"Tell us again about the time you set Augusta up with…" Jay starts.

E.M. just glared at him, and he stopped.

Then Billy Rohrs said, "Mr. Leckner, I've only known your wife for a few days. But I must say, in those few days I have come to learn a few things."

"That she's from a wicked family?"

"Well, perhaps. But also that she's very determined."

"Tell me something I don't know," I said, giving her half a glance.

"She's gonna get even, Royal!" Jay pipes up. "Don't you see? Hot Cha! E.M.'s gonna get even!"

"With who and how?"

"With her sister — Augusta Gallucci Somebody Somebody Carter. It was all she talked about all the way back home, ain't that right, Jay?" Hardy says. "And the way she's going to do it…" At this he stops, thinks about the 'how' part, then looks at E.M. and says, "Yeah. How?"

E.M. looks her wickedest and replies, “At her own game, that’s how. Oh yes, she’s going to post the pony on this one.”

At this point I took control and demanded that right there and now we get us an accounting of the Four Arrows situation, monies and assets and everything. ’Course, Lou(ella) jumped up and went with E.M. into the house and brought out some books and then they runs some numbers up and and down and maybe even inside out, and then they gave me the big final fiduciary picture.

Four Arrows assets was five hundred dollars in the bank, a crop of wheat seed on order, 500 heada cattle to see through the winter, all our extra hay donated and gone to the Spokane Indians, 13 full-time hands, 15 out on their holidays expecting work come next month, and now 12 washed-out, hung-out, fizzled-out base-ball players.

And oh yes, about 225 sheeps, eacha them named and not one sheave to bring in betwixt us.

I set down on the top step of the porch and wondered how I was gonna hang onto alla Four Arrows, after all I’d done the last thirteen years to keep it intact. E.M. come up, set down next to me, put her arm around me.

“Don’t worry, Roy,” she said, putting her head on my shoulder like that was gonna relieve my burden some, which it didn’t. “I have an idea…”

nine

Yeah. Me too. I was *damned* scardt. You may wonder why the hell, if I wasn't owner, if I'd always wanted to move on to my own spread, if I had some money set aside, why I didn't just turn my back and walk out on the whole outfit.

Well, maybe my people understood me better'n I thought, for no sooner had they announced our inventories than they all just got up, each to their own direction, and this is what happened:

Jay went to saddle Buck, so named for his favorite passtime, then brought him out to me.

Hardy went to find the fence stretcher and snips, and put 'em in my saddlebag.

E.M. pours me some rye in a flask and puts it with some sandwiches in a flour sack.

Leviticus brings me his pillow — never really got the meaning of that one, but he tied it to my saddle and I nodded him my thanks.

Lou(ella) brings me out her latest tally of the fence posts — which she had numbered.

Billy Rohrs just stood and watched from the front porch, probably wondering what the heck all this silent fetching was about. I put on a paira chaps, got my working Stetson, and mounted up.

"How long you reckon this time, Roy?" E.M. asked from the front porch.

'Course, I wanted to say five or six years, but I could smell the bar be que fire being lit up out back and it'd been a while since we'd had us bar be que.

"Chicken or ribs?" I asked.

"Both," she answers.

I considered this like maybe I was deciding whether or not to order swords or pistols for a duel, then tipped my hat and replied, "Five o'clock?"

"That'd be fine," she answered, leaving me to ride out alone to my fence-mending, and the five a' 'em waving fare-thee-well.

The fence line I picked, the one that ran 'round back of the house where I could ride the ridge and still keep a eye on the happenings down below, was, I am glad to report, all in pretty good shape. All tight and all right. Posts was solid, wires was strung good. 'Course, every nowanthen I'd get me a whiff of that bar be que and the mesquite Anita had stacked on it, and I hafta tell you, I hadn't eaten me much breakfast that day.

But I had me some executive-like thinking to do on this new rhubarb we was in, and I never subscribed to doing high thinking on a low stomach, so I set down and unwrapped a sandwich, which turned out to be a repeater sandwich. Can you believe it? And when you're thinking bar be que ribs and chickens and steamed corn, a plain ol' bean sandwich just don't cut it. So I gave mosta the sandwich to Buck, but even he turned his nose up at it.

Well, hungry or not I started to back'n'fill on my dilemma. This is what comes to me: I had me some money, but it was all tied up in places where E.M. said I couldn't get at it, and even if I could, well I wouldn't know much about it. Stocks, bonds, land, she said. This money came to me just before we was married, and E.M. used to laugh and call it my dowry. She told me to sign right here and I did, and I ain't seen that money ever again. When I first asked for something in the way of an accounting, you'd think I was asking her to give me her virginity all over again. "Well, because it just can't be done, that's why!" was her explanation.

But E.M. had some dowry too, and she did a right good job of mixing up his'n'hers, and I gotta admit, betwixt her and Lou(ella) we seemed to be doing just fine. So after a while I didn't ask and she didn't tell and she said I didn't have to worry one thing about it, so I didn't. Incept for a coupla fe-as-kos alongst the way.

But things was different now. I looked out over that smack of land I loved so much: the Four Arrows spread — wheat fields, timber tracks, cattle ranges, fishing streams, even the L & L Shortline. How could it be that we might stood to lose it all, just onaccounta I told Leviticus he could handle the cattle sale.

Then I remember what I told him at the train station in Idlehour last week: I told him Lou(ella) would buy him a base-ball. Who was the Big Weee Geee then? I wondered. Me. Royal R. Leckner — the big foreteller of things to come. Hell, he got not only the base-ball, but a whole damn team to go with it! And I didn't say he couldn't, so in a way I blamed myownself. I was the grouthead responsible for the tragedy which was befalling us. Well, me and Augusta.

Things was starting to get active down in our big yard below. I saw the bar be que smoke come a-wandering up my direction — by the way, smoke don't follow beauty, it follows a hungry man. Anita and E.M. had put out the red-and-white checkered table clothes on the picnic tables, and they was bringing chairs and benches out from the house and bunkhouse. There was some horses tied off, lazy-like under the big willers, the grass was nice'n green from the water wagon that I had the boys run over the ground every other day or so. In fact, looking down on all that bucolic activity sorta made my heart flop. Had it not been for our immediate danger, I thought, it was maybe one of the prettiest sights I ever saw.

But I had a whole hour to get back down there, and I didn't want E.M. to think I was doing anything less than a full think about this current fe-as-ko.

I noticed lots of the hands coming in now. That smoke musta been working its way all the way to Idlehour, onaccounta I saw some of the holidaying hands come in.

I started to mount up, thinking I'd just wind myself down the Boskey Ridge. Buck seemed to agree on my choice of trails. I don't care what you tell me, horses know a shindig is brewing as well as a dog does, and he was looking forward to his slug of beer and slice of watermelon.

We was winding down closer and could hear men's voices, dogs barking, and I think I could even make out Anita's high-C instructions above it all. Then, as we was just coming into the clearing, WHANG! a ball shot past Buck's feet, and of all the things I'd taught him not to fear, a base-ball chewing the grass wasn't one of 'em.

Well, Buck blew up and came apart just like his name says, and me being a little more rye-laxed than a cowpoke should oughta be, I lost a rein. He started acting up like he knew he had a audience, and did his best to rearrange my innards. Well, I knew Buck. I knew he wasn't gonna settle for anything less than a total flame out. I was gonna just set back and let him run down his mainspring, which he did, but by way of my backyard, pretty much breaking up the base-ball game that was just getting underway.

Well, I was trying to grab the rein before Buck could find it with his hoof. Men was running, food was flying, we tipped over the beer table and took some hollering for that. Then some tied-up horses get spooked. Horses are that way, you know. One runs amok and boils over and they all gotta join in, so's Buck had him some mean company. All that backyard serenity was now a backyard brouhaha. And it appeared Buck was heading right for the back door — maybe thinking he could short-cut it through the house to get him faster to the barn.

That's when E.M. stepped into it. She was a expert horsewoman and had something of a barnyard reputation amongst the troublemaker livestocks, including one incident involving Buck and some fulla wrath'n'cabbage geese. So E.M. takes a stance infronta the food table and holds up a big soup ladle like she was Moses and the ladle was her Red-Sea-parting staff. Well, Buck took one look at her, slammed on the brakes, and stopped faster'n a colt on gelding day. Maybe that ladle did look something like a nut-loper at that. Point is, Royal comes flying over that saddle horn like he was a blue-nosed, raw-heeled daisy hand fresh offa the immigrant train!

I landed smack dab on a slab of white rubber, and there to greet me was Leviticus, holding the base-ball. And guess what he hollered for everyone — my men, our guests, Buck, my wife, and God — to hear.

"YER OUT!"

ten

Now, you may think I'd lost control of the situation onaccounta friend and foe, family and foreigner, wife and horse was all standing 'round me having a good laugh at my expense.

E.M. gives me the automatical, "Oh, Roy, are you all right?"

Leviticus follows me around and keeps calling me Out! Out!, Buck knows he's in big trouble and tries to look remorseful, but doesn't fool me one bit, Lou(ella) just stands there with her hand over her mouth, and of course Jay and Hardy come waltzing up like they're drunk-dancing and having to hold each other up for the comedy of it all. Then Anita will have none of this foofaraw and just comes blasting through the crowd, holding a bowl about the size of Pilot Rock over her head, hollering, "Por favor! Coming through! Move it, ju beeeg ox! I'm coming through! Por favor!" I am not sure which one of us was the beeeg ox, but it better'a been Buck.

Sore? Well, South of my pants I was sore and North of my collar I was even sorer. You know how it is when you sail so high in the air you could write your will and then land on your afterpiece, how your innards starts to collywobble? Additional, I was sporting a fine gravel rash in places I was afraid to look. And I was dang upset. Didn't know who to yell at first. E.M. was closest, so I gave her my narrow eyes.

"Oh, Royal, you should have seen the look on your face. The closer the house got, the bigger your eyes..." The way she was holding back her laughter made me even hotter.

"You enjoy approaching widderhood a inch at a time, do you, E.M.?"

I wasn't joking, but she musta thought I was. She just laughs and says, "Well, I'd rather go an inch at a time than a limb at a time."

I got up and dusted myself off. Hearing all them Bulldogs laughing at me chapped me Royal. "What the hell kinda picnic is this, E.M.?" I growled.

She looks around and answered, "Just your common backyard variety of picnic, I guess. Why?"

"What're they all doing on all my nice green grass?"

"Well, it seems perfectly obvious, Royal. They're playing base-ball. Or trying to play base-ball, until you and Buck decided to break things up."

I looked over and they was all going back to their bases and positions in the field, I mean in my yard.

"What for?" I asked. "Don't we got enough troubles without fully growed men playing games?"

E.M. put the ladle into the big bowl of cold slaw and looked me straight on. "Well, these men *are* base-ball players, Royal. It's what they do for a living. They're professionals."

"Well, lookit all my hands! Jay's over there and hell, there's Myron, Greg, Rich, Al, Jon, Kent, and Curt." I pointed to each one a' my hands that I saw partaking of the game. "Ain't they got better things to do?"

"I know who the men are, Royal. Can I get you a cold beer?"

I followed her to the beer keg, which someone re-set in the tub-o-ice, and waited whilst she drew me a extra frothy one.

"Besides, they're all having so much fun. Haven't you always allowed as how the men should oughta have theirselfs some fun now'n'then?" she asked, sounding more like me than I.

"Well, they sure as hell don't look like they're having fun," I said, watching the rivalry on the grass.

E.M. looked over the two teams and said, "Well, boys will be boys. You name me one cowpoke who doesn't think he's stronger and smarter than the average yap."

"Royal R. Leckner," I said. That cold beer sure felt good, and I wisht I coulda set my hindquarters down in that ice tub.

"Ha, ha, and ha," E.M. allowed. "And ego? You name me one athlete who doesn't think he's a real he-man." She pointed to the Bulldogs out on the field and added, "Look, any one of them could build a whole new wing on the words 'I got it!' So don't expect any of them to be happy. A base-ball game isn't a game at all, Royal."

"It ain't? Then what is it?"

"Well, it's more like chess. More like war."

To prove her point, she walked us to a coupla chairs. I set myself down, easy-like, thinking I was gonna need a damp bourbon poultice that night. We drank beer and set under a willer tree and watched us some backyard base-ball. You know, before I'd even heard the crack of the bat, I was liking this. Cool shade, warm September day, ice cold beer in my hand, a pretty girl by my side. So far, so good, I was thinking.

Of course, E.M. was right about the he-manning. There was nothing but alota big talk and look-at-me swaggers out there, and I was wondering whose idea it was that the cowpokes was set to measure bats against the Bulldogs. 'Course, it was my cowpokes' idea and I thought, well, that's the best way they can learn a little humbleness. Ain't nothing worse than a chesty cowpoke.

Well, maybe there is one thing worse: a cadavered base-ball team that can't get outa its way. No fooling, if I had not been previously informed that this was a *professional* team, then I gotta tell you, I couldn't have known for their antics on the field. Although I didn't know much about base-ball, I did know that having a smack of ability to hit and/or throw a ball was a primary requirement.

I just shook my head. "What's the score to this thing?" I asked.

"Bulldogs six. The boys five," she answers.

"Wouldn't you think maybe them what profess to be profess-ionals might be doing better agin the novies?"

E.M. didn't answer and sorta lost her grin as Bulldog after Bulldog either tripped, fell, missed, swore, drank, swung and, in the case of one of 'em, passed out, making my hands look less'n'less like cowpokes and more'n'more like base-ball boys. Or at least better drinkers.

"Now, Royal, give them the benefit of the doubt," E.M. allows. "Remember, they've been up all night and most are either hung over or still drunk."

"Al out there's been digging me a ditch down at the southern water hole. Curt's been breaking in a few new horses. Rich, he's…" I allowed her back. E.M. takes my pointing hand down and shushes me 'cause one of the Bulldogs is coming up to bat.

"Shhhs. Watch this. That's Corky O'Toole. He's quite a utility man."

I looked at her, having never quite heard that word in reference to a man who plays with a base-ball for a living. "Utility?"

"You know. All-arounder. Artist. Corker. That's where he gets his nickname. Corky."

So I looked over at this utility-Corky character and I saw he was the big-talker I'd seen earlier — the one with the handlebar mustache so long you coulda tied the ends in loops and used 'em for stirrups. I watched E.M. watch him and I didn't like that look one bit. Just onaccounta he was unlike them other

Bulldogs in that he had a full heada hair, not much of a bay window, was almost as tall as me and, come to take a closer look, he had him a handsome tanned face under all that mustachio.

"He used to be a Giant!" E.M. glosses.

"Looks like he shrunk some," I mumbled back.

"Shush and watch."

Jay was the pitcher and he pitched him a easy high one. This Corky feller took a slug at the ball and missed it clean. He then goes to the bench, takes a slug of beer, and comes back to the plate just in time to miss him a second pitch, which came in real low.

I leant into E.M. and said, "Hell, E.M., I don't know whether to holler 'fore!' or 'pull!'"

She jabbed me and told me quiet.

He goes back for another beer and then returns to miss him his third pitch. Well, you'd think that woulda been fine with him, so's he could go finish his beer, but this Corky the slug-smith got so mad that he walked out to Jay and he takes a swing and pastes the kid.

"Well, at least he made contact with *some*thing," I grumbled to E.M., handing her my beer and going out to break up the pile of men which was now rolling around the pitcher's mound.

Now, my hands enjoyed a good fist-frolic just as much as the next buncha hoodlums from any faction, I reckon. Probably more. What struck me as odd was that them ball players was a little too good at the sport of fisticuffs. Fact is, they was, in general, lots better fighters than they was ball players.

Well, I got 'em separated with the help of Billy Rohrs and E.M., and this is what I said:

"Now, I want alla you Bowery boys to stand on this line and I want alla you Four Arrows boys over on that one!"

They grumbled, picked up their hats and gloves and spurs and mugs of beer and other whatnots, and did like I was warning 'em to do. Leviticus was the only one having trouble deciding which line to stand in, and he jogged back'n'forth until I told him to come outa both those lines onaccounta he needed to be in the middle with me.

"Ahh, Roy..." he grumbled.

I had me some major decision-making to do in the next coupla days. What the heck, I thought, no need to get all frothy about this. They all gotta know things was gonna loggerhead, resulting in employments being waived. Let 'em enjoy their picnic and tomorrow we'll settle the hashes.

So all I said was 'food's on.' On this matter, it seems the cowpunchers and the ballpunchers all agreed, and watching 'em consume the spread, well, I knew we was gonna have to do something fast.

I stayed up that night working some numbers around. Fact is, I couldn't sleep. Maybe it was the cayenne in Anita's bar be que sauce, but more likely it was the problems facing Four Arrows. I walked through the house, studying my options. I had decided I was gonna hafta stand pat with Leviticus and tell him that this wasn't no place for sports like the Bulldogs and we was gonna have to give 'em their liberties, then lick our wounds, count our losses, and pull in our beltstraps to get us through the winter. We'd hafta let go the newer hands and hope the older ones would maybe work on a crop commission rather than wages, and that way ... hell, it was like starting over from '93, but what could we do?

I heard a knock at the front door and wondered who the hell else couldn't sleep. Thought maybe it was Hardy. Sometimes he'd come over when he saw the light on in my study, knowing I would need his wisdom or the company of another bending elbow.

But it wasn't Hardy. It was Billy Rohrs.

"I hope you'll pardon this intrusion," he said, holding his cap in his hand. "I thought you and I better have a talk before things get any worse than they already are."

I invited him into my study and offered him a toddy, which he turned down. He started things off with, "Look, Mr. Leckner..."

"It's after ten, call me Royal," I allowed.

"Royal, believe me, no one knows more than I the problem my team represents," he said. "I mean, I've been their skipper now for six years. Six hard, long, horrible, losing years."

With each adjective his voice got a little softer.

"Can't no one accuse you a' quittin' when you're down," I said.

"No," he replied, sorta smiling at my backsided compliment. "No, they can't. I have to tell you, when I learned we'd been traded to your boss, Mr. Perrault, well, I can't tell you how elated the boys and I were. Once we got over the sting of being traded for..." Here he took a swaller. "...cows."

"Would it make you feel better to think of them as cattle?" I asked.

He went on. "Yes, thank you. But I'm a gentleman, so good manners prevents me from speaking candidly about our previous owner, Mrs. Carter. Suffice to say, she's ... she's..."

"She's a cranked-out, money-grabbin', man-eatin' California Widder who don't know nothin' about base-ball 'cept it comes with alota men?"

He watched me rattle off my adjectives. Then he goes on saying what he come to say: "Well, I just wanted you to know we *were* a good team. Once. Went all the way to the quarter finals of the Long Island League. Oh, I know that's nothing compared to the big leagues, but we were just starting out. Had a lot of talent. We *still* do. Don't judge us by what you saw today. The boys have been so happy about coming here, well, they stayed up all night on the train celebrating. Sure, we're only bushers, but all we need is a good coach, some breaks and — well, who couldn't use a better pitcher?"

"So how do you get from the quarter finals of the Long Island League into the clutches of a female owner out on the frontier?"

"Maybe I *will* take you up on that drink," he said. Apparently, I was in for some lengthy explanations. Billy informs me they was on a road tour. Some big-spending, High Ol' Genius tycoon bought the team, thought maybe they had some potential, brought 'em out west to season 'em, and then ends up married to the Augusta divorcee.

"That woman was our downfall," Billy says, tragic-like. "Had some indiscretions with some of the players. Well, I should apologize for spreading rumors about your sister-in-law…"

"Sister-*half*-in-law," I corrected him, like that made the situation only half as bad.

He smiled a little, like he understood. "Mrs. Carter is a beautiful, charming woman, so I can't blame…" He stopped, looked at me, and then added, "Yes, I can. And I *do* blame her. Anyway, Carter found out, divorced her, and I guess decided the best way to get even with her was to make sure she got the team in the settlement. Well, we haven't had a decent game since. Made us into a laughing stock. Signed us to play the local ladies' teams or kids' teams before a hometown game. Heck," he adds, "we were nothing more than a Barnum and Bailey clown act. Worse. Clowns live for laughter. It killed us. Some of the boys took to drink. A couple just don't give a hurrah in hell. Some of the better men moved on. Had to fill in with whoever we could get." Then he finished off with, "Women sure do have mean ways of taking their revenges."

Not only did I have firsthand knowledge of that, I was always fearing for what was to come in my years ahead with E.M.

Then Billy added, "Now, a man would have made sure we were a winning team. A man would understand what goes on deep down inside. A man would have made us into something."

I knew he was right. But my loyalty was to Leviticus and his well-being and the well-being of the ranch, so all I could say was, "Billy, I'm sorry..."

He stood up and said, "I know, Royal. You can't afford to take us on. Oh, at first we had hopes that Leviticus was richer'n God, trading all those cows ... cattle ... on just a whim. And he was so..." Now here I could see he was struggling for the right word. I, of course, coulda offered him a coupla hundred. But here's the word he finally come up with: "...sincere. Yes, that's it ... sincere. But I know things are tight for you here. Well, I just thought I'd leave these with you. You might find them interesting." He pulls out some papers from his pocket and sets them before me.

"What's these?"

"This is a team roster. Tells you who is who, what position he plays. This book has all the batting and fielding averages. I'm afraid, unless you know something about base-ball, these figures won't mean much."

I took a paper outa the pile he'd handed me. "What's this?"

"Oh that," he said, his face almost melting when he saw the photograph. "That's us in Chicago. 1892. Our first year on the road. That's Adrian C. Anson, manager and captain of the White Stockings. Turn it over."

On the back of the photograph was some writing. It said,

To Billy Rohrs and the Bowery Bulldogs, a terrific team!
Lose some tempers, find some pitchers
and we'll be seeing you become
a franchise all to yourselves!
Best wishes, Cap.

"Well, thought you'd like to see that. Those were the days. Just didn't want you to think we've always been flunked-out has-beens."

He thanked me for the drink, shook my hand, and said it had been a pleasure and the picnic was really good and not to be too hard on all the men for being boys out there in that mound pile-up.

Walking around the house, turning off the lights, my head and my heart was in a heated discussion. Billy Rohrs had said some words that was high priority to me — words that I was real familiar with. Words like 'downfall,' 'laughing stock,' 'has-beens,' 'potential.' Hell, I had a real close acquaintance with all them words. Real good I knew what it was like to go up like a rocket and come down like a heavy stick.

I ended up back in my study, and E.M. was there waiting for me. She never looked better to me than when her long black hair was undone acrost her shoulders, and bare feet sticking out from under her night dress, providing me with a brief diverti-mento from my worries. She was looking over Billy's small stack of good memories.

She opened with, "About the sorriest bunch of ball players west of the Hudson, eh Roy?"

I turned off my corner lamp and said, "Uh huh."

She looked at the open ledger on my desk and said, "We're setting on the ragged edge of poor, aren't we?"

I simply closed the ledger, put it in my drawer, and answered, "Yep."

E.M. then holds up the team photograph, looks at me, and deduces, "Reckon you'd rather ride an ass than chase a horse, eh?"

"Uh-huh."

"We're keeping the Bulldogs, aren't we?"

I turned off the desk lamp and we was in the dark when I replied, "Reckon so."

PART 2

one

Now there's ol' Royal, onct again, setting on the horns of a dilemma. But ticklish spots is where, you may recall, I do my finest thinking.

I was on the front porch, attaching my spurs. Now don't get me wrong, Buck was usually a right smart safety conveyance. I hardly ever needed grapplin' irons with Buck, but after he uncorked hisself the day previous, I thought I might need to remind him of the current chain of command. Besides, I always liked the sound the rowels made against the wrrring of Buck's fiddler and the squeak of my new saddle. So there you have two more admissions — yep, Buck was jumpy enough to need a fiddler on his bit to distract him, and yep, I had recently bought me a new saddle. Some cowpokes don't like to admit to either. Anyhow, there I was on the porch and E.M. comes out, flops down on the chair next to me, and hands me the ranch books.

"All right, Royal, I have everything figured out," she announces.

I looked at her and just blinked.

"I laid awake half the night, but here it is in black and white."

"No red?" I asked, giving the books a onct over.

"Oh here, give me those books," she says, clipping her

pincher glasses to her nose. Always fascinated me when she did that. "Look, this is what we have to do: cancel the wheat order, let the newer hands go, buy hay *today* (she said it like tomorrow was gonna be too late) for the cattle, and get rid of the sheep and every horse you don't absolutely need."

I looked up from my spurs and glanced off toward the quarter-mile track I'd drug last spring. "Every horse I don't need?"

She touched my hand, kind-like, and said, "You'll get your racehorses back someday, Roy, it's just..."

"Today ain't that someday," I replied, knowing I was gonna sell my mares and studs back to the breeder down in La Grande. "Then what?"

"Well, you can see right here, we can afford stores if we don't have so much stock to winter over. That's what's going to kill us, Roy. It'll be a hard winter and that means too many mouths and not enough feed."

"Sounds like something the late Miss Weee Geee mighta come up with," I grumbled, attaching my other can opener.

'Course, bringing up the dearly departed maybe wasn't real smart of me, onaccounta E.M. glanced me a cool one and just said, "Well, Miss Weee Geee's friend, Mr. Tarot thinks..." E.M. says.

"Dammit, E.M., ain't nothing mystical about solving our current ... what's that I-talian word you use?" I buckled my left spur, making note I was getting a little fleshy 'round the middle.

"Fiasco," she said.

"Yeah. Fe-as-ko! What was I saying?"

"Royal, last night you were steeped to the nose with pity for that base-ball team. Said you thought they should maybe get their chance."

"I don't know, E.M. What the hell do we know about baseball?"

"Well," she said, unclipping her nippers and smiling at me, "I know more about human nature than Augusta does, and I'll be damned if she's going to get the better of me on this one!"

"You know, E.M., I been meaning to talk to you about her and you and this family get-even game of yours. Do I hafta remind you your daddy's setting in the State Pen for his get-evening?"

It was like she didn't even hear me, she just kept on talking. "How many times have you told me the best way to get even?"

See, here E.M. was a real master of the game. Anytime she wanted to put a idea over with me, she'd somehow get 'how many times have you told me' into the equation. That way, I learnt, she could damn well say it was my idea. You gotta watch E.M. that way. But hell, back in 1897 I was still a greenhorn to the he-she wars, and sad am I to report I onct again fell for her logic by answering, "Best way to get even is to get success."

"There! Yes! A thousand times you've told me that. You know, Royal, you really are wise beyond your years." (Note that one: two compliments for the price of one — wise *and* young all in the same breath. Damn, she was good.) She goes on, "I admit, *I'd* rather get even by using my natural born kill-ese."

"Kill-ese, E.M.?"

"You know — go for the throat."

She takes a pause and sorta blinks, sighs some, and then finishes, "But I guess that could get me in trouble. Like Daddy."

"And don't you forget it, neither," the young'n'sage saphead added.

"Oh, Royal, I won't. I could serve a lot of things, but a sentence isn't one of them," she said. "So, how can we make the team a success?"

That's E.M. for you: from staying outa jail to parlaying a base-ball team, all in one thought. She put her chin on her elbowed-up hands and set back, and I thought she was asking one of them rhetorical questions wherein the answer don't really mean that much. But I could tell by her silence and her looking at me that she was expecting some more of my wisdom.

Again, I fell for it. "Well, I suppose if we was to want the Bulldogs to succeed, we'd have to train 'em, sorta. Just like you'd train a racehorse. Get some wind into 'em. Hell, they run like they're totin' horse collars, so mosta 'em gotta lose those swag-bellies. 'Cept Billy, but he ain't a player. Then I reckon I'd see who was best doing what. You know, sorta like I had to do when Leviticus and Lou(ella) come on board. I mean, we alla us gots talents. Just a matter of locating 'em and boiling 'em down to something useful. Then I think I'd..."

Well, E.M. was far too attentive for my liking. How many times had I gone out hunting bear and come back with my foot in the trap and *her* having to hold it open whilst I pulled my boot out?

But it was too late. She had me. She had me with her facts and her figures, and I *did* my very ownself just last night tell her, in so many words, that I woulda loved to see them broke-down Bulldogs make something of theirselfs. I made a note to be careful in the future which articles of entrapment to discuss whilst lying in the arms of my wife.

So I took another look at the list of 'better dos' my wife had worked up. I looked over to her and said, "E.M., you ever think about you and me just leaving? I mean, the hell with alla this and alla them and alla everything, and you and me just hoppin' a boat to the South Seas or Europe or anywheres just to see the world and not have no cares incept who's gonna get up to let the cat out?"

E.M. smiles sorta dreamy. "Sure I do, Roy. And we will. But what about them?" She points to Leviticus and Lou(ella), who was supposed to be picking apples in the side orchard.

Don't know why E.M. ever put them two to work doing that, onaccounta it always ended up with every third apple getting a bite taken out and then their own version of this ol' school yard chestnut:

"Hey Lou! Apple core!"

"Four plus four!"

"Who you know?"

Then Heaven help whoever was watching 'cause if Lou called your name, chances are you couldn'ta outrun Levi's throw and you'd be wearing applesauce the resta the day.

I waited to make sure Levi wasn't making a apple core, then asked E.M., "What about them two?"

"Neither of us can turn our backs on them, and no matter how many 'fe-as-kos' they get us into, we owe it to them to see them through."

"But it ain't like they's kin, E.M.," I said, giving my spur rowel a spin. "What if they never grow up?"

"I don't expect they will. But that's why you're working hard as you are to groom Jay and Hardy."

"So, you ain't scart about this base-ball team draining our resources? It ain't all just to get even with Augusta?"

"Heavens no, Royal! It's the challenge, the dreams, the possibilities and…"

I pointed to the ledger and asked, "But do you think we'll be okay?"

"It'll be a hard winter."

"Gonna be hard selling my quarter horses so soon. Haven't even had a chance to get to know 'em proper."

"Well, that's for the best."

"Good thing I didn't brand 'em yet."

"I'm sure they're grateful."

She now had her arm around me.

"Still, it's gonna be hard," I said, wondering if she could tell my lips was a little pout-like.

"Going to be hard sending my new hats back to Meier and Frank's," she whispered to me.

I looked at her and asked, "You'd do that, E.M.? You'd send back all them hats to Meier and Frank's?"

"Consider it my contribution to the cause."

"And it'll be a sizable one," I said, right impressed.

Sacrifice hates to be alone. I think I was feeling a little better.

It was just then, like as though the Upstairs Ump wasn't about to let me have a minute's ease with this one, that Sully come walking up, humming. The problem with a hummer is you never get the idea trouble is coming. Sully was carrying a piece of paper. He comes up the steps, takes his hat off to the missus, and hands me the paper.

"What's this?" I ask. E.M. pinches her specs back on, sees 'Bill' at the top, and takes the paper from me.

"Bill of Lading for the lumber shipment I just picked up. All five cattle cars are loaded with it. Where do you want it?" Sully further states.

E.M. and me look at each other, and I think we mighta been starting to look a little alike, like they say folks hitched good tend to do. Our mouths drop open identical and we each state to the other, "The new barn."

Sully was looking 'round and he noticed a few new faces milling around. "Who're they?" he asked.

I grabbed the bill from E.M., who was still in a state of shock. "How much?"

"Everything," E.M. said. There at the bottom, stamped C.O.D. Paid in Full, was the amount — $499.00.

Sully sees our faces and says, "Royal, I was with you when

you ordered this wood a month ago. You *did* say to just go to the bank and arrange payment, didn't you? Royal?"

"Ain't your fault, Sully. It's all my fault."

"Think maybe it can go back?" E.M. asked, her head in her lap.

"Hell no, it can't go back! Since when does things happen that simple to Royal Leckner? Cripes, it's all cut to order and from our own damn trees, I might add!"

I looked skyward. The Trap Door Puller and me didn't communicate real often, but I did have to say, "Seems to me someone of Your caliber might find Hisself a nice little war or a famine somewheres and quit picking on us!"

There was no immediate reply, but E.M. jumps up, pulls me with her, and explains to the clouds, "He didn't mean that!" Then to me, she urges, "Spit and say you're sorry, Royal! Right now, quick, before..."

"I'll do no such thing!" says me, thereby insuring that every tragedy that was to befall us from that point onward was gonna be my fault and my fault alone ... not to mention a coupla months later McKinley had us in a nice little war with Spain, but I ain't taking the blame for that one.

Sully was watching this and he just walked away humming "The Battle Hymn of the Republic," and you know, I didn't blame him, either.

So I was onct again wrong about our list of Four Arrows assets. Add to it: five cattle cars fulla cut-to-order lumber for the new barn for the horses that I was gonna have to now sell in order to pay for the wood for the barn which, if you don't count the prepositions, was just about worthless to me now. Somehow it just didn't make much sense, and yet somehow it made perfect sense.

two

The first order of business was to unload the lumber. No matter what the second order of business was, we was gonna need them cattle cars empty. I called all my hands, yep, including the Bowery boys, and had 'em start the process. Now, to my hands, hell, work was work and it didn't much matter to them what commodities they was toting. But you should have heard the opera uproar a coupla them base-ball players set up. It was that rakish-looking one named Corky that barked the loudest.

"Ain't nuttin' in my contract about man-u-al labor. Hell, if I wanted to woik like dis, I wudda stayed in Hell's Kitchen!" Corky had one a' them deep New York accents which we didn't hear too often out west. Sweartagod, it was so thick he made *me* sound like a elocutionist.

Mosta my boys look up, being right curious about this Hell's Kitchen. 'Course, I'd heard of it, but knew all eyes was on me, so I answered, "Totin' lumber's better'n washing dishes in *anyone's* kitchen, I reckon. With or without a wage."

He dropped the board he was toting and it made a right good CLONK! on the loading platform. That sound musta been what the resta the team was waiting for, because all of a sudden mosta the ball boys was right there waiting for the other board to drop. Corky looked at me and said, "*Widout* a wage? Well, I ain't woikin' for nuttin'!"

"'Course not. I wouldn't expect any man to 'woik for nuttin'."

"All right den," he grumbles.

I now had everyone's attentions and thought, cripes, may as well be here and now as there and later that I made a few points clear.

"You boys is all, as of midnight last night, working for your chuck and your piller."

That brought about a general milling and grumbling, so I climbed me up on top of a cattle car and asked for them to hear me out.

Here's the gist of my speech, and I'm gonna hafta stand to say it just right, like I screed it back then:

"Boys, ain't no use glossin' things over. Like alla you mighta noticed, we got some extra mouths, not much hay, too many sheeps and, now, alota lumber. Don't take no Ivory League bean-counter to figure out things is about to come undone if we don't batten down our hatches and up our cinches a coupla notches."

They was all looking at each other and scratching their heads, and I figured I taken the wrong tact, so I tried another:

"Let me put it to you this way, men: We got no money, no feed for the stocks we have, and all this lumber for a barn which I have to sell my stocks in order to keep..."

They wasn't getting that one either. So I cut me the most direct trail I could think of:

"Okay, alla you boys who can work for your chuck and who can do so all winter without much gripin' or pitchin' of fits, would you please take your hats off?"

It took some doing, but mosta my boys who'd been with me a coupla years took their hats off. Jay hesitated and Hardy finally whopped him a few strokes with his hat until he like-wise doffed his.

Now the Bulldogs, they didn't a one of 'em remove their caps. They formed their own little remuda and was talking amongst theirselfs, with Billy Rohrs trying to get a word in side-wise.

"You mean you want us … professional at-el-etes to do ranch woik?" Corky asks me. "For beans an' straw beds?" Then he takes his hat off, sorta prances around and slaps his rear with his hat, and says to his fellow players, "Hey, lookit me! I'm a cow-boy, I'm a cow-boy!"

The Bulldogs thought that was pretty dang funny, but my hands did not. There was almost another fist-fest right there amongst the barn timber.

I called out, "Is that hat on or off?"

He put his hat back on with a big tug and says, "On!"

Billy then comes up and asks, "Ah, Royal, what is your intention toward *us?* I mean, surely you can see we are anything but cowboys."

Then Jay hollers, "Well, we're anything but ball players, but yesterday we sure as hell gave all you a run for your money!"

Hardy told him to slap shut. Poor ol' Hardy. No sooner had he finished nurse-maiding me when I'd first come to Four Arrows, he was now getting, as his reward, the nurse-maiding of Jay.

I again spoke out. "Now hold on, those're all good thoughts. Here's some more: We gotta cut our losses and develop our assets. I know we hold the contract on you Bulldogs and legally we gots rights that can damn well make you boys stay on. But that ain't the way we run Four Arrows and that ain't gonna be the way we run a ball team. So if any a' you boys want to pull up stakes, then ain't no one gonna get legal on you." I looked around and made sure E.M. wasn't around to hear me offer freedom for free.

I went on. "But we think with training and some good hard work, we can get you Bulldogs up to snuff, wherein we can get you back on the road and see if maybe we can't all recoup some of our funds."

"Our funds?" one of my newer cowpokes asked. "All I know, Mr. Leckner, is I was guaranteed work this winter. If you can't produce, then I gotta get back out on the grub line."

"Yeah, me too," another one comes up. "I got a sick mother in Cinci." That one came from Al. He'd been with us for five years and we all knew his momma joined the majority two or three years previous, but that line had worked so good for him, he just kept on using it.

"Well, now it ain't that there's a wantage of work. There's just a wantage of pay," I allowed.

That brought about some more grumbling and shifting of feet on the platform. "But those of you who was here '93 and '94 know I'm always good for my word. You'll get paid, it's just…"

It was then Leviticus came to join me on top the car, and those of us who knew him got a bit edgy when we saw him. He was real athletical, don't get me wrong. It's just he could be a little show-offy, and seeing him up so high and sporting that lookit-me-Roy-grin of his made us a little nervous.

Sure enough, he calls out, standing square and tall, "Lookit me, Roy!"

In a odd way, I was proud of him. It's like he was at last figuring out that he was really and truly and legally the boss of the outfit, and needed to be seen and heard as such.

I pulled him toward me where I could latch onto his belt in case he started getting dizzy up so high. Then he whispers in my ear. Now that made the Bulldogs laugh, onaccounta they had no idea that Levi was … well, like he was.

"Ooooohh," Corky calls up, pointing at us, "Lookie! Secrets!"

But here's what Leviticus whispered to me … not because

it was a secret, but because he was too shy to talk out loud to the congregation. Leviticus whispered to me, "Sell the sheeps."

I looked at him to make sure he was serious. He was dead serious. In fact, I think he was about to cry.

All I could do was put my hand on his shoulder and tell him, "Suffer Your Age, Levi, that's real straight thinkin'." His sweet grin came back. "You wanna tell 'em or shall I?" I asked him, indicating the hands.

He sorta got all beside hisself like he does onct in a while, couldn't hold it in any longer and so busted out real loud, "I'm selling the sheeps!"

Well, now you'd think he'd just announced to my cowboys that Jesus H. Christ was back on the speaking circuit and handing out celestial vouchers just for the asking.

Some of the boys shouted up that they was with us if Leviticus could sell his pets — all 225 and counting of 'em. A few more hats came off in the crowd. But I still had me several yet to convert, including all of the Bulldogs.

Then Billy Rohrs comes sorta center stage of his team and he says to 'em, "Look, boys, I know I haven't managed you the best I could. But with Mrs. Carter it's no wonder we're all run into the ground and beaten to doll rags. And wouldn't you rather be owned by someone who has pure love for the game rather than someone who just wants a … a toy?" He was circling one of his Bulldogs. "Cal?"

Cal looked down like maybe he'd been a toy for Augusta. Billy went to another man and said, "And what about you, Jack?" Then another. "Hank?"

I was thinking that sister-half-in-law of mine was quite a … team owner. No wonder the Bulldogs was in such a state of disrepair. Betwixt the toying and the jealousy factor, which naturally has to come into play, then hell … it was a wonder any of 'em was talking to each other.

Billy continued, "Besides, wintering here will give us the chance to train up to our potential! So what if we're asked to lift a little lumber, maybe work some cattle? Forget the past! Dammit, we have a future!" He then, sorta dramatical as I recall, turned towards me and took off his cap.

"I'm obliged, Billy," I said down to him. "I'm gonna tell you straight, men, it ain't gonna be no cake walk!" I'd rather they all knew what we was up against than to have a mutiny comes the tightest time. "Now, I've always held that it's better to have a poor horse than a empty stall. No offense to you eastern boys. We just gotta make do with what we got."

"Well, *some*thing's gotta go, Roy," Hardy says.

"Oh, something's gonna go, all right," I said. "First off, you regulars gotta pick your two best mounts and return the others to the remuda. Gonna sell off all we can." I hated telling 'em that. A cowpoke can work for years developing a loyal string of beasts and picking two meant most of my hands was gonna be saying fare-thee-well to some right good friends.

"That go for you too, Royal?" one of my boys asked.

"Damn rights. Even my..." Dang it, was I ever gonna get my dream to breed me my racehorses? "Even my new stud and his harem. Got a deal from the man I bought 'em from to return 'em at my buying price. Ain't none of us gonna go without a sacrifice or two."

From my vantage point, I could make out E.M. driving up in a wagon fulla what looked like hat boxes. Yes, they *was* hat boxes. She climbed out and right away recognized a storm a-brewing, and she wasn't gonna miss any more'n she already had.

"What's going on here?" she asked everyone, including me. "Royal, do you have a tailholt on Levi?"

I showed her I was holding onto his belt and then answered, "We're just seeing who's gonna stay on and stick it out with us this winter."

E.M. looks out over the crowd. Of course, the Bulldogs didn't know to look down and hem and haw a little, but my band of regulars did.

"I'm selling my sheeps, E.M.!" Leviticus hollers down, leaning a little forward knowing I had a grip his belt.

"Them with their hats off is staying on to see us through," I explained to E.M.

E.M. takes a little stroll amongst the men, then comes forward and takes off her hat, one of her favorites, I will add. Hell, even *I* liked it. She tossed it and it sailed like a dried out cow paddy — whinnnnnng — and landed on topa the wagon load of other hats.

Then she narrows her glance at the Bulldogs, who all had their caps still on, 'cepting Billy Rohrs.

"Well, if this isn't the most down-right, out-and-out ingratitude for you!" she barks.

'Course, we was well outa the way, but even Levi and me backed up a step.

Then she reaches into her purse and pulls out a handful of papers, and she holds 'em up high above her head.

"And after all I've done for you!" She picks out a Bulldog, and I knew E.M. always subscribed to the weakest-one-in-the-herd theory. "Do you know what these are?"

Well, of course, none of 'em did and she knew that, but she apparently wanted someone to guess anyhow. But not a man had the spuzz to say nothing, so E.M. goes on, "These, it may interest you to know, are confirmations of appearances on the Spring Circuit!"

"What're you getting at, Mrs. Leckner?" Billy asked.

"I've been on the telephone all morning long, and these are notes of interest from ball parks all over the Northwest."

"Interest in *us*?" Billy asked.

E.M. was still holding 'em up high and flashing 'em a little back and forth like as to get my attention. I leant down and snatched 'em away from her and looked at them.

"Yes, exhibition games," she goes on to say. "So, as you can see, we have every intention of getting you Bulldogs back to the work you were intended for! Come spring."

"So who's with us?" I called out again.

This was the final tally: alla my men who'd been with me stayed on, alla the new boys, the grub liners mostly, signed off and, insteada their wages, I gave 'em their pick of the remuda in addition to their regular mount. And the Bulldogs? Well, nine all tolled had their hats off. But it was that handsome one, the one called Corky, the one that E.M. had even eyeballed more'n a married woman oughta, who set his cap down even harder on his head and said, "I'm headin' back ta Noo Yo-ork! The resta yous losers can dig doit and play cowboy all ya want! Just pay me my back wages an' I'll leave."

"You can your pick a horse outa the remuda," I advised him.

"And what da hell am I supposed to do wid a horse?" he growled back up at me.

"Reckon you'll need it to get back to Noo Yo-ork," I further stated.

He got mad and swore some Bowery words and huffed off. Sully, who had been leaning against the puffer belly during alla this, musta said something to Corky as he stomped by, onaccounta they exchanged some mean words. As long as Sully's hat was off when he did it, I didn't care if he popped that blowhardin' blatherskite in the nose.

So we had us a plan of action and we had us a crew to put it into play. But what we didn't have was any such thing in the way of commitments from anyone on the so-called spring exhibition tour. The pieces of paper E.M. handed up to me was, I am sad to report, just the sales receipts for her wagon load of hats which she was returning to Portland.

It don't matter. Somehow we turned a mass desertion into a mass conversion. We was alla us gonna send things back — sheeps, hats, horses, and three disloyal Bulldogs. Guilt makes for fine sacrificing all around, so what the hell! As long as heaven wasn't being run by hat sellers or base-ball men or sheeps for that matter, what the hell!

three

Leviticus held up pretty damn tight as he watched his sheeps being marched into the cattle cars. I'd promised him they would go to greener pastures, and so I found a buyer down south where the land is better for sheeps anyhow. I said they'd stay wearables and not become eatables, and I know that made him feel better. But all in all, I was damn proud of him and I think my hands was too. Each one come up and said something nice to Leviticus and Lou(ella) as they checked each critter offa their tally sheet.

Looking back, I think learning to let go them sheeps, especially the youngsters, was one of the most growed-up things he'd ever done, 'cept maybe taking him a wife.

In case you forgot, when Levi and Lou come to us, they was sharing sheets anyhow, so it just seemed natural that they slip on the nooses and make it legal. 'Course, I dilly-dallied giving Levi the B'n'B Lecture, onaccounta it was hard enough for me to learn them delicate things, let alone teach 'em, and to a fully growed man. But E.M. and me agreed, before they met the preacher I would talk to Levi and she would talk to Lou, and so we set the stage shortly before they was to get hitched.

We had us a nice dinner, just the four of us, discussing wedding plans and arranging a coupla days for a honeymoon up to Walla Walla Wash. We was talking about buying some things in the way of wedding presents, and I'll be damned if it wasn't over berry pie that Lou provided us with the opener.

"Baby clothes. I need baby clothes."

Well, we'd been working with Levi all that summer to get him not to talk with his mouth full, and there went all our good work onaccounta the words 'baby clothes' made him start laughing hisself right outa his berry pie.

"You're too big for baby clothes," he said. "Roy. E.M. Lou says..."

"I heard what she said," I said, looking over the table to E.M. Our combined looks said it was time to split up the party and get our pieces said.

I took Levi into my study so's we could discuss things over a brandy (well, I had brandy), and E.M. took Lou into the kitchen so's they could chat over dish water.

Here's how my part went:

"Set down, Leviticus. There's something you should oughta know about babies and such."

He looked real concerned. Baby critters was high priority in his eyes. "Got us some good calfs this spring, huh, Roy?"

"Yep. Now, you know how them calfs come to be?"

His smile faded some. He walked to the fireplace and looked up at the big photograph some traveling picture-man had took of the Four Arrows herds drinking at the river. Levi just stared at it and said, "No." Then he looked like he was maybe counting 'em, then he turned, his face real serious-like and he asked, "No. Where?"

"A... a..." I begin. "A... well, the baby calf comes from its momma."

Then he walked to my cow-chair and ran his hand over the hide seat, almost like he was remembering something. "Where's the momma come from?"

"A... a..." I begin. "A... well, the momma calf comes from *its* momma."

"Where's *its* momma come from?"

Well, I could see where that was going ... hell, Leviticus could probably work that question right on back to the cows what wore the Eden Brand, and none of us was gonna live that long.

So then I think sometimes it's better to use a blunt edge insteada a sharp knife, so I said, "Levi, 'member you helping with calving last spring? 'Member how them babies come right outa their momma's ... their momma's..."

"Pee pees?"

"Okay," I allowed, thinking no need to get real technical here. "Anyhow, them babies grow in their mommas onaccounta the daddy bull comes around some nice spring day and he..."

"Marries the momma?"

"Okay," I again allowed. "So they gets married and then the daddy bull, he sorta takes it upon hisself to..."

"Take it upon *her* self?" he asked, his eyes wide and innocent.

'Course, I thought that was downright inspiring and I said, "Why sure, then you seen all that? Happens all the time, don't it?"

"A pair a nently," he replied. (That was his way of saying 'apparently' back then.)

"So, you think you know where babies come from now?" I asked.

He looked at me and I wasn't sure if he was gonna laugh or cry. His face was ruddy and his eyes was the brightest blue and his hair was always undone. If I had a brother, I couldn'ta loved him more.

"From cows," he concludes.

Well, maybe I wasn't quite there yet. "Only human babies come from humans, right?"

He set and thought on that. We figured Leviticus, on a good day, operated with maybe the mind of a twelve-year old, 'cept I'll be damned if sometimes he didn't harbor deep insida him a wise old man. This is what he returned me with:

"If you ain't sure, Roy, Lou's got a book." He then stood up and asked if there was more pie.

I let him go find out.

E.M. and me met in the keeping room, so-called onaccounta we always would keep it clean, which required keeping everyone outa it. It was a quiet, dark place to compare wounds.

"How'd you do?" she asked.

"Dibby, just dibby," I replied, nonchalant-like. "How's about you?"

"Wow," she said, nodding big. "I learned a lot."

"Reckon we can borrow that book?"

"I think we better."

And that was the end of the facts-of-life lesson all foura us learnt that night.

Why do you let me get side-tracked like that?

Anyhow, we said goodbye to the sheeps. The last to go was ol' Cornie-Cakes. She was the first baby born in his flock, and I know just one sheep is about as useful as a four-card flush, but I touched Levi's shoulder and smiled.

He smiled back. Him and Lou put a tether on her and pulled ol' Cornie-Cakes back to the barn, where she would live a happily-ever-after life with the goat and the milking cows and the dogs and the cats and the rodents and a coupla tame rabbits, and only God'n'Noah ever really did know what other pets them two harbored.

Onct the sheeps was off, that left me to pick out the horses I had to sell. Hell, if you thought Levi was a little weepy over his sheeps, you shoulda seen ol' Royal explaining things to his horses. But I got the job done and Buck damn near stuck his tongue out at the horses which was leaving us. I reminded him of the bucking episode not one week earlier and he sorta lowered his head, sweartagod, even heaved him a deep sigh, like maybe he wanted me to think he was feeling a little colicky. But I didn't fall for it.

Now we was getting things done. It was late September and already I could feel the winds start to change. Things can get mighty coldish in those parts and I was just as glad that our head counts was going down and at least we had us a little cash onct again in our operating accounts.

'Course, there was still the matter of what to do with alla that wood, stacked up neat as you like on our loading dock. E.M.'s crack 'bout it making good firewood for the next coupla hundred years got no smiles from me. Lou's calculations that she thought we'd been short-changed a coupla board feet didn't make me feel any better, either.

Jay thought maybe we oughta cross fence the lower pastures, onaccounta it looked so nice when it was all painted white. Hardy said he thought I could maybe sell it off to other folks, taking a loss, of course, but getting ridda it all the same.

It was Leviticus who come up with the humdinger:

"Got me a idea, Roy."

"Shoot."

"Gonna build me a barn, Roy."

It was times like that I coulda just ground my teeth to itty bits'a sand, holding in my temper and my patience. Apparently, he didn't have a firm holt of the situation. So I onct again said, "No need for another barn, Leviticus. The horses are gone. Old barn will do us fine."

He nodded like he understood. Then he comes up with, "Got me a idea, Roy."

"Oh, shoot," I said, weary-like.

"Gonna build me a *base-ball* barn, Roy."

"Now that's just downright..."

"Brilliant!" my wife insinuendoed from behind. E.M. always was a eavesdropper and I don't know why I was ever surprised when she just deposited herself into the middle of a conversation.

"A *base-ball* barn?" I asked E.M. "What's a *base-ball* barn?"

She whirled around my chair, kneeled down, and put her face to mine. "A base-ball barn is a place where out-of-shape, under-trained, over-weight and over-wrought base-ball players can train."

"Huh?"

And she gives me three words, and she sorta drug 'em all out so's I'd get the plan: "All ... winter ... long!"

Guess I was a little weary and maybe still a little sad saying goodbye onct again to my dream of breeding racehorses. So I looked at her and said, "What the hell you talking about?"

"Take the wood, build the barn, only instead of training horses in it, train Bulldogs! That's it, Royal! Leviticus, you're a genius!"

"E.M., we can't just go building..."

"Of course we can! We have the wood! We have the labor! With a base-ball barn, we can train those Bulldogs all winter long so that, come spring..."

"Royal will have his horse barn," I finished for her, seeing the light and maybe hearing some celestial poultry singing me a chorus of "Hallelujah Lilly, Papa's Been Paroled!"

She was right. Leviticus *was* a genius.

four

I pulled out the blueprints for my horse barn. Now, I'd been planning this barn since I'd been planning on breeding racehorses, which was then about three serious years. 'Course, this was *my* dream, not a Four Arrows dream, but I figured if I could get Leviticus a good, strong stable of quarter horses, we could always use the non-racers as cow ponies. Quarter horses make fine whittlin' ponies, some so good they can cut fly specks outa a pepper can, and such a pony is worth his weight in oats. 'Course, a good racer is worth his weight in gold — both of which — oats and gold — I knew Levi would be needing.

Now, when I say 'barn,' don't go thinking of the usual nice red barn you see on the Currier'n'Ives prints, feed store calendars, Farmers' Home Journals and the like. This barn I was planning was gonna also be an arena of sorts. I was gonna have a breaking corral, rows of stalls, a big tack room, and then of course a training arena. I was gonna fill the arena with sawdust and we'd have us all sorts of work to get done all winter long, weather be damned. We could break horses and train horses. Hell, I thought we could even do us some indoor rodeo work or maybe some cow-poke polo even. Betwixt the arena and the quarter-mile track south of the apple orchard, there's no telling the kinda champions ol' Royal could train.

Pretty damn bright, eh? 'Course, it never in a million years woulda occurred to me to still build me the barn, only maybe with some slight modifications and without the horses to go in it.

But that's what I had a wife and boss for.

So there we was, the committee and me — I called in Billy and Hardy so E.M. and me could announce our plans.

Billy confirmed our genius when he looked at the barn plans and heard our ideas of training the players in it all winter long.

"It's one of the reasons why some of the big East Coast teams are going south for the winter now. So they can train all winter long. It's brilliant and yet so simple."

Anita came in with some coffee and cakes, and I made note that she served Billy first and I thought damn! wouldn't that be a strange match. Anita was a sizable woman and I reckon she could snap a man the size of Billy right in half, but hell, who was I to contradict the Jack Sprat Theory? Who in their right mind would think I would end up with a fire-breathing, number-hating accountant with a family tree fulla names that read like the roster of The Thieves, Extortionists, Blackmailers, and Over-Married Sisters Society? So I wasn't gonna go throwing any stones unless romance got in the way of the work we all had to do and do fast.

"So how long do you think it would take to build this?" Billy asked. "I mean, it looks very complex."

"I reckon a solid month of hammering, onct we get our crews set up. I don't suppose any of your Bulldogs can swing a hammer better'n they can swing a bat."

"None of us talk too much about our pasts," Billy said.

Anita heard that on her way back to the kitchen, stopped, turned around, and glared at him, and so he added, "Except *me*. Nothing in my past worth hiding."

"'Course, the weather is our main factor. We've been lucky

up to now. Things turn fast around here. We gotta start this today, if not yesterday," I say.

"You know, Roy," Hardy begins, looking at the barn plans, "if your idea is to make this area here (he was pointing to the arena) this wide, then how're you going to get those beams hoisted?"

"Horse power, like always," I said. "We'll borrow some logging cables and ... the hell we will! We'll use the steam engine! The dang train! Sure, we'll build the barn where the corrals are, next to the spur!"

"Where're you going, Roy?" E.M. asked as I grabbed my hat.

"To the blacksmith!" I said, halfway out of the house.

Yes, Sully, I think. He's the one with the Engineering degree and he's the one who knows about joists and joints and fulcrums and steam power!

I went into the smithy shed and not only did I not see Sully, I also noticed his fire wasn't fired up. So I went around to the workshop in back and thought maybe I'd find him there, maybe wrapping hisself up fly for his next fishing trip. He was not there, either.

So I went to the bunkhouse for the long-termers. Now this was not your regular dice house. Asking men to stay with a outfit more'n a season or two meant you had to treat 'em more like family. So our bunkhouse was more like a big house fulla small rooms with a coupla community areas. My year-round hands each got his private room.

Sully was in his. He was packing his plunder. Didn't recognize the tune he was humming, but it shoulda been "Carry Me Back to Old Virginny."

"You going somewheres, Sully?" I inquired, thinking he was sure packing alota grip for a fishing trip.

"Time to move on, Royal," he said. Then he handed me a piece of paper.

"What's this?" I asked.

"Operating instructions for ol' Bess. I suggest you give Hardy the job. Bess is fussy sometimes. Needs a patient man."

"Sully, what you leaving for?" I asked. "I thought you was happy here."

He looked at me and said, "I'll miss the fishing."

"If it's onaccounta I can't pay you, if you got pressing financial matters, maybe we could work something out…"

"No," he said, emptying his shaving kit into his satchel.

"Now wait, Sully, it ain't just the operation of ol' Bess. What about me finding another smithy?"

"Anyone can shoe a horse."

"Not like you they can't. Besides, I need you to help with the barn."

"What barn?"

"The base-ball barn we're gonna build. I thought you being a engineer and all, you could help us…"

His face changed some. I knew that onaccounta I was watching him in the mirror over his dresser.

He asked me, "You're building a barn for that base-ball team?"

"What else can I do? I'm stuck with 'em and gotta train 'em into something I can trade on. Sure as I fatten my cattle before market, I gotta muckle up those Bulldogs before I can unload 'em."

He wadded up a shirt and tossed it onto his bed. "It's going to take more'n 'muckle' to help that team."

"Then you seen some base-ball, have you?"

As a answer, he goes over to his dresser, pulls out the bottom drawer, and empties its contents on his bed.

Here's what fell out: A coupla well-worn base-balls, a wedding cake sorta hat, a tin of pine tar, and a whole buncha little cards with pictures on 'em. I picked one up and looked at the face. Compared it to Sully. The card read, Sullivan 'Savvy McTavvy' McTavish.

"*You*?" I asked. "*You* was a base-ball player?"

"Pitcher," he said, gathering up his memorabilia and stuffing it into another grip. "Four years with Philly, two with Louisville."

I had to set on the bed to come to some conclusions. "But Sully … or Savvy … a pitcher's just what we was needin'!"

How could I be so damn plug lucky, I was thinking. All in one man I had me a regular roustabout, a jacka all trades — someone to run my train engine, someone to shoe my horses, someone to engineer me a new barn, someone to go fishing with, and someone to pitch for my base-ball team! I had me, in the immortal words of my own E.M., one helluva utility man.

"Well, Sully, you can't leave us then for sure! What the hell you leaving us for?" I think I was getting roiled. I hate deserters more'n I hate conquerors. "Cripes, Sully, I can sell some things if you got debts…"

He said, "It's not the money, Royal. It's this." And he hands me a old newspaper. Acrost the top it read 'The Sporting News.' And the headline, in the biggest print I think I'd ever seen printed was,

SAVVY McTAVVY BANNED FOR LIFE!

five

I know my mouth was probably wide open. All I could think to ask was, "For the life a' what?"

He took the article from me, looked at it sorta sad-like, like a cowpoke might gaze at a wore-out tintype of his first sweetheart. "For the life of *me*," he answered.

It was then I learnt even more about Sully. He played baseball in college, got hisself a job hurling base-balls for money, his family of uppercrusts decided that wasn't no fitting pastime for a McTavish — yes, that was his real name — and like them New York 400's is wont to do, took him outa the line-up for the family fortune, thereby bringing the count down to 399.

"I was young. Stupid. Arrogant. But hell, could I fling a ball!" he said.

"Seems damn mean, a family tossin' away their son just for doin' something he loves and for doin' it well," I spouts.

He just kept his eyes glued to the article and said, "Looks like maybe they were right."

"Is this here the demise of which you spoke when you said women and booze can downfall a man?" I asked.

"I took the blame to keep the team owner's daughter out of a scandal. But when you're drunk, broke, and in love…"

"Yep, I reckon all three a' those places are covered with thin ice," I said. And I added, "Sully, you don't hafta explain nothing to me."

"Thanks, Royal. But you can see, I need to stay as far away from base-ball as I can."

"No, I can't see. So you're banned from what? Pitching? Playing? *Dreaming* about base-ball?" Sweartagod, it made no sense to me.

He goes on to tell me he can't have nothing to do with professional base-ball ever again.

"Or else what?" I asked. "A big bat comes outa heaven and whonks you on your head? Hell, we're smack dab in the middle of nowhere. Who in the name of Aunt Sadie's corset's gonna know?"

"Corky O'Toole," Sully answered.

"That half-rate, swellheaded, fulla hisself fly swatter?" I asked. "So what?"

Sully just nodded like he'd been listening to someone else, and placed the article and the tobacco cards into his pack. "That's the price of fame," he said.

"Sully, hell, that Cork-head is probably halfway to the outshirts of Who-Cares-Ville," argues me. "Man like him's all gurgle and no guts and goin' nowhere but downhill fast."

Sully looks at me finally and replies, "Doesn't matter. From Who-Cares-Ville to New York City, my name is Mudd in base-ball. I think it's best for everyone I just leave."

"Well, it *ain't* best for everyone. It ain't best for my horses' feet, it ain't best for my barn's cross-joints, and it ain't best for ol' Bess's disposition! Hell, base-ball is new to me and I'll be damned if I'm gonna let a franchise like you leave when you can help make something outa nine men who need to have something made outa 'em." It was quite a speech and I thought it was having an effect.

"Royal, I couldn't be even vaguely *associated* with your team! Not even the lackey who empties the spittoons in the club-house."

"Sully, where the hell was this judgment made? New York? Kentucky? Timbuktu? Where?"

"It doesn't matter, Royal. Whether I deserved it or not, whether it's fair or not, banned for life is banned for life. And if that two-bit Corky recognized me, then it's just a matter of time until somebody else recognizes me."

Although I admired him for carrying out his sentence with such a fierce loyalty, it didn't make no logic to me that he hisownself slapped on the shackle and threw away the key. So I tried this slant with him: "You know, Sully, you're about as far west as a man can get. Sometimes even God forgets where we set. Out here we got us a different code."

Sully looks at me and says, "I know, I know. Look, Royal, what if we … what if *you* do get the Bulldogs in shape? What if they play some locals? What if they even win a few games? Anyone finds out I've been involved and they'll pull your ticket! You'll lose everything and then *your* name will be Mudd, right down there next to mine!"

Now you know me, I've never worried much about being called Mudd or having my tickets pulled. Maybe it comes from my years being ranahan to cowpokes. Hell, a man's gotta stab the law onct in awhile just to make sure it still works. So I told Savvy, I mean Sully, that "onct you've faced outa-sorts Indians, stood a-totterin' on the brink of financial disaster, gazed crost-eyed down the barrel of a six-shooter, settled a range war or two, and even survived a few rocky years a' marriage to a female the likes of E.M., then hell, how scardt could I be about name-callin' and ticket pullin'?" He smiled a little when I finished off my spiel with, "And besides, it's only a *game*."

He looked at me like as to say, a lot I knew about the important things in life. "It's … only … THE … game," he corrected.

"Well then, if *I* don't tell and *you* don't tell and no one else around here knows, then why the hell can't you stay on and teach us more about … THE game?" I picked up one of the base-balls and I sorta rolt it in my hand. Fit perfect.

He took the ball from me and smelt it. He closed his eyes and said, "I can still smell the grass." He then opened his eyes and looked at me. It was that same look he had given me when he suggested we fish the Little Minnie.

"Well, maybe just until you get the barn finished."

"Good enough," I said, offering him my hand so's we could shake on it.

'Course, Sully took one look at my scribbled-up plans for the base-ball barn and probably knew right then and there he was with us. He asked for some coffee, some sharpened pencils, and a buncha paper, and before the end of the day he, me, and Billy was out walking the land down by our cattle loading area where I thought the land was the flattest.

Hell, by the talk and the walking off of distances and the pointing and the brainstorming going on, you'd think we was Moses H. Pharaoh and a coupla his pyramid boys a-charting out the next Wonder-o-the-World.

By nightfall we was hammering stakes and stringing rope to lay out our perimeters.

By the following afternoon we'd set up a cement-mixing operation, and by that night we'd built the forms for the foundation.

By the following week we'd poured a foundation and commenced hammering us up a frame.

By the middle of October we'd connected the frames with walls.

By the end of October we'd got the roof up and started shingling.

By the start of November we was up to our nosehairs in snow and I had to send my hands out to break up the watering hole ice for the cattle and move the herd down lower and spread out some of our precious feed.

By the start of December we all worked inside putting the fine touches on the barn, including stringing wire for lights and even a telephone line.

By Christmas Eve, here's what you saw as you walked into the base-ball barn:

You saw strings of overhead lights dancing in the breeze. Yes, breeze. I don't care what you build a barn with, how you build a barn, or which engineers tell you it's impossible, a barn is a barn and it will always have a breeze in it. The rafters was high and I knew we'd have us a million barn swallows, maybe a committee of owls, onct the word got out. I didn't care. I always allowed as how owls was lucky. I can't recall the exact dimensions, but maybe if you was to equate our barn with a ice rink for hockey players, you'll get a idea of the size. Well, maybe one-and-a-half rinks, come to think of it. Damn it was big! Anyhow, the wood was still new and golden and crackling as it settled, and the gentle reflections the hanging lights gave was warm and honey-like. The earth was still dampish and, by then, well-trodden and clean-smelling.

Leviticus and Lou(ella) and Jay — the closest things we had to kids on the ranch — got all overboard excited about Christmas decorations, and so they hammered up small trees on the cross joints and, even though they hung upside down, it had a real crackerjack effect. Then they hammered up swags of tree boughs and holly on the railing. E.M. brought out her ribbon box, Anita made some colorful yarn things she called God's Eyes and hung them down offa the upside-down trees and, I gotta tell you, you ain't smelt Christmas till you walked into a brand new barn, with the smella new pine being punctuated by fresh-cut evergreens!

You know, to this day, when I smell wood chips I still think of that night, walking into our new base-ball barn, everything all aglow and scented with sweet memories, the decorated picnic tables set all about, E.M.'s organ set up in the corner, with one of the boys pumping out "Silent Night," and all my hands a-setting at the picnic tables, glassa cheer uplifted, awaiting my dedication speech.

six

I gotta admit, walking into the base-ball barn that first evening with everything all aglow, especially me, I was fulla hope for our futures. The only thing that had gone right for any of us that whole fall was the putting up of that barn.

I was damn proud of every man, woman, and horse that'd had a hand in it. And I intended on stating so, just as soon as I downed the glassa eggnog which Hardy had handed me on my way in.

The hands all around started to clap at me and I don't remember being so applauded in all my life. Hell, you'd think my barn was the Augean Stables all spick'n'span and I was ol' Hercules walking through for the white-glove inspection. Some boys set me up on a coupla crates so's I could speak my piece.

When they all settled back down to their seats, I cleared my throat, onaccounta my voice tends to go scrabbly when I'm needing it most.

I said, "Men, ladies (I said that down to the three ladies who was eacha 'em toting in a fresh-cooked turkey), this here sure has been a project. But no one got much hurt and I reckon we set us some sort of record in barn-raising time … leastwise for something of this magnitude."

Clappning and more egg nog.

I go on. "But more'n anything, this here barn says something about who we are and what we can do when we all work together. Now like you know, but maybe forget what with all the hammering and toting and hoisting and cement pouring, this barn is gonna be where we get you Bulldogs on the road to success."

"Say, Royal," Jay calls up at me. "this here's more'n a barn. What you reckon you gonna call this place?"

Well, I hadn't thought about that.

"Yeah," Hardy adds, "a place this high'n'mighty ought to have its own name."

"Place this big oughta have its own county!" someone called out.

That set about some opinionating back'n'forth and name suggestions.

"What say we let Leviticus name it?" I called out, hating to put him in the tight seat, but thinking he was gonna be the one having to live with it for the next hundred years.

"Don't know, Roy," he says up to me.

"Come on, Levi, what would you call a palace like this?" I prodded him.

We was all silent, onaccounta you never knew what he could come up with — might be as simpletonian as the "Not OK Corral" or as inspiring as what he did call out, the "Royal Horse Palace!" which brought on another fit of clappning.

I waited for the men to say it back'n'forth some and then got control over things. "Well, the Royal Horse Palace it is. Somebody make a sign. Now, men, we all worked hard and I'm hereby declaring next week a ranch holiday..."

I did that nowanthen — declared a ranch holiday — and it was always met with approval. Men could do pretty much what they wanted. Go hunting or fishing or into town. Hell, some boys just slept and read and whittled and wrote letters.

"But I am also declaring the 2nd of January the first day of base-ball training. So get your eating and your drinking and your smoking in whilst ye may, for come a week's time you're gonna think you're living in the poor corner a' Sparta and I ain't referring to that one in New York State."

That made some of 'em laugh.

"And don't you regulars think you're getting off the conditioning, neither. Fact is, I've been noticing how maybe we alla us can lose some poundage and work some wind into our pipes. So we may not have operating cash, we may not have much in the way of beasts to tend, but I'll tell you this, we'll have us the best damned, most beefed-up gang of men west of the..." I took a pause. "What was that river?"

All together, the Bulldogs called out, "Hudson!"

"West of the Hudson!" I called back.

We raised us a glass of nog and then I added, "Well, I reckon that about..."

"Wait, Royal!" E.M. shouts, tearing off her apron and joining me on the crates. "I have an announcement to make."

"Well, I think I pretty much covered..."

But she ignored me and said in a voice louder'n I thought she coulda mustered, "Everyone! We have a special surprise!"

I took E.M. by the arm to keep her from teetering off the boxes and asked her, suspecious-like, "What special surprise?"

She shushed me over her shoulder and continued, "Tomorrow of course is Christmas Day and I, we, have extended an invitation to the people of Idlehour to come out, celebrate our new barn, dance, eat, drink and be merry!"

That didn't meet with as much approval as she was hoping, but she quickly added the *coup de grace*, "There'll be lots of *ladies*!" That one worked and they all cheered.

"So the plan is to take ol' Bess into town, load her up, and bring back our guests. We'll all meet at the platform at 8, after breakfast, to doll up the cattle cars and maybe even decorate ol' Bess. It'll be a great party and we want you all to be there!"

We both climbed down as one of the hands went to the organ and played us a hymn, which we all sang whilst the turkeys was being carved, and I gotta tell you, it was one helluva Christmas Eve, even though in the back forty of my mind I had me a wee concern about all them Idlehour guests coming the very next day, and the cost of entertaining 'em.

Now you might need a little review of the town of Idlehour and who these folks was. First off, it had widely been held that, if it wasn't for the Four Arrows operation, there wouldn't be a town of Idlehour. Having alota cowpokes around made the building of a drinking establishment necessary, and so alongst came the Idle Hour Glass Saloon. Well, it was one hot shop early on. I recollect hearing ol' Hardy say the saloon was so rough in those days that you got a free scorpion with every shota booze. So naturally, a place as rough as that made it necessary for day conversions, and so alongst comes a church. Then they needed a store to buy hangover reliefs and Bibles, then a stable to hock a horse so's a cowpoke could start the process all over again. They just kept building all around the 'Glass, and so the town was finally founded and named, rightly so, after the saloon that started the whole ball rolling. In a way, I've come to affectionately think of Idlehour as the Town That Booze'n'Bibles Built.

Anyhow, Idlehour had grown over the years, again thanks mostly to our operation and, of course, a few other big outfits around our corner. Adding the rail spur was a big help, and even though I had a hand in that one, I didn't want to be elected mayor or nothing. 'Course, I'd myownself donated money for public improvements, but I didn't want no statue of me in the park, which even sported a cement pond.

You know that saying: so falls Wichita, so falls Wichita Falls? Well, apply it to Four Arrows and Idlehour and you know why I was a little edgy. But you know human nature. Folks will be folks. I was a little concerned that if word got out that we was onct again on shaky financial ground, townsfolks might get a tad nervous. Might find getting credit for the necessaries a little tough. Now, I'd worked real hard establishing our creditability and our credibility.

Although I thought maybe we should sorta keep to ourownselfs for the winter, we wanted 'em to think everything with us was cracking along just fine, specially where food and spirits was involved, and I wasn't thinking of them Weee Geee spirits.

seven

That night, Christmas Eve or not, was sheet-changing night, and I know that's woman's work, but E.M. trained me early and, I hafta admit, it's a damn sight easier when there's a person on both sides of the bed.

Anyhow, I was a little concerned about the costs of entertaining a whole trainload of folks from Idlehour and thought that needed a little discussion, like as though at that point I coulda done much to reverse the situation anyhow.

But to keep up appearances I asked, "How many you reckon will come from Idlehour?"

She shrugged and replied, "I don't know. Forty. Maybe fifty. Lots of folks will be other places."

"What's on the bill-o-fare?"

"Just sandwiches and beer. Nothing fancy."

"How we paying for it?"

"I'll worry about that next summer," she said, barely looking at me.

"Dammit, E.M.! You know how I feel about eating on credit! Thought we all agreed we up our..."

"...cinches," she finished for me. "I know, I know. But we really need to put on a good show tomorrow."

"Show?" I helped her with a corner and asked her to explain that.

"Well, when folks see that grand new barn and the Bulldogs, then maybe some of them might be interested in — oh,

I don't know — making a small investment in the future of the club."

"What club?" I asked, looking at her.

"Our ball club," she returned.

"It ain't no club."

"Don't be silly, they call it a club and that's what we have. A ball club."

"And you want to unload memberships on those nice, unsuspecting folks of Idlehour?"

"Those same nice folks who'd wait in line a week if Four Arrows went to auction. Smooth out that corner."

I did like she said, but kept talking to her. "So what're you thinking? Selling stock in the team?"

"Well, we need the cash."

"So you think when all them folks come out to eat our sandwiches and drink our beer, you can sell 'em on the idea of investing in our team? Sorta, 'Welcome to our house, here have a sandwich, a coupla drinks, lookit all our good fortune and oh, by the way, did you bring your pocketbook?'"

E.M. snacked out the top sheet, and boy could she make it crack! I looked over to her after it had floated down onto the bed.

"Do you have a better idea?"

"Cripes, E.M., putting on financial airs ain't our style, even when there *is* ham in our beans. I say just be honest with them folks. Tell 'em that we're … that we're…" I put the piller case under my chin and E.M. did the same, like as though I couldn't talk and stuff a piller at the same time. I don't know how them pillers get fatter every time we wash sheets. But we got 'em stuffed.

"What was I saying?" I asked.

"I don't know, something about ham'n'beans," she advised me, fluffing the pillers.

"No, I got it. I oughta just tell those townsfolks we're..."

She was right. I couldn't tell 'em we was on shaky ground. Falling Wichita Falls came again to mind. So did pride which, as I recalled, someone said also comes before a fall. But all I asked was, "What kinda sandwiches?"

"Turkey. What else?"

"There go all my leftovers," I grumbled. "Townsfolk get turkey sandwiches, bet ol' Royal gets nothing but bean sandwiches — no ham — all winter long."

E.M. looks at me and just tisks me some and says, "Poor, poor thing."

She lights a candle on the dresser and switches off the overlight. "There. Isn't that Christmasy-er?"

I'd been so concerned about sandwiches, that I'd plumb forgot it was Christmas Eve. E.M. came back to the fresh-made bed and smiled. I leant acrost the bed and pulled her down upon it. She sorta pretended she was mad, but I canoodled her some and pretty soon we was just giggling like kids.

"Oh, I forgot!" she said, jumping up and going to her dresser. "Your present!"

"E.M.! We agreed we wasn't gonna do gifts," I said, jumping up myownself and going to my dresser drawer.

We met back at the bed and handed each other our gifts.

"You go first," I said.

E.M. always loved her presents. She unwrapped not like a lot of ladies do — a flap at a time, like maybe the wrap was the best part. No, E.M. tore into it like a dog tears into a binfulla beef scraps. Now, women just know by instinct when jewelry is in the offering, I don't care how well you think you've disguised it within a wrapping. E.M. got through to the box and then she slows down and looks at me, and that's the part I love most. What's she thinking, I always wonder. She thinking black pearl necklace or mother-of-pearl cameo? Am I gonna catch the common scold for spending too much or too little?

She opened it and beheld the broach. My heart was about as big and ready to bust as a over-blowed balloon. I watched her face as she gently pulled it outa the black velvet box. It was all polished and in our candlelit bedroom looked twice as expensive as it really was ... it was like a gold bouquet, a coupla small diamonds and a few ruby chips to offset it. It was beautiful. It really was. I fell in love with it at first glance in a Portland pawnshop way last spring.

"Oh, Roy," she cooed, holding it up to the light. "Where..."

But her 'where' trailed off as she took a even closer look.

"Now don't yap me out, E.M.," I said, still fulla pride I'd kept the thing a secret for damn near nine months. "You like it?"

"I always did!" she growled, looking at me like I'd stole it offa her granny's corpse.

"Huh?"

"Damn it all to hell, Roy! You tell me how you got this broach!"

Well, so much for the spirit of Peace on Earth and Goodwill Toward Me.

"Oh hell, E.M., you know I like pawnshops," I confessed.

"Ha!" she said, circling me now with the broach in her held-out hand. "You got this from Augusta!"

"I did not!" I said, backing away from her a little.

"Well, it's hers! I ought to know! Daddy gave it to *her* when he should have given it to *me*!"

"Oh, then all's well that end's well," I said, thinking I was being a little cute.

"So just how the hell did *you* get it?"

"Sweartagod, E.M., at Eddie's Pawnshop offa Burnside when I was to Portland last March! Eddie said it was the centerpiece of a whole collection! I even have the receipt. Somewheres." And I ran to my dresser drawer and began tearing through it for the evidence.

Then she softens up some and says, "Oh, Royal, I'm sorry. Stop looking. I believe you." I turned and saw her big, sorta wicked smile coming back. "Poor, poor Gus." And she says 'Guuuus' sorta long and gurgly. "So down. So out. Pawning her jewelry. How *hor*rible."

By now E.M. was examining the broach up close and under her dresser lamp. If she'd pulled out one of them jeweler's glasses and stuck it in her eye-sock, well I wouldn'ta been surprised. She then sneezed, as I knew she would. E.M. had a way of recognizing value by running it under her fine, empirical nose and issuing a sneeze of recognition. I had stopped making fun of this talent when she sneezed smack dab perfect over the spot to sink a new water well for the kitchen.

She sorta snaps outa it and says, "Oh, I forgot. Your turn." She hands me my gift, which was, I made note, a hat box.

"You giving me your favorite hat, E.M.?" I asked, joking.

"No, that was for your birthday," she replied. "Open it!"

The ribbon was big and pink and fluffy, and when I took too much time undoing it E.M. just snapped it right off like a magician snacks the cloth from under a fully set table. I took the lid off, undid the tissue paper, and there at the bottom of the hat box was one of them new leather gloves with a baseball — all new and creamy and bright — resting inside like a big egg resting in a nest, cozy and safe-like. I pulled 'em out and smelt the leather of the glove. I tried it on my right hand, but she had to inform me you put it on your opposite-to-good hand, which I did.

"They call it a mitten," she said, "but the boys just call it a mitt. All the latest. You like it?"

"I do, E.M.," I said, throwing the ball into the mitt like I'd seen the Bulldog boys do. It was a good sound. A *good* sound.

"Look at the name of the ball," she says, taking the ball from the mitt and pointing to the trademark.

The ball was from a company called Spaulding and the brand of the ball was 'Professional Dead.' No kidding. Painted in black ink right acrost the center.

"Isn't that a laugh?" she asked.

"Yeah," I said. "A real hoot'n'holler." I sorta swallered cautious-like. You know me and omens.

"Merry Christmas, Roy," she finishes, kissing me.

"You too, E.M," I said, kissing her back. I took off my base-ball mitten and placed the ball into it, wishting to hell E.M. had washed off that base-ball name or, better yet, maybe found me one that touted 'Amateur Alive' instead.

I sure didn't want no reminders that we, alla us, might be Professionally Dead real soon.

eight

It might interest you to know, E.M. slept that night with her new broach, the one she claimed was rightfully hers, pinned to her night dress, and I slept that night with my new ball and mitt on my bed stand. It's nice to be a kid onct in awhile, and there's nothing like the glow of Christmas to make it happen.

It snowed that night and by the time I got to the window and looked out, I was alla ten years old. Christmas Day! Snow! And already the crews was outside throwing snowballs and hitching horses up to sleds.

"Get up, E.M.!" I hollered, ripping the covers off my wife. "We're expecting company!"

"Whoa!" she said, hauling the quilt back around her. "Light the damn fire!"

"Come on, E.M.," I said, pulling on my longjohns. "Merry Christmas! We're meeting everyone at the train, remember? It's snowing! You know where my sled is?"

"You gave it to Leviticus about two years ago," she said, yawning and pulling herself outa bed. "Merry Christmas."

I couldn't help myself. Snow made me a kid, and you know what? It still does. I was outa the house in nothing flat and no sooner had I opened the front door when WHAM!!! I got about sixteen snowballs in the face.

If you think cowpokes can hurl a snowball, you should oughta see how them base-ball boys could hurl one. Pretty soon, it was out-and-out war. The snow was just perfect for packing

— after you squeezed some juice out, damn, it was downright dangerous. It wasn't until E.M. came out that things got organized for the decorating of the Idlehour Christmas train.

She told who to do what, and I stood next to her, holding in my smile and looking like I was her bodyguard or something. But every man there knew there was one man and one man only who could fling a snowball at my wife, and that was me.

E.M. was holding a clipboard of notes and lists of names and things to do, and when she'd finished her task-calling, she turned to me and asked me if I would hold the clipboard for her. Like a sap I did, and she swiped a scoop of snow offa the porch railing and stuffed it down my back before I knew what hit me.

She was off and running and we alla us had another free-for-all on our way to the train.

I did not take notice of Leviticus and Lou(ella) though, figuring maybe they'd slept in some. Knowing them, they'd stayed up half the night raiding the kitchen and watching it snow and maybe even working on a Perrault heir.

We set about decorating the train, and even that work was fun.

Finally, I see Lou and Levi come walking towards us. No mistaking them two approaching, even from the distance it was.

I was waving my arms to them so they could see I saw them, and then went back to my work of stringing the red-white-and-blue bunting around the top of the cattle car.

Well, I got smashed a good one right on the back of my head and I dang near fell offa my ladder. I whipped around ready to tell my attacker that was no fair onaccounta my back was turned and I had my hands full, and on toppa that I was on toppa a ladder.

But there wasn't no one around. I went back to my work,

thinking I'll find the joker outa the corner of my eye and then I'll attack. Onct again, I got me another snowball — only this time it was smack dab on the side of my face. It hit so hard, in fact, that it was a little stingey, and now I was roiled.

"That does it!" I said. I climbed down the ladder and loaded my hands with snow and packed me a good one. But still for the lifa me, I couldn't see who the hell was sportin' after my hat. I walked to the edge of the platform and could only see Levi and Lou still off in the distance. I turned my back looking toward the fronta the train. Every man there was busy doing his task and then WHAP! for the third time I got one square in the back of my head, knocking my hat clean off.

I whirled around, just in time to see Leviticus make him a fourth snowball. I warned him to put it down — he was too far away for me to see the siza his grin — but he sorta gave a wind up.

I tossed my ball toward him with alla my might, and it fell so short that a few of the boys who was now watching me started to laugh and call me noodle-arm.

Sully came around the platform and said, "Engine's all warmed up and…"

He got the snowball this time and you shoulda seen the look of surprise on his face! It turned all red and I think the snow mighta hissed as it melted offa his mad-hot cheeks.

"Who did that?" he calls out.

I pointed to Leviticus and suggested Sully get a little closer so's he'd have a chance to hit him back.

But his maddning seemed to vanish as he looked out over the clearing and he saw the distance ol' Levi had hurled his cannonballs.

This is what he did: He stood out on the platform, called to him, and asked him to hit his hand, which he was holding up high. Levi was only too happy to accommodate him. The snowball hit his hand so hard it dang near evaporated through his fingers.

Sully brought his hand down and rubbed it. "Ow," he said sorta low-like. Then he looked at me and asked, "You teach him that?"

"No, I taught him to never aim for a unarmed man. Reckon he needs him a lesson taught again," I said, scooping up a handful of ammunition. "Let's get him."

I jumped off the loading dock, and Leviticus and Lou(ella) started to laugh and even taunt me some with a nah-nah-nahnah-nah! and then each runs a direction opposite. But Sully was still watching Leviticus run in the halfa foot of heavy-wet snow.

Well, I coulda spent all morning chasing them two and flinging snowballs, but E.M. whistles at me from the train and reminds me I'm the boss and it don't look good for the boss to be chasing the owner and his wife over hill'n'dale with a snowball.

So I went back to work. But Sully, he just stood there on the loading dock, watching Leviticus run like a colt, dripping down to scoop up snow on the fly and throwing snowballs.

"Come on, Sully, let's get ol' Bess on the road. I'm riding up with you. Come on. Give the horn a tootning and Levi will come runnin' like a jackrabbit. Gotta whole town waitin' for us."

I started walking toward the engine to pull myself aboard. The resta the hands was left to help get things going in the barn in preparation for our town holiday.

Sully tooted the whistle and, sure enough, Leviticus was right there, climbing aboard the engine. 'Course, he was looking mighty sheepish at us.

"Got you good, Royal," he said, grinning.

"So you did," I allowed.

"Got you, too," he said to Sully, laughing now. "Gonna get even, Roy?" he asked, hardly able to contain hisself.

"Yep," I allowed. I just pointed upwards and there, setting on top of the engine cab, was Jay.

Leviticus looked up and got a box fulla snow dumped on him square and fair.

He hooped and hollered and he mighta even swore, but we was alla us laughing, so he had no choice but to join us. All I saged him with was, "Live by the snowball, die by the snowball."

He didn't get it, but we alla us laughed anyhow. After all, it was Christmas and even though I didn't know it then, I'd gotten me the best present I ever coulda.

nine

Now don't go getting too comfy or too nostalgic or too Ho Ho Hoey about this Christmas train thing. Sure, folks was singing carols and being jovial, and sure, all my men had gussied up for the guests and was standing by the train, waving. And some even had picked evergreen branches as sorta flowerless bouquets for the ladies. So, if you was to paint a picture of the prettiest Christmas Day package, then I reckon that was it, chugging through the outshirts of Four Arrows land. But I know you ain't a painter, so your writ-up words'll have to do.

Nope, things looked peaceful and all, but you know the her-ricane that follows me around, and onct she arrived and introduced her guests, E.M. had put me onct again front'n-'center in the direct path of foul weather.

Here's how it happened. We got the folks unloaded and we walked over to the Palace. Oh, you shoulda heard the oohs and aahs when they saw the place! I got my back slapped and my hand pumped so much you'd think I was running for governor and these folks was all unemployed. We had us the usual town assortment … maybe 40 in all, including widders and old men who didn't have no folks to Christmas with.

And, like E.M. had promised, there was alota single ladies, most prominent and, I will add, threatening of alla 'em was those who I refer to as the Seven Vestal Burnbaums. Now these girls had passed eligible singlehood several years previous and was all pretty much setting in spinsterhood, several of 'em at their last prayers regarding marriage. They was the issuettes of our deceased banker, ol' Silas T. Burnbaum who, try as he could (and apparently he did), just couldn't throw a decent-looking or otherwise marriageable filly. Take the expression, 'she was so ugly she could make a stuffed bird squawk,' and multiply it times seven and that was the Burnbaum girls. Now I know that's not nice, but since I myownself am about as handsome as Aunt Tilly's corpse, I can throw stones and say there wasn't a parlor ornament in the whole crop.

Anyhow, their names was all innocent-sounding enough. Alphabetical-speaking, they was:

Sadie
Sally
Sarah
Sue Ann
Sue Ellen
Sue Lynn
and Verna.

The former six being one of the best representations of the female "S" names ever on record and the lattermost being maybe to break the pattern and the luck. But don't get too concerned if you lose track of which Burnbaum was which, onaccounta you'll more often'n not hear me refer to 'em collectively and not individually. I hate to break up a collection, which is why I onct thought maybe the girls might wanna go looking for one good, sturdy Mormon husband, insteada picking on seven separate men.

'Course, my hands, confirmed batch's all, stayed well away from 'em, having been there in matters of homely Burnbaum girls and E.M.'s match-making. But you shoulda seen the Precious Seven as they entered the barn. It was like they could smell a new brand of hair tonic and, like well-trained cat-hounds, they followed that scent right over to the Bulldogs. Sweartagod, faster'n lawyers to a train wreck, the girls beheld the new material and sized up the odds, and there couldn't be no fightin', onaccounta there was even two Bulldog leftovers. E.M. was probably counting *coup*. And I don't think that was all she was counting.

Remember what she said about selling subscriptions to the team? Well, what Silas T. had been unable to provide the girls in the way of pulchritude, he did make up for in financial standing. Yes, mosta his wealth was commonly known to have come by means of razzle-dazzle scalping and scoff-lawing and other banker-type chiseling, but the girls' sizable feets was all well-shod, of that you may be sure.

I reckon ol' E.M.'s plan musta been to get them Burnbaums financially and maybe even romantically concerned with our guests. I did nothing to stop it, onaccounta them Bulldogs wasn't much to behold as a lot, either. They paired up and I thought maybe E.M. was a genius until, of course, someone thought we should play us a little game of base-ball.

Now the barn wasn't the right dimensions to accommodate a regulation base-ball field. So we made a rule that if a ball hit the sides to just keep playing, and if a ball hit the back wall it was a automatical home run.

Reckon all that beer didn't help none. Well, before you could say 'Royal, you idiot!' them seven Burnbaums was hitching up their skirts, pulling 'em through their legs, and cinching 'em into their belts. 'Course, I do not need to tell you that the other two players them women enlisted was two of my very own: E.M. and Anita. Nor do I need to tell you that it wasn't gonna be a friendly mixed he-and-she game. Nope, ours was to be a b'hoys agin the g'hals.

'Course, even E.M. had no way of knowing them girls all played funsies ball at their fancy back-east boarding schools, and when I pulled E.M. outa the action after she'd struck herself out for the second time, I said, "E.M., don't these women know nothing about men? Tell 'em to be more oh-dear-me-ish and less athletical, for cryinoutloud! You don't got a chance of a snowball in hell the girls'll wanna buy stock in a team they maybe could score against! I think you got your spurs tangled, E.M."

E.M. eyeballs me, then the Burnbaums, and then the Bulldogs, and allowed, "Oh."

She looks at me for a minute and, of course, I hadn't been Mr. Elijah Marie Gallucci for long enough to recognize that look and what was gonna come after it.

"You know, Royal, you're smart as a cutting horse."

Careful, Royal, I warn myself.

"Yes, you are. I hadn't thought a think about that."

"About what?" I asked, but she pulls me away from the crowd and into the … well, I thought of it as my office, but it was already becoming the training room for the team.

Onct we're inside, E.M. says, "I never in a million years would have thought of that, Roy!" she gushes. "Now, what are you thinking?"

"You tell me what *you're* thinking," I returned, giving her my half-glance.

"No, I want to hear *your* idea."

See that right there? See how she did that? She goes from whooping hostess to marriage broker to setting on a bench, awaiting me to spill my wisdom marbles like I was Solomon, Rockerfeller, and Teddy Roosevelt all rolt into one.

And I fell for it.

"Well, I suppose if the girls thought maybe they had a bit of hope regarding how them boys might someday add up, then I can see how's they might want to invest a few coins of the realm."

We heard a crack of the bat, followed by some cheering,

and we both come to the window to witness yet another Burnbaum take her a base.

"Wouldja lookit her run," I muttered. "Which one is she?"

But E.M. wasn't there to answer my question. I watched her stomp out amongst the infield until the play all came to a halt. Before long, she had gathered all the Bulldogs and the Burnbaums about her. From where I stood watching, it looked just like this:

A line of boys facing a line of girls. E.M. in the middle pacing betwixt the two, wearing her think face, like maybe a schoolmarm setting up her spelling bee teams. Then she starts mixing the herd — moving men and women around like — you here, you stay there, you stand next to him, and you just smile. She finally had arranged two new teams on the boy-girl-boy-girl-program.

'Course, you and I both know what she was really doing was undoing martial material and matching marital material. (Them two words — martial and marital — is so close-related for a reason, you know.)

But them semantics is neither here nor there, onaccounta the upswing of that whole Christmas Day was E.M. got the Burnbaum girls to do just what she thought was my idea: Each one wrote out a sponsor chit to a player. Now, if that sounds a little off-colored to you and maybe even a little on the illegal side, well who the hell knows! I didn't know how the professional base-ball teams back east set these things up, but as far as any of us was concerned, why couldn't a gal kick in some funds to see a guy develop his potential? It ain't slavery or Montgomery Ward Marriage or nothing like that.

And I reckoned, hell, after about a billion years of men picking up the tabs on women, why not reverse the situation a little? Now, don't ask me the peculiars of the set-up. Alls I know is what I witnessed at the auction, and by the end of Christmas Day 1897, each Bulldog had him his own personal investress, each of the Seven Vestal Burnbaums had her own personal base-ball player, and I had money to buy feed for my critters.

Ho Ho Ho.

Could you pass that bottle? Thanks. Now, I reckon I'll take a nap before this gets any worse. Feel free to wander 'round, but steer clear of the kitchen come cooking time or you'll get a belly-cheat slapped around you and end up totin' a mixing bowl.

PART 3

one

Ready? Yeah, I slept some. But mostly I just tossed and wondered how the hell to begin this next part. I know how much you like a eye-popper to recommence things proper. So how's this?

It was the 2nd of January 1898. As I had warned my crews, this was the first day of training. So I go out, and damn it was cold. I woulda preferred to do book work by the fire, but no, I go out and clang the clanger, and I reckon even the bears hibernating in the hills grumbled awake.

I went back in the house for another cup of coffee and waited for my hands to get into their line ups. By the time I returned, here's who was in that line up:

Billy Rohrs and Leviticus. Yep. After all my warning, after all my planning, after everything, only two men (and their talents at great question) lined up to be counted.

I'da been steamed, but it was too dang cold.

"Billy, you round up your Bulldogs and I'll round up my hands," I said, whipping my muffler around my neck.

"Who you want me to round up, Roy?" Levi asked, hopping around to keep warm.

"You take yourself inside where it's warm and see what Anita has cooking," I said. I protected him like a daddy.

"Aw, Roy, can't I play?" he asked. "Wanna be me a baseballer, Roy."

"You come on down later, Levi. Now go as in git before you freeze." He did, but he slammed the door, grumbling, "Suffer my age!" I made note to talk to him about that.

So I go into the bunkhouse. I could tell by the remnants of a card game still spread out on the table that the boys had been up late. The spittoons wasn't emptied, there was half-smoked cigars and cigarettes poking outa ashtrays, and a heavy smella Happy New Year! hung over the room. There was still whiskey bottles half full here and there, and I picked 'em all up. This further agitated me, onaccounta they all knew our conditioning program was to commence today. So I went down the hall and started knocking on doors, calling out, "Rise'n'-shine, you sapheaded border ruffians! New year, darlin's!"

Not even a break in the snoring did I hear. So I then hollered, "Get your miserable asses outa bed!"

That always worked. You shoulda heard the swearwords. But I kept a-pulling bodies outa bunks, slapping lights on, and being loud and troublesome.

I finally got 'em all mustered in a general line in the living area. What a sight they was! They was all yawns and itching and holey longjohns and pink ugly feets and puffy eyes and hairs askew, and the smell wasn't pretty, neither. Not a likely looking buncha anythings.

This is how I got their attentions: I took the gathered up bottles of hooch and I walked to the window, opened it, and poured the whiskey out in the snow.

Well, that woke 'em up! One even tried to stop me, but I'd already had me two cups of java and so I was quicker'n he.

"Roy! What you doing that for?" Al asked. "My Momma sent me that from Cinci..."

"Men," I begin, "you are now officially offa the whiskey wagon and onto the water wagon."

"What for?"

I went to the calendar on the wall and pulled off January 1, exposing January 2nd. "This here is the first day of our training, that's what for."

It was like I'd said a joke and they was all relieved, and they just sorta 'Oh, that. Yeah, ha ha ha, I'm going back to bed. Tell us another one, Roy.' You get the idea.

"Hold it!" I called out, bringing 'em back. "Thought we agreed. Thought we was all in this together."

"In what?" Jay asked. He was downright comical-looking in his droopy, new-for-Christmas long-handles. His momma always sent him ones that was a coupla sizes too large, onaccounta she knew he'd shrink 'em down in the first wash — somewheres around April — anyhow.

"Are you boys forgettin' about our current situation? Now you may think throwin' a ball ain't got nothing to do with throwin' a calf or throwin' a leg over a saddle, but you better damn well believe one thing: them buncha Bulldogs is all we got this year in the way of barterable goods, and gettin' 'em up to snuff *is* the immediate plan."

"So how's me getting up at this hour gonna make that happen?" one man asked. It was met with a general "Yeah, explain that, Roy."

I don't think I held a finger Godwards when I quoted 'United We Stand, Divided We Fall,' but I'll bet I looked just like ol' Abe anyhow. Then I gave 'em the pitch about no wonder they was all bachelors.

I think they mighta thought they was in the Army by the way I walked the inspection line saying something to each man, alongst the line of: "Lookit that gut! You call that muscle? You look older'n Adam. And don't laugh, onaccounta *you* look older'n the serpent! Ain't it been a while since you got a letter from your sweetie?"

Then I summarized to the boys, "Besides, don't you all think it's better to wear out than rust out?"

My men started looking at each other. I finally had 'em taking note of their state of disrepair, and pretty soon they was pointing out their shortfalls to each other. Then they come silent as alla their eyes land on me. It was Hardy, onaccounta he was the senior, who comes up, pokes my middle, and asks, "Say, looks like you been putting on the tallow too, huh Roy?"

I took the kind of breath that comes from the toes, so's I could suck it in, but I made note my belt buckle didn't move much. Well, I knew I had gained me a few pounds, which is natural onct the knot gets tied and a female starts arranging your life.

I said, "Ain't my style to ask my men to do something I ain't willing to do. You boys know that about me. Ain't I always the first one in the line of fire? I'm on the program right alongst with you."

"You giving up the panther sweat too, Royal?" another boy asked.

I thought of how much I enjoyed a libation after dinner. How much a cold beer made a bean sandwich livable. How much elderberry wine Anita had put up last year. How much … but I said, "Damn rights I am."

"Well, if you can, I can," someone else came up.

Now to understand how cowpokes' natures are, this last comment takes off, expands, blows up, and the next thing you know the hands had shook hands all 'round on a bunkhouse bet on who could hold out the longest. Then Hardy goes to the cupboard and pulls out a big jar of pickled pigs' feet, empties the contents out into the garbage pail, rinses out the jar, and then sets it center stage on the table.

"What's that for?" I ask.

"Every man who slips up has to put a two bits into the kitty," Hardy said.

"Who gets the money?" Jay asked. "I always wanted to buy me a diamond mine!"

The boys laughed and then we all agreed that the money would go to a good cause to be determined later.

"So, we all in this together?" I asked. Each man, like in a jury, each said 'in'. I then go into Hardy's room and come out with a bottle of rye.

"Royal, that's my private juice…" Hardy protested.

"Tell you what," I said. "To keep us honest, we'll set Hardy's juice right here next to the money jar. That way, we'll be reminded we're all in this together. Now, you men got five minutes to report to the Palace."

They grumbled, but went off to their rooms to dress for the new program. That left me alone with the bottle of rye. I looked around, took a short shota grit, poured a shot of water back in, recorked the bottle, and then dug into my pocket and pulled out a quarter.

It was my pleasure to seed the No Juice Jar, and I will also mention that by the end of the week that bottle a' rye had miraculously turned into a bottle a' gin.

two

I took myself over to the Horse Palace. I always loved walking in the early, early morning, before the sun was risen, no matter what the season. There is something about the hills with the sun thinking about appearing, the sky gently coming pink, the stars bowing out and the day sounds bowing in. 'Course that morning it was cold as a cave at midnight and just about as light. There wasn't much of a moon left over and the air was crisp and my breath came out like dragon's puffs. My boots crunched in some leftover snow and I come to wonder how it was I got so lucky to be plunked down in such a beautiful parta the world.

I paused to look at the gigantic silhouette of the new barn. Someone had painted a sign and put it up, and I could barely make it out, but of course I knew what it said: Royal's Horse Palace, Established 1897. I pushed open the heavy doors and walked through the dark passageway that led to the arena.

I turned the corner and saw a light on in the training room and wondered who the hell was earlier'n me.

There was a fire already going in the big cast iron stove and it felt real comfy walking outa the cool and into the warm. At the back of the room the closet doors was open. I approached careful like. There, at the end of the room, gazing at hisself in a long mirror was Sully. He was dressed in one of them baseball uniforms that come with the team. He was holding a bat on his shoulder.

I watched him watch hisself in the mirror for just a moment — you know how men don't generally eavesdrop in cases such at that. Then he took a stance, like maybe he was facing a pitching foe, and then he takes a swing infronta the mirror and he watches hisself every stepa the way. Then I heard him say to hisself, "No, more hips. Use your hips." Then he took another swing and I'll tell you, his control was damn good, onaccounta I think I woulda hit everything within a twenty-foot radius, including the mirror.

It was before his third strike that I thought I oughta announce my presence. But he was so damn smooth and good to watch, I waited until he'd taken his third swing before saying, "Thought hips was only useful on a woman."

Sully didn't look surprised or embarrassed being caught by me. He just kept looking at hisself in the mirror and practicing his battning swing. He said, "You'd be amazed how handy hips are when swatting balls. See?" And he sorta took his batter's stance and swished his hips back'n'forth like he was a-rotating in the middle of a gyroscope. "Helps with the transference of weight."

He then offers me the bat and asked, "Want to try?"

"Hell, I couldn't swing nothing more'n a lariat," I said.

"No, come on. I'll show you what I mean."

"Nope, I think too mucha that new mirror," I allowed, indicating its closeness.

Sully said he saw what I meant and then put the bat down. Then he adds, "I hope you don't mind I put the uniform on."

"Looks right smart, Sully."

He touched the shirt, which was without a collar, and the neckline was open pretty low and only connected with a leather lace. He looked back at his reflection and allowed, "Been a while since I've worn the wools."

"So, can I take that as a yes, you'll help us build the team now that we built us a place to build the team in?" I helped myself to the pot of coffee on the stove.

He joined me and said, "It's so risky, Royal. If just one man recognizes me, it's..."

I looked at him closer and asked, "You forget to shave today?"

He put his hand to his face, felt his whiskers, and said, "I hate shaving on a cold morning."

"Me too, but then I ain't thinking about growing me no face lace. My missus just wouldn't allow it. I miss that about being single. A batch can go around changing his appearance and no one barks him out about it."

Sully's face broadened with a grin. "A beard, huh?" he asked.

"Another bother about wifes is they're always pushing a man to slick up some. Hell, onct E.M. even gave me some henna hair coloring and said lotsa men was turning gray a lot slower these days. Imagine that?"

"Yeah. Imagine that," Sully said. Then he grinned at me and added, "Looks like you *are* getting a little something around the temples there, Roy. I wouldn't go throwing out that henna just yet."

I heard some of the men start to lumber in and I asked Sully, "How you reckon we explain to them others how it is you're a good base-baller?"

"Tell them the truth."

"Huh?"

"Tell them I played ball in college."

"Oh. *That* truth."

One by one, the men all came into the training room. They was all grumbling about the cold and the hour and the whole idea of being pulled awake just to make their hearts pound. At the head of the room was me, Billy, and Sully. I started things off with:

"Men, this here is the first day of training."

"No it ain't, it's the first *night* of training," Jay grumbled, wrapping his arms acrost his chest. Then he takes note of Sully's uniform and asked, "Hey! How come Sully gets a uniform?"

"Well, just so's you know that Providence is smiling on us, come to find out Sully here played him some base-ball in college. So he has kindly consented to helping us with our training."

"Well, do *we* get uniforms?" Hardy asked, sounding more kid-like than Jay.

My answer was, "Stand up and touch your toes, Hardy."

He started to but could only get just a little past his knees.

"I can't," he said. "My belt's too tight."

"Does that answer your question?" I returned. "If I'm gonna ask you to touch your toes and run and jump and all, then sure as hell you ain't gonna do it in denim and belts and boots."

That was met with a general approval. Then Hardy asked, "You too, Royal? You putting on a paira them field-pajamas?"

I knew all eyes was on me and so I answered, "Sure, why not," and if ol' Buck had any opinions about it he could just go hang hisself. But betwixt you and me and that buffalo head on the wall over there, I didn't much relish the idea of getting outa my jeans and my boots and my hickory shirt. But already that 'united we stand' line was coming back to smack me in the face. So I held with the rest of the crowd.

Uniforms was handed out and they all went to the locker room and before long we was, Billy, Sully, and me, standing in the middle of the arena, surrounded by our recruits.

Billy started 'em off with some deep knee bends and then some jumper jacks, and you shoulda seen all the breath-smoke filling the place.

Then, just as we was ready to do some laps around the place, in comes two more players.

"I'm here! Roy, I'm here!" shouts Leviticus, running barefoot and holding up Lou(ella) as he ran.

Now here's a sight: Leviticus standing tall and grinning infronta me with a uniform only half cinched up. And here's the kicker: Lou(ella) was all uniformed up too, but I'da paid any man a dollar if he coulda made out who was inside all that wool uniform. I reckon being last, alls they could muster up was the extra-extra larges, and you shoulda heard the laughs and the guffaws when they come to a halt infronta me.

"Howdy, Leviticus," I said.

"Lou too," he said.

"Lou too what?"

"Lou too wants to play."

I walked to her and crouched down. I picked up the uniform sleeve, which was damn near dragging the ground, and I began to roll, roll, roll it up till her tiny hand finally appeared.

"That so, Lou? You fancy yourself a base-baller?"

I loved it when you could watch her face go all askew and she was thinking whatever wild assortment of thoughts she was accustomed to thinking. Someday they'll have a window on minds like hers and I want to be first in line to take a gander inside.

All she did was nod 'yes' and look up at Levi. But after all was said and done, after alla the screaming and the shouting was over, at the end of the day she *was* the owner's wife and damn, if she wanted to join the conditioning program, then, well, why not?

And so we began. The cowboys, the Bulldogs, the owners, the coaches, and two dogs was a part of our program. I am sad to report that, all uniformed up and all, it was damn hard to tell which one a' the boys was a Bulldog and which one was a bulldogger. That's how frayed alla our cinches was.

There was, you may be interested to know, not one single drop of horse liniment or muscle plaster anywhere to be found in alla Four Arrows land by the end of the week. And you couldn't walk from here to there without smelling some of it, all in the accompaniment of moans or groans or so deep-asleep snoring that you'd think ol' Bess and three of her cousins was roaring through the bunkhouse.

three

As we had decided, the coaches, that is me, Billy, and now Sully, would all meet in our house onct a week so's we could assess the progress of the conditioning program. Here we allowed Leviticus and Lou to set in on the session and, of course, onct Anita served us all something desserty, she'd pull up a chair and help herself to our conversations and our plans. Do I need to make mention that E.M. set at the head of the table?

That first week's end, things seemed pretty hopeless.

Now you would think that cow punchers and ball players mighta been in a better state of condition. Factually, we was alla us pretty damn pitiful.

We had called the YMCA men up to Walla Walla Wash to see if maybe they could mail us some exercise books. So, thinking we would get the latest in the art, we was disappointed to see that there was nothing much new in the set-up, jumper jack, and deep knee bend regimen. They also sent us down a Bible, which mighta been standard procedure, but I often wondered in the months what was to follow if maybe them YMCA boys didn't do a little Weee Geeeing theirownselfs.

"Tic Tac Toe, Lou! One dollar!" Levi called out whilst we was discussing the YMCA plan. Levi and Lou'd been playing that damn nine-square game for a hour, and the same ol' dollar bill had been slid back'n'forth from eacha their custodies. I was thinking maybe I'd snatch me that dollar and go make a coupla offerings to the No Juice Jar in the bunkhouse.

"Cheat!" Lou said back.

Now, how you can cheat in that game is beyond me, but they was happy, so I kept outa it.

Next came a issue a little more urgent and one that I was gonna be damn interested in seeing how those assembled would solve.

You see, what none of us had put into the equation was some 25 man-eating appetites three times a day, not to mention various snuck snacks. So I brought E.M.'s book work to my face and here's something: Lou(ella) snapped right out of her Tic Tac Toe game.

"Reckon even with that Burnbaum conglomeration we aren't gonna have the funds to see us through. The weather keeps this up, we'll need more feed by March," I said, looking at the figures. As a courtesy, I handed the book of numbers to Lou(ella) and she nodded as she added, divided, and multiplied. What a wonder she was. All in her head she comes up with a cost per man, and she woulda tossed in a cost per pound of man but E.M. kept her still.

Well, all my managers was silent. I looked at each one whilst they thought of bringing more cash into the flow. Sully was silent. Billy was silent. Anita had gone for more coffee. And Leviticus was now playing the game amongst hisself, and in the spirit of good sportsmanship losing every other game.

Then my eyes fell on my wife. I always knew when her wheels was chuggin' up-hill. She'd contort her lips — pull 'em in, then to the side, the other side, maybe take a pout. All the whilst staring at some object far off into space.

I was starting to worry, the silence had been surrounding us for so long. Then E.M. pops outa it and announces, "Daddy!"

"E.M., you know perfectly well your Daddy is…" and here I just mouthed the words, onaccounta who the hell was prouda the fact her daddy was "in … the … Big House."

"Of course, Royal! And you can say it right out loud. There are no secrets here." Then she announces to the table, and a little too casual-like I thought, "Daddy's in the Big House." And she scoots back her chair and starts to clear the plates, saying she thought we'd covered just about everything.

Billy and Sully wasn't sure how to react, but I just wanted to stay on the subject at hand and steer her away from anything to do with her daddy. Well, I knew we'd only just started, but thought why scare the hell outa my two allies, and so early in the fe-as-ko at that? So I agreed to our adjournment, knowing E.M. and me was heading for a Battle Royal about 'Daddy.'

I will mention that Sully, Billy, and I all waited for the others to leave the room before attempting to get up ourownselfs. When it was just us three, we sorta looked at each other and, being gentlemen, all said, "Go ahead, after you."

Seeing we could be waiting that one out all night, I just said, "Okay, on the counta three. One. Two. Three." At which point we each pushed our chairs away from the table and unfolded ourselfs, slow and creaky-like, to a standing position. I reckon we had, betwixt us, a whole team of Charley Horses. They limped to the door and I limped toward my bedroom.

Even the sleeping dogs around the room lifted their heads and wondered about all the ouching and ooching as we eacha us shuffled out.

four

It was no use me trying to change her mind. E.M. started packing that very night, mumbling things like, Why hadn't she thoughta this before? Her mind was made up and "Besides," she said, "the 14th is his birthday and Daddy owes me."

"He owes you a punch in that long, beautiful nose a' yours," I said, setting on topa her luggage so's she could buckle it shut. "As I recall, it was your testimony brought the jury to tears. Your daddy wants to see you like a snake wants to see a mongoose. I tell you, E.M., don't go troubling trouble till trouble troubles you."

She starts looking through her remaining hat inventory and replies, "Pish posh. Daddy will be thrilled to see me. Poor thing. In that big horrible jail with none of the comforts of home. I'll bet he didn't even get the pool cue and macasar I sent him for Christmas. The warden probably gets first pick of all the Christmas presents. Well, I'll make sure he gets his birthday present."

"Which'll be what? You asking him for money? I tell you, E.M., no wife of mine is..."

"Who said anything about asking him for money?"

"You did."

"I did no such thing." Then she holds up two hats and asks me, "Which one?"

I point to one, like as though I could tell the difference, and continued, "E.M., think I..."

Then, like as though the ghost of Miss Weee Geee had given her the insider's information on my thoughts, E.M. cuts me off and says, "Fine, then pack your things."

"What for?"

"Well, you think you should come along, right?"

"I think you oughta think this whole thing through."

She folded her arms, cocked her head, pursed her lips like this, looked real thought-like for two whole seconds, then said, "There, I thought it through again and I tell you, Royal, Daddy will be delighted. Now, I know for a fact that his firm is always needing extra help at the end of January to close out all last year's books."

Well, she lost me. I asked her to set down, and when she said she didn't have time onaccounta she had to catch a train, I just said, "E.M., it's *our* train. It ain't going nowhere till we tell it to. Now set down and tell me what you're thinking."

She didn't set down, but kept on packing and talking as she went. I was listening to her plan and I didn't take much notice it was *my* things she was now packing.

"Okay, here's my idea. I'm going to bring Howell, Powell & Gallucci the best book balancer west of the Rio."

"Lou?" I ask.

"Of course Lou. With Daddy in jail, the company is shorthanded, and who better to help out than Lou? Besides, she'll make good money for a few days and will be in seventh heaven with all those numbers." She then holds up two of my sweaters and asks which one, the blue or the brown. I say brown and she throws the blue into my valise.

"E.M., now I'm getting confused..."

"I know you are. That's why I chose the blue."

"Not the dang sweater, your dang plan!"

"Well, by me taking Lou to Portland to help out the company, I'll score a few runs with Daddy. Then I'll go down to

Salem and see Daddy for his birthday and sluice his worries some."

"You're gonna get him drunk?"

"No, Royal! I'm going to salve him over — let him know that everything with the company is just fine and for him not to worry, and then I'll ask him if he wants in on the ground floor of financing a winning base-ball team."

"Winning?"

"You don't expect me to tell him the *truth*, do you?"

"Just how many subscriptions can you sell on one team?"

She looks at me like I was dumb as a door jamb and said, "You realize, of course, he's going to just give us the money. He won't even have a dotted line for me to sign on."

"That ain't a loan, E.M.! Ain't an investment, neither. That's just downright charity and you know what I feel about charity!"

"Yes. You feel it begins at home."

"Damn rights," I agreed, before I could think better.

"And that's just where I'm going to bring the money — home!"

"E.M., I got…"

"Royal, listen, after a few days with Lou doing the company books, don't you think we'll find *something* to hold over his head?"

"Now there you go again!"

"What?"

"Blackmailing your own kin! I tell you, E.M., that's just not a real comeatable trait and I think you oughta work on fixing it!"

"Well, you have a few traits *you* might want to think about repairing."

"Like what?"

"Like how you always think you're six feet above contradictions, for starters."

"The hell I do!"

"See! There you go again!"

We glared each other some, then E.M. softens and says, "Oh now, Royal, let's not get into it."

Well, we'd botha us been filing our teeth for a fight for some time. But she was right. Maybe we best stick to the real problem at hand. But you can damn well believe we also both made us little bookmarks on the trait-mending list and was gonna, no doubt, take it up at a later date, when we had nothing better to argue about.

She looked at me like she was reading my mind. So she then pulls me to our bed, sets down next to me, and says, soft-like, "Now, Royal, I know my father. It's really not blackmail if it's all in the family. He would — he *has* — done it to me. It doesn't mean we don't love each other. Some families are built on trust, faith, and gentle guidance. Ours is built more on holding things over heads, oneupsmanships, and gentle grudges. It's all love. Just communicated a different way, that's all."

"Makes me worry for *our* family. What're we built on, E.M.?"

She puts her arm around me and says, "The best of everything."

"So what if the books're all in working order at H.P. & G.? What if you can't find anything to one-up the man for?"

"Impossible. Daddy's books are crooked as a Virginia fence."

"I don't know, E.M. Do they got a ladies' wing at that Salem Penitentiary? Seems like the moth is a-fluttering mighty close to the flame. You walk in there delivering blackmail, you just might end up in your own suite, thereby sparing the state the cost of a judge, jury, *and* transportation charges."

She gets up and swishes away that notion with, "Really, Royal, you're so dramatic. This is going to be family helping family and nothing more. Besides, I haven't seen Daddy since the sentencing and I'm worried about him."

"Yeah, I noticed you been so hope-sick for him you been tossin' and turnin' nights for the agony of it all," I said, standing up and going to my dresser drawer.

I pulled out my brown sweater, exchanged it for the blue in my valise, and asked, "So how long you reckon we'll be gone?" That wasn't resignation you heard in my voice — that was a simple cry-pax and nothing more. I was learning.

"How much money you reckon we'll need to get by?" she asked me right back.

"Three thousand, halfa which's gotta go to feed. Soon as we can order it. Before it goes sky-high."

She then makes some sorta money + feed = how long formula and says, "We better plan on a week. A day to get there, three days in Portland, two days down to Salem and back, and a day back home."

"My feed broker's gonna laugh his fool head off me coming back to buy the hay I sold him last year. Wonder how much extra he's gonna charge in the way of a 'dummy fee.'"

E.M. whirled around and laughed at my words. "Maybe we'll get lucky and find out he has Howell, Powell & Gallucci do his bookkeeping!"

"You just concentrate on one blackmail at a time, Mrs. Royal R. Leckner," I warned, stacking our baggages next to the door.

Well, she looks at me as if I was issuing my go-aheads to her, and says, "Yes, dear. Anything you say."

Whoever said eyes are the windows to the soul was never onct married, I can tell you that. I could never onct figure out E.M.'s flashy eyes at times like that. Sorta fleer-like, sorta come-hithery, sorta go-away-I'm-scheming all in the same glance.

Women.

five

So, for the third time in less than one year, I was onct again walking down the streets of Portland, Oregon. I remember thinking, for a man who hated cities as much as me, I sure was spending alota time in one.

We set up at a central hotel, then E.M. and Lou went to visit the accounting firm of Howell, Powell & Gallucci. Wisht I coulda seen the faces of Howell and Powell as they beheld ol' E.M. and her book-balancing act walk in.

So the girls set up shop and I set out to make the feed-on-credit arrangements for our Four Arrows critters, gritting my teeth the whole way.

Ernie, the feed broker, joshed me some, but tell you the truth, it wasn't the joshing that had me worried. You see, Ernie starts out with, "Well, Royal, I was wondering when you'd be in."

"You was?" I asked, setting my hat on his desk and helping myself to a cup of coffee from his stove. I loved the smell of his warehouse — rich smells of new burlap, molasses'n'oats and, of course, one of my most favorite smells in the whole wide world — hay.

"Well, we're hearing that Four Arrows is on shaky ground," he said. "Once again."

Well, he had my attention there. "That so? Who you been listening to?"

"Oh, just the gossip on the corner. Are you, Roy? Your

outfit in trouble?" Ernie asked, concerned like a good friend should oughta be.

I leant against the window and warmed my legs by his fire. "Well, damn Ernie, we started out real fine last fall. Then it all went to hell."

Ernie nodded, and he was good enough a friend to not beat no bushes. "Ever since your boss traded your herd for that ball team, eh?"

"How'd you know about that?" I asked.

He sorta indicated the area around him and said, "Big town, big ears, big mouths."

"Small minds," I allowed. "You taken to reading the chatter-mucker columns, have you?"

Ernie just opened a drawer and pulled out the very same thing and a leather-covered flask. He walked over, put some fortifier into my coffee, and handed me the paper. He'd circled the article in red pencil.

It read: "What San Francisco socialite, part-time Portland resident, and daughter of an incarcerated accountant is now free of her infamous base-ball team known as the Bowery Bulldogs? And what ex-Portland resident and daughter of an incarcerated accountant who is married to the foreman of one of the state's largest cattle ranches was seen escorting the same base-ball team out of town?" He handed me the article and added, "Of course, it doesn't mention any names."

I sipped my coffee and then handed the article back to him. "'Course not. That might be considered actual journalism."

Ernie smiled and said, "You know, we always used to get such a kick out of the goings on of the Gallucci Girls. Portland lore is filled with the battles those two sisters have had over the years. Every summer when Augusta came to visit her father — but I'm sure you already know."

I shook my head no, and I think he was gonna tell me one

of those Portland lores, but he caught my eye, wiped the smile offa his face, and just said, "Well, it's all in the archives. At the library."

He smiled big and I remembered why I liked him so much. He was long-married hisownself, real friendsome, and his smile wasn't aimed at me, it was to match my own. Yes, I was smiling. I wouldn'ta expected anything less than a wicked childhood outa my E.M. And hell, we had the rest of our lifes to open the archives. Besides, I hadn't been one-hundred percent honest with her about a few broken feathers in my wings.

So Ernie goes on to tell me he'd been awaiting my arrival for a few weeks. You know what he did? He walked me into his warehouse and pointed to stacks and stacks of baled-up hay and bagged-up feed.

"Recognize that?" he asked me.

I took me a deep inhalation and replied, "It's from Four Arrows land. Northwest section…" I took a deeper smell and added, "Third field up from the Big Minnie."

"Well, it ain't as good as the usual stuff, so I'm willing to let it go at my cost."

He handed me the already writ-up invoice and said he'd ship it out today. I told him I'd pay him soon as I could, and he said he wasn't worried. I gave him one of E.M.'s daddy's birthday cigars, which I'd stole from the box. Where E.M.'d found Cubans in Portland (on credit no less) when we was having problems with Cuba, Spain and all, I preferred not to know. But I sure as hell was gonna pocket a few for myownself.

"Tell me, Roy, that team half as bad as they say?"

I, not lying, replied him with, "Nope."

"Worse, huh?"

All I did was give him a sly one and say, "I'll send you a ticket when the Bulldogs come to play Portland."

He lit him his cigar and said, "I'll alert *The Sporting News.*"

*

Two days later I rested easier. I'd got confirmation from Hardy that the feed had arrived and that they was hauling it back to the ranch.

"So how's things going there with the training and all?" I asked.

E.M. looked at me from the setting room in our hotel. She watched me nod my head with three huh-uhs and one uh-oh whilst Hardy filled me in.

After I hung up, E.M. queried me, and I told her what Hardy had told me.

"Snow's melted."

"That's good."

"Feed arrived."

"That's good."

"Bulldogs all lost a total of 17 pounds last week."

"That's good. So why do you have that look on your face?"

"Augusta called."

E.M. whipped around like she was expecting me to draw a gun on her. 'Course, I knew what she was gonna ask and so I just fired off the answers: "Called Tuesday, again today. Anita said you was in Portland, and she's in Klamath Falls."

E.M. goes to the mirror like as though she needed two of her to figure out the right combination of Augusta's plans. She turns back around at me and orders, "Royal, call the train station and get us three tickets for Salem!"

I mighta hesitated just a second, 'cause then she bellows, "Royal, now! There's not a second to lose! We have to be on the next train!"

"What's the all-fired rush?"

"She's working her way up to Daddy, that's what!"

You shoulda seen me move.

six

Now, I don't care what you call it — calaboose, stir, clink, cooler, brig, bullpen or *husgado*. What it was was the State Penitentiary and the one in Salem, Oregon — the one my father-in-law was setting in — was a damn big one. Getting there wasn't a problem, being as how Salem is the state capital and only a coupla hours by train south of Portland. The road into the prison was even macadamed, indicating to me we musta had us a whole lota crime in Oregon. Additional, you sure couldn't miss the joint. Sweartagod, whoever the man was who owned the local cement factory musta made his fortune. The walls around the prison was at least 20 feet high all 'round, maybe higher. Wasn't no one climbing those walls to freedom.

I'd rented us a hack and we'd loaded up the presents E.M. had picked out for her father. E.M. was quick to make note how many of the Cubans had gone missing. Sweartagod, damn near called *me* a thief right there on our way to visit her father serving two to five.

Lou set in the back keeping her nose buried in the ledger books E.M. had brought for her to enjoy on the trip. And enjoy 'em she did.

I looked over to E.M. as we approached the gate and asked, "You think you oughta be totin' that jewelry, considering where we're heading?" I pointed to the Christmas broach which was pinned to her coat.

E.M.'s hand goes to it and says, "Not on your life! Just in case Daddy's in one of his ... *moods,* I might need to bring this little matter to his attention."

"If I'da known you was gonna use that broach as blackmail, I'da bought you the accordion instead," I grumbled, pulling the horse up to a halt.

The front gate was manned by a guard, a-settin' easy-goin'-like in a guard booth, feet propped up, and you shoulda seen the way E.M. took his casual words.

"What do you mean, 'Do I have special clearance?'" E.M. asked. "My father is in there and it's his birthday and I want to see him!"

"Well, lady, visiting days is Sundays. Any day other'n Sunday and you gotta have special clearance from either one of the bigwigs or the warden himself. Now it ain't Sunday, so where's your special clearance?"

I just held the reins and looked around, thinking E.M. had control of the situation, but I woulda been stupid to let the horse have a slack rein, under the circumstances.

"Well, call the warden!" she commands. Damn uppity for a woman who had a past that included a few peccadilloes that coulda landed her in the ladies' wing.

"Warden's in California. Convention."

E.M. slaps me and says, "How do you like that? The warden's off conventioneering in sunny California, leaving the lunatics to run the asylum."

All I said was I was sure someone was in charge in his absence and nicely asked the guard man if maybe we could see the next man in charge to get us our special clearances.

"He's in Nevada. Testimonial dinner," the guard answered.

"There, you see?" E.M. barked. "Just drive in, Royal."

"Lady, you go one step further and I'll shoot that horse out from infronta you. And I recognize that there nag as a

Quimby rental, and you got no idea how much value he attaches to his nags. Not to mention it's a long walk back pulling a carriage," he said, leaning back in his chair and making sure E.M. could see his rifle leaning in the corner of his guard booth.

When I turned to see how E.M. was taking this piece of information, surprised was I to see she wasn't there, but had jumped down and was tromping around the back of the carriage to speak to the guard man up close. She was toting the box of Cubans and she handed a few to the guard, bringing a gasp a' horror to my lips. Then with a great long strike of a lucifer alongst the booth, E.M. lights one for the man.

"Thanks, lady," he says, puffing the cigar to life. "But you still need special clearance."

Then she tries the pouty face routine alongst with the ghost story, "But we've come *so* far and only have today and it *is* his birthday and poor daddy isn't getting any *younger*." Now here I must admit I thought she was doing pretty damn good. She even sounded a little bit southern. But it wasn't working on the guard man.

"I heard 'em all, lady, and you could cry tears big as millstones, but it ain't gonna make no matter with me."

Good as E.M. was, he was better. I was taking some notes, of that you may be sure. I had yet to offer a vote one way or another. Lou was too far into her columns of numbers to even take notice of the situation. The guard man looked up at me and asked, "Mister, this your wife?"

I nodded. No use lying.

"Well, can't you do something about her?"

I looked down at him and just said, "Nope, stopped trying last Easter."

E.M. shoots me a mean one, takes a suspiration, and asks the guard man just who is it she has to talk to get her some of that special clearance.

He then scribbles down a telephone number.

So she asks to use his phone in his booth and he tells her that's for official business only and the closest phone for her to use would be back in Salem.

"You mean to tell me I have to go all the way back there" — she points from whence we came — "just to call over there?" She points straight ahead.

The guard man nodded and took a puff from his cigar.

E.M. looks at him like he was the riddler feller at the base of the Finx. She blows out a big breath and stands with her hands on her hips. I recognized that to be her last-ditch think pose.

So she says to me to start handing her down the presents for her daddy. "Then the least you could do is make sure my father gets these." And she starts stacking the gifts inside the booth.

"Put those back, lady. I don't get paid to be no delivery service."

"Just what is it you *do* get paid for?" she asks.

Well, even Lou was curious about that and stuck her head outa the carriage. I pushed her back in.

He made his lips into a circle, pushed out little o's of cigar smoke, and said, "I get paid to keep folks like them *in* and folks like you *out*." Then he smiles down at her and says, "Good at it, ain't I?"

E.M. stared at him, then up at me, and demanded what the hell I was gonna do about alla this. I just shrugged and said, sage-like, rules was rules.

He then lifts up a wrapped gift, shakes it a little, and starts to hand it back to my wife. He looked at the card and read aloud, "'To my sweet Daddicums.' Bet it's a hack saw." He picked up another one and shook it, read its card. "'Happy

Birthday, Enrico, from Royal.' Bet it's a..." Then he brings the package closer to his face and rereads the card. "Enrico?"

"Yes, Enrico Gallucci. My father," E.M. informs him.

"Two to five? Two counts embezzlement, two counts fraud?"

"And one count bribing a public official," E.M. adds a little too proud-like for my liking.

"He your old man?"

She nods her head and says, "Why certainly!"

Then he asked me, "He her old man?"

I nodded slow-like, onaccounta I didn't want to appear real happy about it.

Then get this: he jumps outa the booth, tosses the presents back into the carriage, and runs — yes runs — to open the gate for us!

E.M. looks up at me and takes full credit for his change in heart. "See? I told you getting in would be easy as pie." She then takes the handful of cigars back from the guard man's booth and hops back into the carriage. He damn near saluted as we passed through the gates, and I pocketed the Cubans. He pointed to the check-in area and I gotta tell you, seeing that gate close and lock behind us made me a bit edgy. Even as a visitor I hate me lockups and, besides, I wasn't sure that maybe E.M. *hadn't* wrapped up a hacksaw or two for her daddy's birthday.

I reckon the guard had telephoned the check-in man, onaccounta he was there, all smiles and howdies, by the time we tied up our horse.

You would think that not only had E.M. solved the riddle of the Finx, but she was Nefertiti, her handmaiden, and her charioteer all come to pay a call on the head mummy.

Come to find out, in a way, I was right, being as mummies is pretty much captives just like prisoners is, and being as how they get the Grateful Accommodations with all the trimmings, and being as how E.M.'s daddy, Mr. Enrico Gallucci, was better kept in that lockup than I had ever been anywhere, anytime, or for any amount of cash money or barterable goods in my whole entire life.

seven

We was escorted up some stairs, through some halls and, I gotta tell you, prison never looked this good. 'Course, I know we wasn't going through the general quarters — this was the officials' offices and such — but still, I was thinking cold, damp, hard concrete, gray and sullen walls, and black metal bars acrost thick glass windows. Instead we was walking on marble floors and going down a corridor that was warm with wood and had nice hanging lights and high windows which was almost cheery, not tragic.

From somewheres I could smell good food cooking and my stomach reacted with a small whine, onaccounta we'd only had us a small reminder of breakfast that morning.

We passed a library, an infirmary, a game room — I peeked inside and saw tables set up with checkers and chest and even a pool table, for cryinoutloud. We turned left and was welcomed with big windows which sported a view of the outside accommodations. Lou(ella) paused to take a look. Outside there was a large expanse of concrete yard with a few boys playing some handball, and there was a large field beyond. There was a buncha prison boys out on that field, and guess what they was playing? You guessed it — base-ball!

Lou stuck her nose to the window and said, "Look, Roy, base-ball in the lock-up."

"Shush," E.M. advised her. "It's not nice to call it the lock-up when you're *in* it. Someone might hear you."

"But base-ball, E.M.!" she says.

I gotta admit, I was just as amazed as Lou was. Our escorter stopped and watched us. "You got enough prisoners to play base-ball?" I asked.

"We have ten teams," he boasts. "We play all year long, weather permitting."

"Don't say?" I muttered, and we continued alongst our way. At the end of the corridor was a door which had 'Superintendent' painted on the glass. The man opened the door for us and allowed us inside.

Well, if you was thinking that prison work ain't got its upsides, then you ain't never set in a superintendent's office. That's the nice way of saying warden, by the way. No, think of the nicest bank president's office or maybe politician's office or maybe even university president's office if you want a comparison. It was downright voluptuary, and I was wondering what the dang Governor's office musta looked like!

But I didn't have much time to look around and marvel, for no sooner had we walked in than E.M. screeches out to four denim-clad men, "Daddy!" and goes flying not to the man serving the coffee, not to the man with the barber sheers, not to the man making tailor cuts on a coat-racked prison suit, but to the man setting behind the warden's desk.

There he set, looking for all I could see like he was the owner of the whole conglomeration — one Enrico In-The-Dimes Gallucci, my father-in-law and, according to the number on his shirt, prisoner number 23923. The lunatic in charge of the asylum.

"Elijah Marie!" he calls out, but not getting up onaccounta the barber was still trimming his sideburns. He outstretches his arms and E.M. flings herself around the desk, damn near causing the tailor to poke hisself with a needle, damn near spilling the coffee being poured, and damn near making her daddy fall back in his overstuffed leather chair.

"What are you doing here?" he asks. Then he looks at me and acknowledges I was there. "Royal." He leans forward and offers me a handshake. E.M. was already taking up most of his lap.

I shake hands and say, "Sir." Well, he was still my elder.

"Oh, Daddy, happy birthday!" The man who escorted us placed the gifts on the desk and took hisself back out.

"Well, darling, that's kind of you," he said. "You came all the way from … where is it you live?"

"Same place. Four Arrows."

"Oh yes, the farm. You came all the way just to wish me a happy birthday? Why, that's enchanting! Now stand up and let me look at you."

E.M. got up, stood back, and whirled around. I watched her careful like, onaccounta she didn't too often speak so high of her daddy that might justify this giddy, girl-like affect. I was assuming this was all a part of her delicate approach, so I didn't say nothing.

Lou(ella) had found a window where she could keep on watching the base-ball game. "And who is this?" he asked, pointing to her.

"Oh, don't you remember Lou(ella)?"

"Can't say as I do," he said. E.M. pulled Lou away from the base-ball game and introduced them. Lou wasn't good at introductions. She'd put her chin to her chest in shyness and wouldn't look a stranger in the eye.

"Oh, is that the one who can't stop counting things?" he asked, looking a little like maybe he didn't want to get too close to such a person.

"Yes, the same. And guess what she's been counting?"

"What?" he asked, now a look of real concern on his face.

"Oh now, E.M., we just got here," I jumped in. "Let's not talk business just yet. Why don't you let your daddy open his presents!" No use getting kicked outa that nice office before we'd had a chance to have some coffee and maybe one of the bear claws I was spying on a silver tray.

"Yes, sit down! Sit down!" he said. Ever notice, the more fulla hisself a man is he generally repeats hisself? I notice that all the time. All the time.

He dismisses his troops — the tailor, the haircutter, and the coffee server. Now we was just the three of us in the room — well, four if you count Lou, but onct she was distracted by something like a base-ball game, you may as well think of her as occupying a whole other planet somewheres.

Anyway, E.M. pulls up a chair acrost the desk from her daddy and says, "Well, it looks like you have some explaining to do."

I didn't think that was the best way to start out, being as how E.M. was setting him up for a loan. But I took a bear claw and pretended my mouth was too full to say anything.

"Do I?" he asked back, lighting one of the cigars. "Cuban?"

"Naturally. So how do you explain these diggings?" she asked, swooping the room with her arms.

Now I want to say right here, women are well — now I know you ain't hitched and so you may not know this — but women can be different around their daddies than they are with us regular recruits. Most women would deny it, but I've seen it with my own woman. So there I set, witnessing it onct again.

She goes on, "I mean the last I saw you, you were in handcuffs. And look at you now: Enrico G. Potentate! What did you do? Stage a *coup*?"

Now any other daughter asking that of any other father and we'd all think ha ha ha, nice joke, but when E.M. asks it of *her* father, well there was no look of surprise on my face when he answered, "You might say that."

Then she leans into him like maybe she didn't want me to hear this. "Is the warden *really* out of town?" Sweartagod, she said it like maybe she was thinking the warden was tied up in cell block OHG for Off His Guard.

"Of course, Elijah…"

"Daddy, please. Call me E.M. It's the least you could do after naming me that!"

"Your mother named you, not me. All right, E.M.—" then he looks over to me and asks, "What do you call her?"

Well now, there was a tough one. Since he didn't inquire under what circumstances, I just set down my coffee and replied, "I call her what she's askin' for."

Now, Enrico and I hadn't shared too many one-upsman talks, being as how he was a city man and he'd been in jail for maybe half of the time I'd been married to E.M., so it wasn't like we was good friends or nothing. I just wanted to keep my good relations with his daughter and some respect in his eyes at the same time, if that was even possible. But he got my meaning and smiled back at me and offered me a cigar, which I took and pocketed.

I don't think she wanted her daddy and me to get too chummy, onaccounta she said, "This is some coal hole, Daddy. I want to know how it is you're serving time and yet somehow land here, in the Corinthian Corner. Is this the Warden-for-a-Day program or something?"

He laughed. "Well, my dear, since I know you won't get around to whatever it is you have come here to get until I tell you, it seems I have, well, special skills which our prison system needs."

"Such as?" Sweartagod, it was like E.M. demanded to know why the hell her daddy wasn't setting in solitary confinement.

"Since the auditor took french leave to Alaska in search of gold, it seems they needed someone to go over the books," he explained, indicating a huge stack of leather-bound ledgers stacked on the floor next to his desk. Then he sorta whispers, "Seems they've misplaced some funds." He follows that with a big nod and a smile.

"Well, if that isn't sending the fox to catch the chicken thief," E.M. marveled, plopping down some papers infronta her daddy. "We've been doing some auditing ourownselfs," she adds. "You see, I knew H. P. & G. is always shorthanded around the first of the year, so Lou and I stopped in to help out some."

"How are H.and P.?" Enrico asked, looking a little like he was gonna need a belt.

"Fine, and they send their regards," E.M. said. "But Daddy, look right here." And she points to a column of figures. I leant over to try to inspect the numbers, but E.M.'s shoulder got in the way. I hated those puffy balloon sleeves and wisht she'd stop wearing 'em. "You certainly made a wicked blue fist salting this account. Just look what I found." She says it like a little girl holding up a lost puppy. Think I expected her to follow it up with a 'can I keep it?'

Well, Enrico looks over to his daughter and a big grin comes acrost his face. I could see the resemblance betwixt 'em. "You know, daughter — there, can I call you that? — you know, you do me proud. Yes, proud."

E.M. takes the papers, puts them back in her valise, and says, "Thank you, Daddy."

"I have taught you well. Yes, very well. Aren't you proud of her, Royal?"

I just nodded. Now it ain't like I didn't know E.M. had this blackmailey quality from the day I met her. She did not deceive me in any way whatsomever. So I smiled and nodded and said E.M. was a constant source of amazement to me.

"So now, why have you come here?" he asked, folding his hands in front of him sorta resigned-like.

"Well, your birthday of course."

"Oh yes. Now, what's the *real* reason?"

E.M. looked at me and asked, "Do you want to tell him or shall I?"

"This here's been your fe-as-ko from the get-go, E.M. I'm just along to see how it all turns out."

Enrico grinned at me and said, "Smart. Smart man."

"Well, did I tell you we've invested in a base-ball team?" E.M. begins.

He looks at her and stays quiet whilst he runs two plus two equals trouble around in his mind. "Augusta unloaded those Bowery boys on you, did she," he deduces.

"She told you!" E.M. hollers.

Then he starts laughing and says no one had to tell him anything. "I tell you, E.M., she's been waiting for years to get even with you." He's laughing so hard he has to pull out a sneezer to wipe his eyes.

"Laugh it up, Daddy," E.M. begins. "But this is no ordinary base-ball team."

His laugh was real deep-down and I was catching it. "So I hear!"

Well, E.M. knew perfect how to handle her daddy. She joins him laughing, and onct he was winding down she giggles one last giggle and says, her voice all baumy-like, "We need five thousand dollars to see us through the winter."

"Five?" I mouthed to E.M., who mouthed "Five!" right back. Even Lou turned from the base-ball game to see what Enrico's reaction to that would be.

He had stopped laughing and he looked at me. "Five thousand dollars?"

"If you can spare it, sir," I felt I had to add.

"Is this a joke?"

"No, Daddy. We aim to make that team into something. But that takes money and, of course, we still have Four Arrows to run."

"But you kids don't even own Four Arrows, why should you…" he stopped when he looked over to Lou(ella). Enrico wasn't setting in the warden's chair for nothing. It wasn't as though he couldn't make the best outa a bad situation or nothing. He looked at me. He looked at E.M. He looked back at Lou.

"I have the papers all drawn up," E.M. continues, going for her valise onct again, cocky as a blue jay.

Just then there was a knock on the door.

"Come," Enrico said.

The clerk man leant his head in the door and said, "Mr. G., you got another…" he paused to look behind him, then stuck his head back in and finished, "…*daughter* here to see you." Then he winked, big as life at the warden.

E.M. grabbed my hand and gripped it tight, like she'd just been told she had one minute to live.

The *daughter* gushed through the door and called out, "Daddy! Happy birthday!"

It was Lou(ella) who said it best, only she said it about the base-ball game she was watching: "Out! He's out! Strike three! Out, o-u-t, out!"

eight

Augusta damn near couldn't make it through the door what with all her puffy satins, flowing silks, sumptuous feathered hat, and fur around the collar. I reckon she musta stopped all breathing as she walked through that prison, or anywhere else she ever trodded. I stood up and my knees felt a little weak. E.M. whipped around and plastered a tooth-showing smile on her face which, I was to learn in later years, was her cornered tiger smile. Don't know who her eyes burned a deeper hole in, Augusta or me looking at Augusta.

But Augusta rushed right past us and flung herself into Enrico's arms and called out 'Daddy!' just like E.M. done. A prison man, loaded to the teeth with gifts, followed obedient-like behind her. "Happy Birthday, darling! Put those down there." The gift-toter did, Augusta flung him a quarter, and she dismissed him with her swishy hand which, I made note, made quite a rich jangling noise.

'Course, the dandy part was watching my wife watch her sister. I think she probably had calculated the worthlessness of Augusta's whim-whams before she was halfway acrost the room.

"Augusta, my dear, thank you. Did you see who is here?" Enrico said, indicating us whom she had just gushed past.

"Elijah Marie!" she says, coming at E.M. like as to hug her.

E.M. stands up and they sorta gave each other pretend little cheek kisses. She said, flat and whiskey-throated, "Hello. Gus.

Dear." That pretty much set the rhythm for the dance which was to follow.

"Oh, and hello Roy-allll," Gus said, sidling over and crooking elbows with me. She ran her gloved hand down my arm and said, "My, have you been lifting weights?"

Augusta was smiling up at me, and I want to tell you, son, she was a full load-and-a-half of Sheba she-charm and about as easy to look at as any woman I had ever laid my eyes on. I reckon I forgot my name was Royal Leckner and that my wife was standing right next to me in the middle of the superintendent's office of the state penitentiary in Salem, Oregon, U.S. of A. I sucked my stummy in some and replied, "Oh, you know ranch work, there's…'

Well, E.M. wasn't having none of my explanations. She took my other arm, sorta gave me a tug, and said, "Well, in the four years we've been married, Royal just seems to get stronger and stronger."

There was one of them ackward silences. Gus dropped her grip on my arm, Enrico just puffed his cigar and watched, and I smiled weak-like down at my wife.

"Well," Gus finally said, "you look good, too, Elijah Marie. You look so … healthy. Compared to the last time I saw you — let's see, that was when, oh yes, I remember! Portland last fall! Wasn't that fun running into each other like that? Well, you did look a little, well, pasty then."

I took a step back.

"Nothing *pasty* about me now," E.M. said, leading with the shoulder that her Christmas broach was holding up.

Augusta just eyed the broach, gave me a little glance, and said, "Yes, I can see that."

Finally, knowing his two issues like he did, Enrico stands up and says, "Well, this is just a regular family reunion. Imagine, both my girls here at once and no guns drawn."

"Don't be silly, Daddy. You can't bring guns into a prison," E.M. says, and they all laugh. I made note E.M.'s and Gus's laughs was real identical sounding.

Gus took one chair and E.M. took the other infronta their daddy's desk. I was feeling as outa place as a nun at a prize fight, even though I *had* brought in one of the major contenders. So I joined Lou at the window. I was wishing I'd been watching the game out there insteada the game inside.

"Who's winnin'?"

Lou said the boys in blue. I made note that they was alla 'em wearing blue.

"Roy, gotta go look at the crops," Lou whispered up to me.

"Sir, you got a necessary around here?" I asked Enrico.

"Certainly. Go the way you came in. It's just outside the entrance. The sign says 'Visitors Only.'"

"E.M.?" I asked.

"Yes, I think that's a good idea, Roy," E.M. said, only barely casting us a glance. "You take Lou and wait outside. This won't take long. I just want some time to visit."

I didn't need no further explanations. Lou and me was outa there fast.

After using the accommodations, Lou and me was enjoying the fresh air, and alls I did was walk a little way 'round the area and that was enough to lose sight of Lou. I then heard the hollers of the men playing their base-ball game and I knew that's where she'd wandered off to.

It was hard to tell who was who when they was all dressed identical. But it sure was nice standing behind the wire fence and watching probably the original murderer's row of base-ball. Sure beat setting in that office, which was about to ignite in a family flareup. Call me cowardly or call me cleverly — Lou and I both was breathing easier. I looked up to the office onct in a while, like as though I wasn't gonna hear the cannon fire.

There was this feller setting behind the bench where the batting boys was a-waiting their turns to swat. He had him this sorta book on his lap and a stub pencil in his mouth. Get this: every time anything happened to the batter, he jotted something down in this book. Well, it didn't take Lou long to take note of him either, and before I could advise her otherwise she had taken herself through the gate and was standing behind the book feller.

I followed, thinking we was probably already way past the trespassing point. Onct Lou got a close-up look at what the feller was writing down, it was like I'd have to pry her away with a crowbar, and considering where we was, I doubted I could find me one.

"Come on, Lou," I said, sorta pulling her away.

She didn't say nothing, but the feller with the book seemed to think it was perfectly natural that someone was looking over his shoulder and reading what he was writing. He handed it up for her to inspect. Now, I didn't think that was too smart. Then again, he didn't know the lady like I did.

Well, the closest I can describe her face, so's you get the whole picture, is just imagine the expression of a new recruit to say … God. It was like she'd been hit over the head and all prior knowledge gone out and the new knowledge — the knowledge of that Book of Numbers — all come cascading in.

I took the book and looked at it. All it said was 'Statistics.' There was just lists of numbers to names, only in this case eacha the names was a number.

I handed the book back to him and Lou just leant over and took it back. She flipped through it and seemed to be devouring the numbers like they was her last supper.

"Hey. You mind?" he finally said. "Tell your kid sister here she'll have to make her own book."

Lou looked at the batter and mumbled back his chest number. "34333." She looked down at the book and then muttered to the air, "Point 223." Then she looked at the pitcher man's number and repeated that out loud. Then down to the book. Then she looked at me and announced, "Four."

"Four what?"

Or maybe she meant 'fore!' like as in golf, for just then there was a big hit from the batter. We stopped to watch him run the bases all 'round, making him one of those homers.

Lou looked at me and said, "Told you. Four bases."

Well, anyone coulda looked at the batter-man, took in his big size, and reckoned him for a big hitter, so I didn't think nothing about it, even after three more times she'd made a number announcement and each time it came true. Even the man with the book was looking at Lou with a 'I'll be damned' look on his face.

I finally pulled Lou(ella) away, but her lips was moving fast, as she was making some more internal calculations. Well, I figured, what the hell. Leastwise she wasn't gonna count all the telegraph poles on the train ride back home like she did coming west.

I was hoping I could see E.M. signal me from the office upstairs. And in a way she did. The window flew open and out flew that box of Cuban cigars. There was some prison boys in the yard where the cigars fell and they leaped on 'em like ducks on slugs. I thought about asking for 'em back, but looking at them buscaderos, murderers, thieves, and miscellaneous gangsters, I thought it better to just keep my own graveyard and smile at the boys as they was having a guard man light 'em up.

Least I knew one thing: It was time to fetch E.M. and get us back home.

I told Lou to wait at the front doors and that we'd be right back down and on our way. She was still running numbers through her brainpan. Doubt she even heard me.

I go back upstairs and down the hall. It was real quiet. You know how a cowpoke gets nervous when it's *too* quiet? I walked faster. The office door was still closed and I figured, good, no witnesses.

Just as I got to the door, open it flies and out comes both E.M. and Augusta, each pulling the one outa the way so's the other could get through first. They was caterwawing at each other and if you only heard 'em and didn't see 'em, you'd a' thought maybe you was in the ladies' wing of the cooler and there was coupla cats with their tails caught in the cell doors.

"Hurry, Royal!" is all E.M. hollered at me as she ran down the hall, neck'n'furlined neck with her sister.

Well, I didn't like the looks of that one bit. No sir. So I went into the office and ahemed my presence to the father, who was holding his head in his hands and sorta shaking it sadly from side to side.

"Sir?" I asked. "What was that? They damn near run me down flat."

"Well, Royal, you wouldn't have been the first corpse in their wake."

"Sir?"

He grinned me a big one and said, "I imagine the only thing holding this family together is a good grudge. Here. Have a drink?"

It was the first time my father-in-law had offered me a drink, and I took it. "Aren't you gonna join me?" I asked, noting he'd poured only one.

He looked a little sad-like and said, "No, I can't. It's against the rules for inmates to imbibe."

I remembered the No Juice Jar back home and I took a quarter outa my pants pocket and put it with the four other quarters in my vest pocket.

I downed mine, then asked, "You mind telling me what the hell happened?"

He looked out his window. "There they go, all fuss'n'-feathers, my two little girls," he said, a little weary-like. "Don't worry. I'll have you driven back in the prison wagon."

I looked and, sure enough, E.M. was driving our rig back to town, going like sixty, and there right at her side was Augusta driving her own rig. I knew by the look of her ladies' carriage that wherever it was they was racing to, our hack was faster.

He looked back at me and said, weary-voiced and tire-eyed, "For twenty years I've watched those two girls one-up each other like … like … opera prima donnas. For twenty years I've tried my best to get them together. I always said half a sister is better than no sister, but *no* … they didn't see it that way. Always one doing the other better, with me in the middle! Well, today was the last straw! Here it is *my* birthday and do you think for a minute they actually came to see *me*?"

I knew he didn't want a answer, so I let him keep talking.

"Well, your wife, Elijah Marie, came in asking for five thousand dollars, pretty much saying that if I didn't give it to her she was going to blackmail me about some shortages in the Turner and Gates account."

I wondered if I should apologize, but onct again he kept on talking and I think he just needed to get it off his chest.

"So then in comes Augusta! Christ, I got hit from the North *and* the South. I feel like Richmond. Guess what *she* wants for my birthday?"

"Money?" I finally had to ask.

"That's right. Five thousand dollars. At least those girls are alike in one way — they like big, round numbers."

"Sir, we can find another way outa our fix. We can sell the rest of the herd..."

"And deprive me of the joy of seeing how this all turns out?"

"Sir?"

He then tells me what he did to his daughters. He told me he wrote 'em each a check for five thousand dollars. Then, before the ink had dried, he made mention of one tiny little fact.

"What was that?"

"That I only *had* five thousand dollars in the account I wrote their checks from," he answered, finally smiling big. "Your wife says (and he does a right good imitation of E.M.), 'But Daddy, that's i*lleeee*gal. You can't knowingly write twice over what you have in that account!' I just smiled at her and reminded her of where we are sitting. I pulled out my watch and said, 'Jockeys, mount your horses. First one to the bank wins the roses.'"

He was now setting down and laughing.

I know I shoulda been worried, but I wasn't. Enrico's laugh was real catching. I shoulda been wondering what was gonna happen to us if Augusta got her money first, but I wasn't. Pretty soon I'm laughing too. I shoulda wondered what if E.M. couldn't keep a tight holt the reins all the way back to town, but I didn't. Pretty soon we can hardly catch a breath from our laughing.

I finally get control of myself. I took my hat off the rack and could barely squeek out, "I'll send you another box of cigars, Enrico."

He looked at me, wiped his eyes with his sneezer, and said thanks, followed by, "Take my advice: Have sons."

I replied, "I'll keep it on the tapis."

"You do that, whatever a tapis is. Stay in touch. Here's my card."

He gave his nose a big blow.

"Thank you, sir," I said, wondering if he was gonna be all right after his laughing fit.

"And Royal? Don't *ever* get yourself wedged between those two women." He was starting to laugh again. "But if that happens, there's only one thing you can do."

"What's that?" I asked.

"Sit back and just enjoy the ride, son!" He barely got the words out before leaning back in his chair, twirling around, and going back into his ho ho hoing.

nine

I found Lou(ella) right where I left her. You gotta be real careful what you tell folks of her natures, onaccounta when you say 'don't move,' well, you worry they think that might even include don't breathe or blink or swaller or nothing. But since she was still digesting those numbers the base-ball man had shown her, well I knew alls I had to do was get her a pencil and a pad of paper and she would set tight all the train ride back to Portland.

Now, whether or not E.M. was gonna accompany us on that train ride seemed yet to be determined.

Like he promised, Enrico asked for a wagon to come around, and even though we was pressed into setting in the back section and looking, forlorn-like, through the barred windows, it still beat hoofing it to the train depot. Now I imagine there was other sorts of vehicles available and I always meant to ask ol' Enrico if maybe he didn't send out the Black Maria just so's I could get a taste of criminal life. You know, sorta like a wife will let her husband set in the cooler till the hangover sets in, just so's he'll think twice about celebrating every Friday night.

I recall the guard man at the front gate had a comment to make as he inspected us on the way out. "Well, well, well. Lookit you. I ain't never seen a man go in so grand and come out so low. That wife of yours turn you in?"

I was gonna tell him he oughta slap shut and smoke his

cigar, but him and the wagon driver was laughing so hard I didn't think he'd hear me anyhow.

We was deposited at the train depot and I got some leering looks as I jumped outa the back of the wagon. Some woman grabbed her children away from me onaccounta it did sorta look like I was just out on parole. I kept Lou close to me and started to look around for E.M. or, hell, even Augusta, or anyone who looked like they mighta suffered a recent run-in with either of 'em.

Folks was boarding the train and I consulted my pocket watch. We had five more minutes before the conductor was gonna call us aboard, and there was still no sign of my wife. I quick-like got Lou some paper, and I bought myself *The Sporting News* at the newsstand in the depot.

And still no E.M.

One of the first things my wife and I set up as a rule when we was first married and traveled a few times together was, if one got separated from the other — that is, if E.M. wasn't showing up — then the other, me, was supposed to go on ahead and she'd catch up eventually. I reckoned this was gonna be another time we put that rule to the test.

Lou and I went on board and I set myself in the window, looking for E.M. Folks was kissing goodbyes outside my window, but onct they moved on I could see a little ways down the road. I was hoping E.M. would remember this was a real train with a real schedule and not like ol' Bess at home, who could wait forever for her arrival.

There was some tootning of the train whistle and I even felt a little bit of a jerk. Lou looked up from her pad of paper and I had to admit, I was scardt for E.M. How did I know she wasn't lying somewheres in a heap, that carriage overturned and the horse run off? How did I know Augusta didn't run her over?

How did I know she wasn't somewheres else on the train? How did I know anything?

We started to move and I got up. I walked through the car as the car was moving out and it looked like I was walking in place.

Never so happy was I to be jerked offa my feet or to hear that familiar she-holler, "*Hold it!*"

I returned to my seat, Lou looked at me, gave me her crooked smile, and said, "Safe!" I smiled her back.

Well, the whole car knew it was E.M. who had caused our sudden stop so's she could board. And looking at her first-sight, I wasn't so sure maybe that carriage hadn't tipped over and she'd gone hindquarters over teakettle over the horse. She looked like she'd done some serious traveling since I last saw her just a coupla hours ago, and she was damn near the Wreck of the Hesperus … hat half tore off and ribbon a'dangling, dust a-smudging her fine linen coat, only wearing one glove, and her satchel hanging from her arm and looking like it had been used in a fire hall tug-o-war.

She plopped down in the seat opposite us, and a little dust come up as she did. She blew some hair offa her face and said, "Hello."

"Glad you could make it, E.M.," I said, sarcastical.

"You didn't think I would?" she asked, catching her breath.

I looked out the window and saw the horse and carriage we had rented walking hisself, head low, back to the stables, and I knew I'd be hearing from the owner. The horse was, I made note, well lathered.

"You do that to that horse?" I asked E.M., pointing to The Cardinal Sin.

"Well, it was going to be either the horse or me, and I figured you'd rather me riding back to Portland with you," she snapped. "It's a rental horse. He's used to that. Nobody treats a rental horse like they treat their own."

"E.M., a horse is a horse and shouldn't oughta be drove hard and left to wander back all lathered up..."

E.M. stood up. "Fine. I'll catch the next train."

"Where you going?"

"To cool down that horse. I'd say we're only going about twenty. I can jump for it."

Some folks in the car was laughing at that, and I was already damn embarrassed for an assortment of things my wife had gotten me into that day. But I also was learning that every time I blew in the fire, I got me a face fulla sparks for my trouble.

So I loud-whispered, "Set down, E.M.!" She did, but it was with a bit of a huff.

"Don't you even want to know what happened?" she asked.

Well, of course I did, but I also didn't want to lose control of the situation infronta all those strangers.

"Well, Daddy did the strangest thing," she begins before I could invite her to proceed. "There we were talking to Daddy..."

"He told me that part. Tell me if you cashed the damn check, E.M."

She looked at me like maybe she'd been robbed of the moral to her story. "Well, lucky for me, I knew where the closest bank was. Remember how I used to be sent out to audit Daddy's client's books?"

Remember? How could I forget? That's how E.M. and me first met — she was monitoring the Four Arrows' books.

"Well, it didn't take Gus long to figure out where I was heading, and she started following me."

"Who got there first, E.M.?"

"Well, the road was just wide enough for neck'n'neck, but I made sure she couldn't pass. Plus," she added, patting my knee, "you picked out a really good horse for us, Roy. I'm glad we didn't go with the pretty gray one."

"No, that woulda been a mistake," I grumbled.

"*Gus* picked the pretty gray one," she said, smiling like that serves her right. "You know, after being married to that polo player you'd think she'd be a better judge of horseflesh."

"Mrs. Leckner, you gonna tell me who got the damn check cashed?"

I think by now the whole car wanted to know too, onaccounta no one was talking and they was all looking at us.

E.M., in her own dramatical way, opens her valise and pulls out the biggest handful of cash I think I'd ever seen. Not only does she pull it out, but she fans it like maybe they was a deck of aces, and then she swishes her flushed face with it.

"Does that answer your question?" is all she said.

I settled back and breathed a reliever. E.M. gave the money to Lou and told her she could count it, but don't bother memorizing the serial numbers, onaccounta it was all legal cash.

I didn't want to know any more. I decided it was best not knowing if my wife had a duke-fest with her sister in some respectable Salem, Oregon bank. But somehow she'd got us the money we needed to keep Four Arrows and the team afloat until Four Arrows and the team could stay afloat on their owns.

"You know, E.M., whether your daddy made you sign a note or not, we're paying that money back, soon as we can," I said, stern-like. It still didn't set right with me borrowing money from my father-in-law, no matter how much the aristocratic codfishes he swindled it outa mighta deserved it.

She looked at me and said, "But we never pay Daddy back. It's family tradition."

"Well, that's gonna change, E.M.. You're my wife and my responsib..."

Her glare cut me off. She didn't take kindly to being called a commodity like 'a wife' and being anyone's responsibility incepting her own. But I did add, sending her my own deadlight glare, "E.M., no use arguing. I ain't gonna owe no man money — especially your father — and I don't care what prison he thinks he's running or what peanut politics he's been sent there to pay for or how much money he has to do it with!"

I reckoned all that information served the eavesdroppers right. I saw some heads come up, some backs straighten, and the lady in the seat behind ours, I made note, moved acrost the aisle, taking her toddler with her.

I then leant into E.M. and whispered, "'Sides, E.M., calling our Bulldogs a winning team is nothing but a 18-carat lie."

"They might win. A little," she whispered back.

"Might's a long way from owing five thousand dollars. You of all women oughta know you gotta catch the bear before you can sell the hide."

She sorta looked out the window and mumbled, "Guess you've never heard of commodity futures."

"Don't change the subject, E.M. *Our* futures is all that matters. You, me, Lou and Levi. Four Arrows!"

E.M. just stared at me for a spell. Then she smiled and said, why certainly, Roy, anything you say, dear, and Daddy really did look wonderful. Prison life has done him well. And she goes on to say she was proud how he handled the situation onaccounta he usually flies off the handle and derails whenever he's up against both us girls, and Gus (she said it that same low-growly way) looked like a tawdry little bijou totin' all that costume jewelry, and then she added, she hoped that when I was a daddy to daughters (I was remembering Enrico's warning to me) that I would be just like him.

I muttered that we'd just have to wait and see on that one, and I didn't say nothing about the 'tawdry little bijou' looking like a three-round knock-out to this ol' cowboy.

*

The resta the trip was uneventful as hell, and I could not have been happier than setting back and watching the countryside slick past us away from the State Pen. E.M. caught some well-needed snooze and Lou had drawn her some big boxes that looked like a giant tic-tac-toe game and was playing some numbers game amongst herself. She chatterboxed some numeric blather, without giving it a rest all the way to Portland.

Portland came into sight and we was happy to get there. E.M. had her some errands to run, and Lou and I just found the nearest hotel and settled in for the night. Now that we had the cash in hand, no use breaking our necks to get back home.

I called Four Arrows, but no one answered the telephone which, I gotta tell you, concerned me, especially since I had a telephone line strung into the Horse Palace. Well, I knew if we caught the 8 a.m. train the next day, we'd be safe back at home by nightfall, so I just relaxed.

And I'm glad I got my relaxing done whilst I could. It may interest you to know that by then I had two dollars set aside for the No Juice Jar in the bunkhouse back home. I wondered how full it would be by the time I got back, or if the boys was keeping to their water-wagon pledges. I felt a little guilty — there I was, smoking a Cuban cigar, setting in the bar in that nice Portland hotel, having a coupla fingers of rye, whilst my hands was all doing push-ups and jumper jacks and running the quarter-mile track back home.

Oh well, I was management and had me the resta the winter to lose a few pounds.

Looking back, I think if I had it to do all over again, I woulda stayed right there in that bar, in that hotel, in that town.

Or maybe, if I had a second chance to live that day over again, I woulda got on the very first train for home insteada dabbling so long in Portland. I don't know — maybe it wouldn'ta made no never-mind. Things was already too far set into play for Royal or anyone to change ol' Lady Fate and Her Affiliates.

It was dark when we finally pulled into Four Arrows, so we wasn't greeted by the usual assortment of hands, livestocks, and problems. Which ain't to say we wasn't greeted at all. For there a-standing right on our front porch was none other'n Augusta Gallucci Chumsky Wainwright Carter.

She had arrived early that same morning, under the guise of reduced circumstances. Reduced circumstances meaning she was broke, without a home, and hell-bent for vengeance.

E.M. wouldn'ta had it any other way, and I'll be damned if she didn't even hug her sister a welcome-for-as-long-as-you-want-but-if-you-even-so-much-as-*smile*-at-Royal-you're-dead hug.

So there I was, standing on the front porch, my chin somewheres around my knee, our luggages stacked around me, watching my wife put her arm around her sister, who just two days earlier she woulda run over flat, laughing whilst she did it, and saying as they walked in, "Oh, you poor, poor thing. You should have told me you were *so* desperate. Come inside. Gus."

PART 4

one

Now then, this is usually the point where you ask me for a little rundown of the situation. Since you didn't bring it up, I am forced to think one of two things: either One: you're getting used to my fe-as-kos, or Two: you've given up trying to figure 'em out. Either way, it's a sorry state for botha us. And whether you need it or not, I do, and so here's the hand-o-cards that'd been dealt by the first of February 1898. Check off your list and see if I miss anything:

#1: Four Arrows was the first ever ranch to hold in its assets a base-ball team, called — and if you think about it, the name fit — the Bowery Bulldogs.

#2: We had about one dozen hands getting in shape, and even though I chided my wranglers into it, I had a much deeper reason for doing so. I was planning on picking the best, most fit men for the base-ball team, and if that meant a few Bowery boys was gonna get dropped off the roster, then so-be-it-said-Moses. Might be some of 'em could maybe bulldog a dogie better'n they could someone at first base. Anyhow, bulldogging is honest work and wasn't anyone gonna get their waivers in the dead a' winter.

#3: We had us funds to winter us through, which was owed back to my father-in-law, signed note or not. But betwixt E.M.'s nose for bargains and Lou(ella)'s memory and my stingy nature, I reckon five grand was gonna do us fine.

#4: I had me Sullivan 'Savvy McTavvy' McGinty, a banned-for-life player who, thanks to a big red bushy beard and some henna rinse, didn't look nothing like he did when he first come to Four Arrows to be our Director of Transportation.

#5: Love was in full bloom in the middle a' winter, in the form of my cook, Anita, and the base-ball manager, Billy Rohrs, and it was gonna take a heavy hand to keep the two love-strucks in the kitchen and in the training room, preferably Billy in the latter and Anita in the former.

#6: I had the Seven Vestal Burnbaums each having sponsored a ball player, and even though the girls was a good team an' all, I knew to keep things running steady I had to keep 'em off the grounds as much as I could, even though they was at their last hopes in the marriage department. I was dreading the spring when ol' Mother Hope and Her Affiliates springs eternal.

And of course, number 7 was the kicker:

#7: I had me a sister-half-in-law who was body'n'britches *the* feminine conglomeration, now roosting under the same roof as my wife, and onct alla my boys got a gander at her, well, it might make that whole Helen of Troy episode look more like just a cross-town rivalry.

Now I'm no crepe-hanger. You know that about me by now. We did have us a ace up our sleeves, and it was:

#8: We had us Leviticus, who never met a round object he didn't wanna hurl.

Now, you know I'm a pretty damned easy-going sonuvagun. I just sorta like to ride the trail, see where it leads, let my horse have his head, and enjoy me some scenery alongst the way. And I think I'd been pretty 'let's see' about the whole Bulldog situation. I wasn't standing down from my post, I was just waiting for alla E.M.'s shoes to drop.

I didn't have to wait very long. We'd been home maybe fifteen minutes when E.M. and Gus sets down at the dining room table to have tea. 'Course, I knew what they had to say was gonna be just betwixt the two of 'em, but I sure was curious and I'll tell you onct again, I can hear damn good 'round corners. So, since I thought I'd polish my boots and since the supplies was in the pantry and since the pantry was within tongueshot of the dining room and since I'd got yelped at for polishing my boots in the bedroom onct and since there was a chair in the pantry, that's where I set.

Their tea-talk commenced and I could hear just fine, even with the door half closed.

"Well," E.M. started off, "you can imagine my surprise to find you here, Gus."

"Well, you know us Galluccis. When we decide to go, we just go go go," Gus replied.

That was true, I recalled.

"Yes, that we do. And when did you decide to 'go go go' here?" E.M. continued.

"Well, I missed the train out of Salem, but didn't stop over in Portland. I thought I'd see if I could catch up with you. I got to … what's that charming little town … Whittleaway?"

"Idlehour."

"Oh yes, I knew it was something about doing nothing. Anyway, dear, I phoned out here and since there was no answer I just came on out. I've only been here since this morning."

"Sugar?"

"Four."

"Cream?"

"Oh no, I'm watching my waist."

"Oh, you don't have anything to worry about, Gus. About your waist, I mean."

"Thank you, Elijah. Either do you."

I sure was tempted to peek around the door to see the kinda smiles the girls had whilst they was swapping their lies and damning with faint flattery.

There was a silence. Alls I could hear was tea-stirring and cups and saucers clinking. Finally, Gus said, "Isn't it funny, how our paths crisscross? You bursting in on me in Portland and then me bursting in on you in Salem. You'd think we had mystical powers, the way we somehow attract the same things, ideas…"

"Men?" E.M. asked.

Uh-oh, I'm thinking. Here it comes.

"Why no, E.M., I think we're night and day about men," Gus replied.

"Then just make sure you keep your P.M. away from my A.M., Gus. Deal?"

"Elijah … you're my *sister.*"

More tea-sipping, spoon-stirring and, I'll bet you that autographed photo of Teddy Roosevelt over there, lotsa eye-glaring over their cups.

"So tell me, Gus," E.M. then said, "just how reduced *are* your circumstances? I mean, I don't want to pry: [like hell], but from what I recall from your three marriages, you were set pretty high up in the stirrups."

Gus laughs a little and says, "Oh, E.M., I just love how you've adopted all those cute little down-homey expressions. Imagine, me high up in the stirrups when you know perfectly well how much I hate horses."

E.M. said, "Oh, Gus, it's so nice to see you can still laugh after what you've been through."

There was a silence. Then Gus said, "Oh yes. Well, no use crying over spilled milk."

"Cookie?"

"Thank you."

"So, Gus, how will you recover? I mean, fair is fair and I *did* handle that horse better than you to cash that check."

"Oh yes, I know. It was a fair race. But one which unfortunately has brought me here. Well, I wish I could say how I'm going to recover. I have so many … debts."

I stopped polishing and leant closer.

"But, Gus, you got all our cattle — 1200 head!— for the Bulldogs. You sold them, didn't you?"

"Oh yes. That very afternoon. I sold them to my creditors to pay off some of my debts. But … well, you just don't know how much money those Bulldogs cost me."

Then E.M. said, all honey-throated, "I have to say, Gus, us getting that base-ball team is turning into the best investment we have ever made. I just can't thank you enough for…" I couldn't tell if she was grappling for the word or pausing for effect "…sharing. Of course, now I feel just awful. I had no idea things were so bad for you."

"Well, think how I feel. I hope there aren't any hard feelings. After all, Elijah, Daddy always taught us the time to sell is when you have the customer. But I feel bad now, because if it weren't for that base-ball team you wouldn't have had to go to Daddy for five thousand dollars. That must have just *killed* poor Royal."

Now here E.M. laughs. "Is that what you think? That we were borrowing money from Daddy?"

"Well, I'd say by the way you handled that horse all the way into Salem, you needed that money pretty badly."

"Well, I just wanted to secure Daddy's investment."

"Investment?"

"Of course. You see, Gus, that was Daddy's investment in the team, not a loan."

"Well, how come he never wanted to invest in the team when *I* owned them?" Gus asked, sounding a little pouty.

I could hear E.M. stirring her tea. Clink, clink, clink. "Well, I suppose it's because you don't know too much about men."

My head comes up.

"My dear, I've been married three times. I would say I certainly *do* know something about men."

"Oh, please don't get the wrong idea, Gus," E.M. corrected herself. "What I meant to say was you didn't know much about base-ball players. *Those* men."

"Oh."

"Except the ones that…" I was sure E.M. was now a-fiddling with her napkins corners; seen her do it a million times when she was talking to me. "…you know, the ones you…"

Now the talk got so low I couldn't hear anything, but I don't think I had to, for the next thing I heard was high-pitched giggling — the sort that strikes fear in a man's heart onaccounta it usually means the ladies is talking about something you had heretofore thought was only men-talk.

Well, so much for E.M. getting to the bottom of Augusta's visit. They kept laughing and clanking their tea cups and I finally was getting bored. Who the hell polishes working boots in February anyway, for cryinoutloud?

I heard their chairs moving and thought I'd best stay put whilst E.M. showed Augusta to her room. I heard E.M. call out, "That's right, Gus. Second door on the left. I'll send Anita in to help you unpack."

Then the pantry door opened full wide and E.M. stood there. I looked up, red-handed. All she said was, "You can bet those boots that high-stepping saloon chicken is up to something!"

two

Next morning, I set out to the Horse Palace to review my troops. I took note that two mounted men and a pack horse was riding off toward the winter pastures, and of course, since I'd been gone nearly nine days, I wasn't sure where the herd was or how everything else ranch-wise was coming along. They waved at me and I waved back. Had no idea who they was from the distance. Didn't matter. Least they knew I was back and vacation time was over.

When I walked into the Horse Palace I was greeted by the sound of men a-counting one-two-three-four all together, and I'll be damned if that wasn't the very same line of men what only ten days previous couldn't get outa their own ways for being so outa shape.

At the end of the line was Leviticus, and he was looking so serious with alla his counting that I wondered if maybe some of Lou's number-fascination wasn't wearing off on him.

Billy and Sully saw me come in and came over to greet me.

I made note first off of Billy's good healthy complexion and bright eyes behind his spectacles, and I reckoned he'd put some meat on.

We shook hands all 'round and Sully said, "Welcome home, boss."

"That Sully behind all them chin curtains? And is that the same buncha boys?" I asked, pointing to the push-up crew.

"They're coming along nicely, Royal," Billy allowed. "Been working like Turks. Even your cowpokes. Look at them."

We walked closer to the line-up. They was now doing push-ups, and I hardly heard one groan amongst 'em. Jay was doing 'em double time, I made note, and he was being met on both sides with Bulldogs. A little competition is good for a conditioning program.

"You know what has really made the difference?" Billy asked.

"Good food and decent sleep, I reckon. Maybe not smoking and drinking too?"

"Well that, of course," Billy continued. "But there's something else. Something less tangible."

The exercise leader, none other'n ol' Hardy by the way, blew a whistle, and the men commenced to running laps around the arena.

"It's the fact that someone actually believes in them enough to do all this," he said, indicating the Palace. "And the fact that your wife has arranged all those spring games, so the boys have something to train for."

I stopped and had to think. What spring games? I was thinking. Oh. Then I remembered: E.M.'s hat receipts. "Well, Billy, now let me explain about those."

"Oh, don't worry. We know they aren't big games. We don't care. Any games will do. Just so long as it's base-ball and not circus acts." He paused to marvel at the men jogging around us. "You know, it's like night and day."

I knew then that E.M. had better dang well get on the telephone and arrange a base-ball game somewheres, and it better ought not be with them Burnbaums either. All I told Billy was, "I'm looking forward to them games, too."

Then Jay jogged by me and it was like he just remembered who I was and who he was and that I might want to go over a few ranchish things with him. He jogs hisself outa his number one position and comes over to me. He did not stop jogging, I will add, our whole conversation, and it's real annoying talking to someone who's going up and down whilst you're on terra firma.

"So how's things here?" I ask him.

As a answer, he pulls up his shirt and slaps his stomach and says, "Cast iron and double bolted!"

"I mean, how's the ranch?"

"Oh. I don't know. Ask Hardy."

But Hardy was in the middle of the arena tossing a big brown ball that looked like it weighed a ton back'n'forth to Levi. Levi tossed it like it was a cantaloupe and Hardy caught it like it was a watermelon.

"Can I go, Roy? They're lapping me."

You know, looking around that arena I saw plenty of my hands all being athletes and, come to think, a few of the Bulldogs seemed to be missing.

"Say, Sully, I saw two men riding out this morning. Who're they?"

"Oh, that must have been Jack and Hank."

"I don't got hands name Jack and Hank."

Sully smiles at me and says, "Sure you do, Roy. Remember, we're all in this together?"

"Yeah, but…"

"Look, Jack and Hank are pretty dang hopeless fielders, but they can ride a horse and they can string wire fence. Now, on the other hand, there's your Jay and Myron over there. Never in my life have I seen two more natural-born players."

"That's right, Roy," Billy agreed. "We need to put the best man for the job in the right job."

Well, I couldn't argue him there.

"So," Sully said, "how was your trip? Profitable, Roy?"

"Sorta," I answered. "But…"

But Sully interrupted me. "Well now," he says, looking past me, a big grin sprouting from under his mustache, "and who is *that*?"

I turned around and saw E.M. and Augusta come walking into the arena. Billy turned too, saw the pair, and muttered, "Oh no."

Some women makes appearances better'n others. Some women can walk into a place and not one eye casts her way. Augusta coulda walked into the blind man's ward and I reckon every man there woulda still took notice.

But it was one of the Bulldogs who said it best. "What the hell is *she* doing here?"

Before I could get a handle on things, the Bulldogs was all coming toward Augusta, and she was looking right concerned the closer they approached. In fact, she looked sorta like she was facing a herda stampeding cattle, and then E.M. pulled her sister fast-like into the training room. She locked the door, leaving alla the Bulldogs standing infronta the window demanding of everyone else what in the name of Uncle Abe's corpse was *she* doing here?

"If I'd known *she* was in on this whole deal, I would have resigned right along with Corky!" one Bulldog said.

"Who's she?" Jay asked, taking off his cap and slicking down his forelock.

"Yeah, that Mrs. Carter ran us ragged. I demand to know…"

"Who's she?" Hardy asked, edging Jay out for a better look.

"Now boys, now boys," I said.

Then another Bulldog said, "If she's in, I'm out!"

"Who's she?" Leviticus asked, dropping the medicine ball on Hardy's foot.

I finally got a handle on things and got the men to stop their editorializing. E.M. and Augusta was almost like two

Moner Lisers, only one smile betwixt 'em both, with the window framing 'em in.

"Okay, men, now here's the story," I began. "Now, in case you didn't know, Mrs. Carter is my wife's kin."

That was met with more swearing and slapping down of caps and such.

"Now hear me out. We all know you got a rotten deal from Mrs. Carter, but hell, you know women ain't built right to run anything like a base-ball team. So I'm asking you to be a little forgiving." I smiled at Gus behind the glass and she smiled back. I reckon the girls couldn't hear my spiel real good or else E.M. woulda come crashing through that window when I mentioned the women-ain't-being-built-right part.

It was Billy who tipped the scales for me. I reckon he had been hurt most by Gus and her antics with the team, onaccounta he was the manager and everyone blames the manager, no matter what fixes the owner gets the team into.

But Billy said, "Come on, men. When have we had it so good? Remember, Mrs. Carter got us in the divorce. It wasn't as though she came gunning for us."

"And you remember what caused that divorce, don't you?" another player said. "She mettled with more'n the batting order."

Well, dammit, Augusta was just so damn beautiful to look at, it wasn't long before the rabble got to reminiscing about this'n'that, and before long Gus's eyes starts getting full and she could sluff her charm clean through that glass window. 'Course, by then E.M.'s looking all confused, like maybe she was hoping the boys would teach Gus a lesson, but it had all backfired.

"Ahhhh look," one of the Bulldogs said, pointing at Augusta, "she's gonna cry."

Well, I reckon men are like that. One minute they can be thinking tar and feathers, and the next minute, when a beautiful woman enters the melting mood, all bets are off and it's nothing but pity and there-theres all around.

Just like that, she came outa the training room and the men was surrounding her with, We didn't mean it, all is forgiven, and how wonderful you look, and here — she was handed about twelve hankies.

Most attentive of all, I will make mention, was Sully.

E.M. and I stood back from the crowd and just marveled. "Can you stand it?" she asked.

"Stand it? I can't believe it. They was ready to hang that woman and now look."

"Well so much for Plan A."

"Plan A?"

"I was sure the Bulldogs would treat her so mean she'd have to leave. But I should have known she'd charm her way out of it!"

"You got a Plan B?"

"Royal, is your saddle slipping?"

I hiked my pants up and said no.

She nudged me and indicated Sully taking Gus's arm to show her the Horse Palace.

"Of course I have a Plan B, and I think we're looking at it."

three

After that, I needed fresh air, and so I went about doing what I shoulda done in the first place — checking on the ranch. I looked into this'n'that and learnt that onct the snow had melted, the cattle was all doing fine, and there hadn't been no emergencies other'n the ones that naturally follow a Gallucci woman.

The next morning I tracked down Sully at the bunkhouse to see if maybe he'd gotten over meeting Augusta enough to bring me up to snuff about the team. Caught him mid-stroke of slickin' back his hair, looking at hisself in the bathroom mirror.

I made note that he was now humming a new tune. It was all bright, not dirge-like, which was sometimes how he hummed. This tune was light and fun and real catch-onable. I recognized it onaccounta we had the same song on one of the wax cylinders for our phonograph. But I didn't feel like joining his hum in a chorus of "Hot Time in the Old Town Tonight." And I didn't want to talk about Augusta and her influence on his new hum. And I didn't even want to talk about blacksmithing or even ask how ol' Bess was running. I wanted to know about more pressing issues — like how he thought Leviticus was coming as a pitcher.

"You know, it's the strangest thing," he started off, walking with me to the Horse Palace. "For a while there, I thought he was a going to be a genuine 3-H flinger."

"3-H?" I asked. These base-ball boys sure had a language all their own.

"You know — head, heart, and hands," Sully clarifies for me.

I gave that a think, then replied, "Well now, Sully, you know ol' Levi. Even though he might be lackin' for one of them H's, he's damn good at applyin' the other two to make up for it. He can draw his own bucket most times."

Sully grinned sorta sad-like and said, "Yes, but the boy has to remember what he needs the water *for*, Royal. He has to concentrate on base-ball. While you folks were gone, he worried like a widder about to be foreclosed on. Just fell apart. When he thinks base-ball, he's solid gold. When he doesn't…"

He held the door open for me and we went inside. I said, "Well, I reckon all along I've been fearing that. See, folks like Levi, folks with minds like that, can go either one a' two ways. Hot or cold."

"Which makes him just like any other common-run pitcher," Sully commented, shaking his head. "Look, let's get him over here and take a look."

Levi was still up at the house eating lunch, so we called to have him sent down. Now that was a treat. Never in my whole life did I think I would ever be so lazy that I couldn't walk or ride someplace so close to deliver a message. But having that telephone in the Palace was just too damned handy. What a world we was coming into!

Whilst we waited, we watched some of the other boys practicing their base-ball skills. Here's something: At the back of the arena where we had us the breaking corrals, there was some batters practicing their hits. Billy and Sully asked the boys to halt whilst they showed me the ball catcher they was hitting into. Strung from the ceiling to the ground was layers and layers of…

"What is that?"

"Fish net," Sully replied. "I traded some fly-fishing equipment with this ol' Indian in Idlehour."

I looked at him. "Not your Hinckley Special?"

"Ah, who has time to fish these days, anyway," was his reply.

Those layers of Indian fish net had seen its day from the catching of salmon in the Columbia, but was doing a right good job of catching those base-balls and giving the boys lots of good battning practice without the chasing and losing of base-balls, not to mention wrecking havoc on my new barn. But I still felt bad about Sully's Hinckley Special.

About then, Levi came in toting him a slice of cake.

Sully told him to warm up so's we could watch him pitch.

Sully and Billy had rigged this sorta swing-like thing from the rafters at the battning end of the arena. It was like a wagon wheel only without the middle and the spokes, so I guess you could say it was just the iron ring, maybe two feet yea. Anyway, when they unhooked it from a side post, it came swinging down back and forth pendulum-like. And that was one of Levi's warm ups. Throwing balls to see if he could get 'em through the ring. Sully said it was to train his eye so's when he had to throw the ball to someone besides the catcher, he could track him a moving target. Then, after he did that some, Sully stilled the ring and made it hang straight down, and I made note it was at the height that Billy called the strike zone.

Levi set his cake down on the dirt and did some throws. But not onct did Levi make the ball go through the hoop. He hit it a few times, sending it spinning, but he never onct did the expected.

"See?" Billy asked.

Sully added, "So I'm afraid it's back to the drafting table for our pitching."

"Now, boys, are you sure you're talking to him right? Didn't say some bull-sense to set him off, did you? Or maybe did some yack set off some raillery or maybe hurt his feel-bads? Levi can be real odd sometimes. He can hold him a real mean grudge."

"We've treated him just like you said. Haven't yelled at him once," Sully said. "I've always treated him kindly, Roy."

Billy added, "I can't imagine anyone saying anything bad to Leviticus. Why, in some ways, he's just a sweet little kid."

"I know that." I looked over and watched him throwing the ball back'n'forth with Jay. "I just can't reckon it. Before I left, he was flinging 'em balls and hitting bullseyes every damn time."

Then Lou(ella) came in the Palace a-toting her a piece of cake. She walks up to Levi, totally ignorant of the training and the pitching and the throwing of balls going on all around her. Walks right smack dab up the middle of the arena. Doesn't flinch, doesn't stray off course, and all the balls seem to somehow just avoid her.

"Watch, Lou!" Levi said, wiping dirt offa his cake, stuffing it into his mouth, wiping his hands on his pants, and then taking to the pitcher's box.

So Lou sets down right next to him and watches him wind up, and I want to tell you, even if you don't know much about base-ball and pitchers and wind-ups, you'd had to of noticed the way Levi put his life and soul into his wind-up. But dang, you coulda heard that ball WHAPPP! into Jay's mitt from acrost Four Arrows. It was followed by Jay's "Ouch! Not so hard, Levi!"

"Wait a minute," Sully said to me, getting my attention.

"Maybe she shouldn't oughta be settin' out there," I said, thinking Lou might get hit if Levi was to miss a catch.

Levi threw another one, his wind-up even a little more show-offy.

"Strike," Billy said, sorta under his breath.

Well, that ball went back'n'forth several times, each time resulting in Jay rubbing his hand and Billy and Sully walking a little closer to the boys so's they could get a better look-see.

"Hey, Billy!" Jay calls out. "Tell him to lighten up a little. He's hurlin' cannon balls!"

"Watch this, Lou," Levi said, this time doing his wind-up backwards and then switching to frontwards on the last rotation and still throwing a ball that Jay could barely hang onto.

Finally, Jay took off his face cage and put his hands on his hips and shouted, "Here! How do you like it!?!" Then, with all his might, he throws the ball right at Levi like they was playing soak ball, making Jay to rub his shoulder some.

Insteada flinching or running, Levi just sticks his mitt out and catches it like he was picking a peach offa a low branch.

"I don't get it," Billy said. "What do you think, Sully?"

"Maybe he's just been in a slump."

"Do some more for us," Billy called out.

"Okay, but tell him to ease up a bit on the starch or else I'm gonna need to stuff a bale of cotten into this mitten," Jay called over to us.

Back'n'forth they went some more. Lou finished her cake and looks around like she's now getting bored with the catch game. She stands up and goes off somewheres outa sight, but of course we're all so interested in watching Levi pitch, we didn't think nothing of it.

"Let's get a batter in there," Sully suggested. Billy called somebody up to go against Levi's pitches.

Well, you would think he was now back to his ol' childhood habit of throwing rocks at birds, the way he put that ball everywheres but over the plate. This went on with a few more hitters, and not a one did he give a strike to. In fact, I think the total amount of contacts with the ball was three out of a total of four batters up. All the rest was so far, wide, hither and yon that the batters just stood and watched the balls go elsewheres.

"Well, there you have it," Billy said, shaking his head, sad-like.

"I've seen this before. Too bad really," Sully agreed.

"What? Seen what before?" I asked him. "What's the kid doing wrong?"

Sully then informs me that sometimes a man can toss bullets and each one of 'em right acrost the plate… when there's not the pressure of a batter standing there, staring at him.

"It's a clear case of well … anxiety. Kind of like stage fright, only without the stage. But it's not the kid's fault," Billy said. "I should have noticed this a lot sooner. I was just so hopeful."

Then Lou wanders back to start straightening the bats and balls on the ground. That was also a part of her numbers fascination — she couldn't stand it when things was outa order or not set out even-like. She was a real good closet and drawer keeper, and now she was doing it with the team equipment.

Well, guess what? The batter at that moment gets three strong ones right in a row and even though he swung three mighty swings, not a one made contact, and each swing was determined a strike.

"There!" Sully says to us, "Did you see that? He's on again."

'Course, not knowing Levi and Lou the way I did, ol' Sully and Billy go over to Levi to see what made him so good just then.

I go over to Lou and ask her to fetch me some coffee outa the office. About then, Sully has Levi try another batter. Sure enough, Levi throws a buncha wild balls. By now, all the boys was standing on the sidelines watching this.

And sure enough, the minute Lou comes back out with the coffee, we hear the swish-swish-swish of three strikes in a row.

I decided to put Billy and Sully outa their strung-out misery of not having a clue as to the source of Levi's hot and cold spells. I marched Lou out to the pitcher's box and sipped my coffee.

"Sully? Billy?" I said, my hand on Lou's tiny shoulder.

"This is really strange," Sully said to Levi. Then he takes him by the shoulder and asks, "Levi, what's going through your mind when you're facing those batters?"

Well, I knew whatever it was going through his mind wasn't gonna make no sense to anyone but Levi, but more'n that, I knew what *wasn't* going through his mind and that was his wife and buddy, Lou(ella).

"Boys, I think I have the answer right here." They look at me and then down at Lou. "Sully, you recall how good you played when you was a kid, knowing your best girl was watching?" I asked him, a smile on my face.

Billy and Sully looked at each other, and I reckon we alla us knew that the Bulldogs had found theirselfs a team mascot.

four

E.M. grinned ear to ear when I told her about Levi not being able to pitch a lick unless Lou was watching.

"So, you reckon you could make this uniform fit her?" I asked, handing her a outfit.

Well, you'd think I'd just asked her to move the Blue Mountains from our Northeast corner and plunk 'em down somewheres westa Wenatchee. No, come to think, I never had seen E.M. sew up anything. Anita did mosta that, but she was extra busy now cooking.

"Don't worry, Roy," E.M. said. "I think Gus needs to be useful as well as ornamental."

"Hell, E.M., if *you* can't sew, what makes you think *she* can?" I asked.

"Nothing. But she better learn how to do something if she wants to un-reduce her circumstances. After that, I'm putting her to work in the kitchen with Anita."

I had followed her to my office, and she set herself down behind my desk. "You think that's safe? I mean, Anita's temper and all?"

E.M. smiled big and said, "I think it's wonderful. Besides, Billy's too busy with the team now to help her, and she's really wearing herself out."

I sorta looked at my boot tips when I asked it, but I want to go on record as having *had* the guts to ask it: "And what about you, E.M.? What're you doing to help out?"

She had the telephone to her ear and the talking piece in her hand. I knew she wouldn't throw 'em, onaccounta she woulda lost the operator connection she'd clicked up.

"This," was her reply. Then into the phone she said, "Hello Miz Rose, could you get me the Walla Walla YMCA?"

'Course that meant some waiting and so I asked, "You ain't ordering more bibles, are you?"

"Of course not, Roy. I'm finding out how to contact the base-ball team in Walla Walla. I'm contacting all the small town nines and setting up some spring games."

"Try the State Pen in Walla Walla. Bet they have a team," I joked, remembering the boys in blue down to Salem.

E.M. clicked the phone again and got Miz Rose back on the line. "Me again, Miz Rose. While you're at it, I'll need a connection to *The Sporting News* in St. Louis."

"Why you calling them?" I asked.

"Well, Roy, would you ride through hostile Indian territory without knowing who's on first base?"

Now, only E.M. could pull off a sentence like that.

"Huh?" I asked. "What's hostile..."

"I'm taking out a subscription, for heaven's sake!" she sorta snapped back at me.

"Oh," I answered. My wife subscribing to a sporting newspaper. I thought I'd seen just about everything.

She set back in my chair and you know, I have to say that woman, my E.M., looked so perfect natural in that setting — business all around her, leaning back, telephone in her hands. Hell, she'd a been smoking a cigar and putting her feet up on the desk if I wasn't bound to catch her doing it. Come to think, sometimes I think I did smell a stale cigar odor in my office after I'd been gone a coupla days, and I always meant to ask her about that.

Anyway, things was moving now. The team was being

trained, E.M. was booking us games right and left, and even ol' Gus was learning how to sew and cook, and hell, she had a temper! You can't tell me things like tempers isn't inherited. And I made note she had a good throwing arm herownself, same as E.M.

And here I might throw in a little household hint: If you ever want to get all the critters — you know, dogs and cats and bugs and such — all outa a house real fast-like, start a kitchen commotion and just watch 'em crash over each other to get out. I know onaccounta all our critters wasn't ever the same after that first all-three-women-together show-down occurred in our kitchen. It taught alla us, well, the critters and me, the fastest way outa a argument is the back door. From that first flare-up, alls it took was a higher pitched remark and the animals was outa there fast! Worked real good come summer when their flea-scratching would drive you plumb bats. Justa hint.

It was around the Ides of March, and insteada being 'bewarein,' E.M. had booked us our very first game. Now, the winter had been rough and yes, it was always iffy counting on spring to come in when it should. But E.M. said we was gonna play indoors anyhow, since the ground hadn't softened long enough for us to drag out a good field out back.

"What the hell you mean, 'out back'? Where out back? Not my nice backyard lawn out back you don't, E.M.!" I hollered.

"Now, Royal, settle down. We're going to keep the grass. All we're going to do is drag a baseline. Really," she huffs, "you'd think I was asking you to plow it under and grow rocks."

E.M. had been in contact with the base-ball team in Walla Walla Wash. They called theirselfs the Wranglers. It was planned that we'd send the train up to Idlehour to meet 'em and chug 'em on back to the ranch.

We sorta kept this game under the hat onaccounta it being our first game with a club of any kind. If we was to let the Burnbaums know what we was up to, then the whole town of Idlehour might come wandering out, and then if we was a bust, no telling what mighta happened to the Burnbaum-Idlehour economy. No, this was gonna be a test game, just to see how the boys stacked up against a real team. So we arranged a after hours schedule in the hope of playing things down. We offered the Wranglers food and overnight accommodations at the ranch, and they accepted.

Now, I don't think them Wranglers was real happy about the cattle-car-style traveling, but since we was working on the Q.T., and since we'd cleaned it up real good and put in some sofas and chairs and spittoons and even had a crock of lemonade, well, they didn't have too much to gripe about.

And if they was grumbling about the late-hour arrival and the cattle car, well, seeing that lit-up Horse Palace changed their minds real fast.

They was oohing and aahing and saying things like 'we heard, but we didn't believe' and 'ain't this something' and one man even suggested in the deada winter we could ice it over and play us some hockey. The man next to him said forget hockey, how about indoor football? The man next to him said forget hockey and football, they could fill the joint fulla water and do some war-shipping like them Romans used to do.

I gotta admit, we was alla us damn proud of the Horse Palace. But of course, we wasn't all gathered there to pass suggestions and compliments back'n'forth. We was there to play us a base-ball game.

It would be too painful for me to relate the events of that first game, so I'll just say this: Wranglers 22, Bulldogs 2.

'Course, being our first real game, we couldn't be sure if our trouncing was onaccounta the Wranglers was that good or the Bulldogs was that bad. In practice we looked good. Anyway, we asked the Wranglers if they would be so kind as to play us another game the next morning. They said, sure. They needed the practice, being as how they hadn't played together since last fall and this indoor playing was fun.

Now, outa respect for the Wranglers — who all turned out to be good friends and supporters — I will not relate the events of that second game. I'll just say this: Wranglers 4, Bulldogs 6.

The difference? This time, Lou had a whole game's worth of numbers on both teams. Well, I thought she was just doing some big, fancy tic tac toe game — the sort only she coulda come up with in that heada hers. But it wasn't no x's or o's she was cipherin'. It was *statistics.*

So she'd taken those numbers and come up with some numbers of her own. She scampered down to Jay and he just shooed her away.

Levi took some issue with that and beaned him on the next pitch. The Wranglers was all just laughing. 'Course, they knew all about Four Arrows and the crew we usually kept. Hell, looking back, maybe the only reason they came down in the first place was to get a good end-o-winter laugh.

So a few more times Lou goes over to Jay to inform him of some number. I, of course, was watching this real close-like.

"Maybe we better get her out of there," Sully said. "She might get hurt, and she's got Levi all upset."

"But he needs her around to pitch," Billy said.

"So what? I just want this to be over," Sully said.

"Now just wait a bit. I know Lou, and I reckon she's got herself one of her fascinations."

"Fascinations?"

"Think I'll go up there and see what she's running through that little brainpan of hers."

Sully was big disappointed in the team and Billy was taking the grain of salt, but I thought maybe it wasn't all over yet.

I pulled Lou aside and asked her, "What you thinking, Lou?"

She answered me with a string a' numbers and then looked at me like as to ask, why the hell didn't I see that?

"What, Lou? What's it mean?"

"Inside!" she yelped at me. Then she by-passed Jay entirely and hollered the best she could, which wasn't much, to Levi, "Leviticus! Inside!"

"We *are* inside!" he called back.

The Wranglers and even some of the Bulldogs now was damn near rolling in their laughters.

Sully had come up behind me and pulled me back. "Inside?" Then he asked Lou, "You want him to pitch this batter inside?"

Lou looked at him and smiled big and just repeated her string of numbers like *finally* she'd found someone who understood what she was seeing to be so damn obvious.

It had been like playing a game of chest without having any knights. Can't turn a corner without 'em.

From there, we had us all the pieces and the makings of a real team.

five

The next day, after the Wranglers went home and things was back to normal, us managers was going over the two ball games and seeing how well so-and-so played what position and where maybe we could move 'em around to play better.

Well, no one was more surprised than me to see we had won us a ball game. E.M. was acting a little like maybe she'd known it could be all alongst, and the most surprised of all was Augusta.

Sully set acrost from Augusta, Anita set acrost from Billy, E.M. set acrost from me, and Lou set acrost from Levi. I will bet you any amount of money that we was the only equal-sexed base-ball board of managers in the whole world, then, now, or maybe even in the will-be.

"Well, I can still hardly believe it," Augusta said, looking at Billy. "How come you Bulldogs never played like that when I owned you?"

Everyone there had two or three reasons and we all gave 'em to her at onct.

'Course, it was that last reason Billy gave that had me most worried. I hate it when things is finally going alongst without a hitch after one foofaraw after another. You know how it is, you ride through one storm, look on the western horizon, and see red skies, meaning better tomorrows, and then WHAM! the cattle stampedes from a-rears and there you are, riding like sixty just to keep from being squarshed.

So Sully and me looked at each other when Billy said to Gus, "Hiring players like Corky."

"Corky?" E.M. asked, like she had ant-antennae and there was a fresh dollop of maple syrup just spilt on the table.

"I'm sorry, I spoke out of turn," Billy said, gentleman-like and casting Sully a little smile.

But Gus just sets up a little straighter and, of course, alla us men took notice, and she says, "You told me he was a good hitter, Mr. Rohrs."

"He was."

"And you said he could catch and field with the best."

"He could."

"So don't blame me if he couldn't keep his eye on the ball," she finalizes.

I reckon everyone outsida Lou and Levi knew what she was referring to.

Our meeting adjourned and I had to talk to Sully and he had to talk to me. We walked down toward the Horse Palace and he started it out.

"Did you hear that, Roy? Augusta and Corky! Oh, this is too close for comfort. I tell you, Corky knows me, she knows Corky … it's just too risky."

"No, wait, wait, let's just think on this. So she and Corky was —-well, let's just say they was friendly."

"That beautiful woman wasted on that *chump*!" he grumbled.

I had to keep him on tract, so I kept talking. "Look, Corky is long gone. He left way last fall and he's probably back east, where he deserves to be."

"Oooh, I just boil when I think…"

I pulled him back so's he could stop boiling and look me direct. "Sully," I said, "Augusta's had her lots of men like Corky. That goes without saying."

"It does?"

"Why, sure. Now, I know you're smit by her and I don't blame you. She's about as handsome as they come."

"That she is."

"Now, I reckon there's two ways you can look at things. Either Gus's got bad taste in men or else she ain't never had the chance to get to know a decent man."

"I'm decent," he said.

"Damn rights you are."

"Royal, do you think she'd really, I mean really go for someone like me?"

"Why sure, Sully. She's been making eyes at you since she's arrived."

"She really has, hasn't she," he said. Then, like he snaps outa it again, and adds, "No, no, I have to leave. It's too risky. I said I would stay until the barn got built, then I said I'd stay until you got things rolling, and now they're rolling and..." he stopped talking and looked over my shoulder. I could tell by the misty look in his eyes that Augusta was within eyeshot.

I heard her 'Yooo-hooo, Mr. McGinty!'

"Something else you ain't thought of," I said to Sully before he went galloping off to pay his homage.

"What?"

"The more Gus thinks of you, the less she's likely to even remember Corky Somebody from the Bowery."

His face looked like I'd just told him he got a reprieve from the hangman's noose. "You're right!" he said, slapping me on the shoulder and running off to see Gus.

I turned and watched 'em walking, her on his arm close as a kitten to a warm brick, and I wondered what the hell I had done. Maybe I shoulda let Sully leave —- all three times that he'd offered for the sake of the team. After all, Gus wasn't no spring chicken, beautiful as she was. Additional, even though she could charm the rattles off a snake, she was also about as trustable. And Gus had her three notches on her marriage-pistol. Then again, thinks me, she was kin, as much as E.M., Gus, and me wasn't likely to admit it in public.

But E.M. approved my support of her so-called Plan B, getting them two together, even though she herownself didn't know what I knew about Sully and about Corky or what the hell any of 'em had to do with the success of our Bulldogs.

So that spring, which finally came in good and strong and beautiful, we had about the best base-ball training, I reckon, anywheres in the country. The ball field out back trained the boys on the grass, which was the best onaccounta that's what they was gonna be playing for real on. I did whimper some when I saw Hardy dragging that big rake behind his horse to make the base lines, but hell, what's some grass when we had base-ball to play?

When word got out we squeaked by the Walla Walla Wash Wranglers, we got us more commitments to play the small town nines, as E.M. called 'em. That musta been by the end of May, so now all we had to do was schedule the ranch work around the travel and see about getting the Bulldogs around. We agreed to make use of the railroad as best we could, but no one knew nothing about a private train commencing alongst a big-company seta tracks, like the Union Pacific or the Great Northern. E.M. said to just leave it to her, and I musta been occupied with something else at the time, so I just nodded my head and forgot all about it.

Anyway, the money was holding out, and the cases of Spring Fever on the ranch never ceased to amaze me. Even E.M. got a bit kittenish, which wasn't like her when we was setting smack-dab in the middle of a fe-as-ko.

Kittenish or not, I did take issue in her spending the money for the Pullman cars.

"E.M.! They're base-ball players, not congressmen!" I yelped when she announced she'd sent Sully to Idlehour, where the two cars was to be delivered. "Why the hell can't we just fix up the cattle cars more like we was planning?"

"But Royal," she said, "you can't ask the boys to be delivered like so much beef on the hoof. We've spent all this time building up their self-esteem averages as well as their batting averages, so we just can't let them ride in cattle cars!"

"Well, ain't it cheaper to…"

"Really, you're so picayune stingy sometimes it surprises me you ride with two stirrups!"

"Well, two stirrups is a damn sight cheaper'n two Pullmans!"

"Well, you don't expect to twenty-mule-team them around, do you?"

"No. I … Well, how much you spending on those Pullmans?"

She showed me the number and I looked at her knowing there was a P.S. at the end of the statement.

"Now, Royal, I told you it's best to just let me work these things out and save your brain for the important work."

"E.M., you didn't sell more stocks in the team, did you?"

"Only if they win. If they lose, the cars go back to Mr. Easley and all we're out is two hundred dollars. Each."

"Each Bulldog?" I hollered.

"No, each car. That's four hundred dollars, so unless you can think of a better way to haul the team around … Besides, the Bulldogs have their traveling stove and so Anita can go along to cook and we'll save on meals on the barnstorm tour."

That sounded logical, but it did bring me around to a pressing point which I don't think I'd thought of previous. And that point was, "Now, E.M., let's discuss just who all's going along on this barnstorm."

Well, as we checked off the names, it appeared as though just about everyone at Four Arrows was going on the barnstorm, up to and including a brace of our best laying hens.

"And Royal, you just have to go. I mean, you're in charge."

"I'm in charge? Since when? Besides, E.M., Four Arrows needs a ranahan. We can't just all pick up and leave the place. There's too much to do. Who the hell's gonna run this place?"

"Well, I guess I'll have to stay."

Well, I love my E.M. and I think she could run just about anything she set out to run, but she couldn't turn a breech calf, she couldn't turn a runaway herd, and she couldn't turn a roll of wire into a fence.

"I ain't gonna hear of that, E.M. It's too dangerous."

"But Hardy will be here and I'll have — what do we have — eight hands?"

"Nope, ain't gonna happen, E.M. You have to go with the team and I'll have to stay. That's all. Don't say any more. That's the end of the discussion."

I shoulda known by the way she agreed all too easy that my cookie-pushing wife was planning all along that she should go with the team and I should stay on Four Arrows, where I couldn't see first hand the barns she was gonna storm.

So we was settled on almost all accounts. Incept one. Gus.

"Oh, I have that all planned out," she said.

"Well?"

"She's coming with the team."

"What?"

"Sure. I think the best use of Gus is to let her do what she does best."

"Get married?"

"No, let her feather herself out where the opposing teams can see her ophidian charm and let things happen as they may."

"What kinda charm?"

"*Her* kind of charm. You know..." and here she does a hot little hitchy-koo dance, topped off with a Hot Cha!

"Oh, *that* kinda charm," I said. "But ain't they got a distraction rule in base-ball?"

"As a matter of fact, the rules don't even say women can't play. If I was really smart and living up to your expectations of me, I'd have her on the team!" E.M. said.

"E.M.," I said, not one bit liking that glint in her eye, "now you know how I feel about cheating!"

"Well, it did pass through my mind. But I think the Bulldogs are going to win, Royal. All on their own. No cheating, no nothing. With Lou and her numbers, Levi's pitching, Sully and Billy, I can just feel it right here." She tapped the tip of her nose.

"And which medium did you consult to come up with that prognation?" I asked, pulling her on topa my lap and recalling how much E.M.'s new chest of drawers cost me.

"*Farmer's Almanac*," she replied. "Said our area will have a ripe harvest."

"Ripe, huh? As in ripesuck?"

"No. As in ripe for the picking, only *we're* the ones doing the picking this time, Roy. We're going to win. Wait and see."

We kissed, and I thought maybe things was gonna be fine. The Bulldogs was about to be Pullmaned all over the Northwest playing their ball-games, Gus was gonna be offa Four Arrows, we had us the blessing of the *Farmer's Almanac*, and it was gonna be like old times, just me and Hardy and a few hands fending for ourownselfs on Four Arrows.

six

The town of Idlehour was sure decked out that Sunday when we arrived to load the team into the Pullman cars that had arrived just the day before, used but in good order and to E.M. specifications. I gotta tell you, she'd planned it out real good, complete with a little sign on the end touting the Bulldogs Base-Ball team setting inside. The front half of the first car was seats, just like in any other train. The back half was the men's sleeping arrangements. Just bunks with pull-curtains. But the second Pullman was the attraction. The front half was tables and chairs with a long narrow kitchen and the back half was the ladies' accommodations. Since there was only foura them, they each got a separate little room and they was about as snug as bugs in rugs.

E.M. had arranged for the train to hitch on our two Pullmans, and I didn't even have the sand to ask E.M. how much that was gonna cost. E.M. was a real early riser when it came to planning things. When they played the towns that the big railroad boys didn't go to, they'd be deposited on a spur and the small town local would chug out and bring 'em all in. I could see how's that would make it a real holiday for everyone.

The Burnbaum girls was in charge of the bon voyage to-do. Now, if there was one thing them girls was good at it was bon voyages, having, I reckon, seen off more'n their shares of men. Anyhow, they'd got together with the townsmen and had somehow wrangled 'em into putting out the Fourth of July decorations, so the telephone poles was decorated and there was bunting along the stores and we even had us the Idlehour Brass Band to play us a few J. P. Sousa marches. 'Course, arranging that musta been easy, onaccounta there was only two non-Burnbaums in that band. They looked right pert in their uniforms of red and gold, and I made note of the ones that had paired up with a Bulldog. They was actually sorta cute, for Burnbaums, a-tootning their horns so earnest-like and batting their eyes over the glare of their cornets and trombones and such.

'Course, up to then the townsfolks had mostly just rumors of our base-ball team. But onct the Walla Walla Wash Wranglers had passed through town and word of our Bulldogs got out, well, folks was all turning out like it was a real holiday.

It was the Mayor who announced in his little speech — ain't it funny how a politician can take any event and turn it into a speechmaking opportunity — he was the one who announced to the townsfolks that not only was the name of the local team the Bulldogs, but they was now the *Idlehour* Bulldogs! How do you like that? He just sorta claimed the team like they was some of that imminent domain territory and he was ol' Uncle Sam.

Onct he did that — announced to Idlehour they now had their own base-ball team — well, just try to claim otherwise. So, naturally I took advantage of the situation and announced to the crowd right back that I was looking forward to seeing the progress on the Idlehour base-ball grounds, in which they could sport their new-claimed Idlehour Bulldogs.

The Mayor took me aside and told me, "Royal, we don't have any plans for..."

"Can't have a hometown team without a hometown place to play 'em," I gave him.

"But that takes money," he said, already starting to backstep, like voted officials do.

"Well, there's money in the park fund. I know onaccounta I myownself seeded it there back in '93. Pass the hat to the resta the community, Mayor. Ball park'd do us all good."

The rest I left up to his constituents and, knowing how quick-like a friendly crowd can turn ugly on a politician, I knew he'd find the ball park money somewhere in the budget. I was thinking right out past the turnaround, next to the park and the cement pond.

So the team finally got off. There was lots of kissing and hugging and handshaking. It was a very friendly ship-off. E.M. gave me the itinerary and said they would be home from their first barnstorm North by July 30th, providing things went smooth and the God-o-Base-Ball agreed.

Six weeks was a long time to be away from your wife, but we knew it was for the best. 'Course, even though the Walla Walla Wash team was a good team and we'd beat 'em, didn't mean we was gonna make good everywhere. If you want the truth, I looked at the puffy natures of the Bulldogs, yep, even ol' Levi, and I was hoping they'd get some trounces along the way.

E.M. promised to call at each stop and give me the latest results, and I told her to stay away from telegraph offices. She knew damn well why. She instructed me to keep reading *The Sporting News* onaccounta you never knew when they'd print up something about the team. Now, here I thought she was being over-hopeful. I'd read me a few of their issues and I don't think they had a clue that there was civilization westa the Rockies. I'm not sure they do even now.

So there was Hardy and me and a few other hands setting atopt our horses, waving goodbye to the team. It was Sunday, and since we knew we couldn't get a beer at the Glass, we just turned our horses and headed, kinda slow, kinda sad, back to Four Arrows.

Now like you know, even with a reduced herd, early summer ain't no time for settin' back, braiding rope, or admiring the horizon. We was busy, that's sure. Sunrise to sundown. But we'd got by on as few as six hands one year. 'Course, they was seasoned men and this year I was working with three Bulldogs who was still a pale shade of green. But since they liked the work, they learnt fast.

It wasn't long before alla us come to figure out that it sure was a lonely place without the womenfolk around to tell us what to do. When we had spare time, we would gather out back, play us some catch — and you know what — I found out I was a good hitter and I could even run faster'n you'd think a man my age could. I reckon that came from all my years of running down dogies. E.M. always did allow as I musta been a quarter horse myownself in a past life, onaccounta I was so quick-like chasing critters in a pen.

So, whilst the Bulldogs was out barnstorming and playing anyplace E.M. could get a challenge, we was tossing the ball back'n'forth some too.

The No Juice Jar, of course, was damn near full by the time the team'd been gone a week. Hardy counted the money, and even though it was mostly mine, we'd agreed we'd save it for a special purpose.

I was making use of the team office in the Horse Palace as the place I kept track of the team's progress. We'd painted a scoreboard along one wall and Hardy, onaccounta he had real nice printing, had writ the dates and the places they was scheduled to play. Then when E.M. called in the results, he'd post the scores for each five-game series.

Here's a few that I happen to recall of their first swing:

Pasco	Them 2 games to our 3
Kennewick	Them 3 Us 2
Wallula	Them 0 Us 5 (wasn't a real team)
Starbuck	Them 4 Us 1 (took the game serious)
Dayton	Them 1 Us 4

Now, they was all small towns and small teams, as E.M. was quick to remind me each time she called in. The real tests would come if she could wrangle some exhibition matches with Seattle and Tacoma and Portland, she said. Big towns. Big teams. She said after what ol' Gus had left of the Bulldogs' reputations, it was gonna take some work, but Billy was calling in what few favors he'd tallied. Gus, so reported E.M., was helping out by mending her some fences and such. I reckon a woman like Gus has knocked holes in some right high fences.

"I tell you, Roy, she's a changed woman," E.M. said when she called in the Dayton scores. "I don't know if it's this humble living or the team doing so well or Sully, but if you'd told me that a pill like Augusta could go this long without chiseling someone or lying or causing a duel or any of the other things she does so well, well I'd have told you you were crazy."

"Well, I'm glad you two are getting along," I returned. "Your daddy's gonna be real happy about that, E.M."

"It's just I can't help but feel … way down deep … Oh, nothing. I must be crazy," she went on.

I knew that 'way down deep' feeling. I'd had it a few times myownself regarding E.M. She goes on to tell me how Gus sets herself close to the opposing team's line-up. She does her eyes and her swishes and her slathers and she smiles real big. Then Lou can look over the statistics man's shoulders and do some calculations and relay her information out to Levi in ways only the two of 'em could ever decipher.

"Ain't that cheating a little, E.M.?" I asked her.

She says, "No, it's not cheating, Royal. Besides, Lou is getting so good at this, she's not using their statistics that much anymore. I don't know how she does it, but she can glance at the box scores in the paper, then look at a man and tally up his height and his weight, divide it by how he holds his bat and the number of times he blinks, and somehow she has him figured out. She's an absolute genius. Who knows how she does it? She does it!"

Well, E.M. kept wiring home a little money after each game, and with each deposit I cared less'n'less how they got their wins. We was getting some return on our investments.

Reckon it was the other way around with our Bulldogs … their investment didn't have nothing to do with spoondulicks. Nope, money didn't have a lick to do with pride, confidence, and playing the best a man can play.

You can learn a lot from base-ball.

seven

Six weeks later, just before August, they all came back home, and it was a nice surprise to have 'em all back a coupla days early. But E.M. announces to me that they was only just beginning their tour, onaccounta she'd next arranged a swing to the towns down South. I moaned me some at that news, but she allowed they was gonna stay and rest for a week or so, so I agreed. We picnicked and played us another backyard game, only this time what a helluva different game it was! They was what they call in *The Sporting News* 'seasoned,' which I come to think didn't mean they was salt and peppered, but they was playing real good within their base-ball season.

So before we knew it, they'd gone South and we was onct again by our lonesomes. E.M. promised me this time they'd be back in a coupla weeks, so I marked my calendar for August 20th. I did some fishing with Hardy and I loved him like a daddy, but he was tongue enough for two sets a' teeth and could talk the blaze off a horse. He had a bad humming voice to boot.

But E.M. reports more good scores along their way, posting only one losing series. It happened up against the Pendleton team, and E.M. said those Pendleton boys had applied the whitewash fair'n'square.

"The losers had to paint some fences, did they?" I asked her back.

"No, Royal," E.M. snapped back at me. "That means we got drugged'n'drubbed."

'Course, I knew she was talking about getting a big defeat, but she railed me about my speech so often that I thought I'd do it to her for onct.

"Who's been drugged?" I asked, sounding a little disapproving.

"Nobody. Will you listen? We got whipped so bad it took a bloodhound a week just to find our scent."

"Oh, you took a big loss, huh, E.M.? What happened?"

From there she tells me Lou(ella) had caught her a cold and stayed in bed. Well, Levi refused to leave her side and so Jay had to fill in as pitcher, and E.M. said it was a good lesson for them all, and they started that very day training Jay to pitch to the batter and not to the crowd.

They stayed in Pendleton to let Lou get better, and even though they was so close to Four Arrows I just set tight. Lou could take sick real bad, but each year she'd been with us she'd gotten stronger and stronger. But she never grew any more.

They played some more games with the Pendleton team and won each game after Lou joined 'em. 'Course, any time you have a whole team's success relying on one person, be that person a player or not, be that person a midget-mascot or a seven-foot fielder, you got trouble. I tried to pass this along to my wife, but with each phone call from E.M., with each win, I made note her voice got a little more fulla herself and she talked more and more base-bally and less and less wifey.

So, it did not surprise me that her August 20th homecoming deadline came and went. She justified it by telling me she'd sent Billy ahead to the Puget Sound, where Gus had set up some meetings with local ball promoters and such. She then informed me whatever Gus had over these fellers it musta been considerable, onaccounta Billy got some big-town games scheduled for the end of August. Now these still wasn't league games for the Pacific Coast League, which was still in the planning stages. But it was big-town ball as far as E.M. was concerned.

I have to admit, knowing my wife was on the road in small towns, pretty much just good local agrarians, sporting her team of ball players — and no matter what you may think otherwise, they *was* her team — was one thing. But seeing her take on the big cities — Seattle, Everett, Tacoma, Vancouver, Portland — especially in the accompaniment of her sister, well, I was setting more and more ticklish, even though I don't think I was in a full out-and-out dilemma just yet.

Anyhow, they was gonna go north to the Puget Sound area and get their big games. Extending the season, so E.M. said. These was golden opportunities, she added.

"So, you'll be home then when?" I asked her when they was stopped in Chehalis for a coupla games.

"I can't say, Roy. By the time we play the Puget Sound, then drop back down to Vancouver and Portland, probably won't be until the first week or so in September. How are things there?"

"Lonesome," I said. "E.M., you looking for buyers whilst you're barnstorming?"

"Oh, no one's going to buy the Bulldogs based on this one lucky streak, Royal," she said. "Besides, the kind of offers we'll be fielding will be from big Eastern cities."

"You planning on taking the boys east to Spokane, are you?" I asked.

"No, Royal, I mean *real* Eastern cities — the kind that can afford and support their own team. There really aren't any ball club opportunities here out west."

"Well, if the boys are going east, then you can just damn well stop off here at Four Arrows and deposit Anita, Sully, Levi, and Lou," I said. "And I want Jay back whilst you're at it!" I reckon I was still roiled that they wasn't coming home for awhile.

"What about me, Roy?" she asked, a little huffy.

"Hell, E.M., I'm lonely," I griped, losing my upper hand in the conversation.

"I am too. Don't you think it's been hard for me — Anita and Billy are all gooey-eyed, Levi and Lou are all gooey-eyed, Sully and Gus are all gooey-eyed. Everyone's gooey-eyed but me!"

Well, she'd done it again. Swapped saddles so that it was *me* now having to coo the tears outa *her*. So I now-nowed her, and before you know it she was all cheery again and we was right back to where we'd started our conversation. We ended it by me wishing her good luck and her telling me she'd call us after their first Tacoma game.

Don't even ask me about our phone bill that summer. I think I'm still making payments on it.

Now here's the run-down: E.M. didn't even have to call me the scores anymore, onaccounta I got the *Portland Oregonian* and their sport-writer man was talking up big the Bulldogs and following their come-outa-nowhere successes.

The Bulldogs won their series with Tacoma, even won in their series with Seattle. They took only two games offa Everett, but they took four offa Vancouver. (The one in South Washington, not South British Columbia. Whoever the hell named them two cities identical was either too fulla starch or too fulla hooch, and he shoulda known better!) So they finally light in Portland and here also they posted wins in three outa the five games they played.

Winning or no, it was the middle of September and damn I wanted 'em back! This was no way for cowfolks to live, and

I know I was real short with E.M. when she calls me from the Howell, Powell and Gallucci office to tell me of their phenomenal pheats. I asked her if maybe *now* wasn't it time to think about getting the Bulldogs sold, so's they could continue on the way they was meant to and she could continue on the way she was meant to, which was as my wife.

"What do you mean, Roy?"

"Well, E.M., we agreed we'd get the team shaped up — which they is — and make 'em a base-ball concern — which they is —then we'd sell the team and make back our expenses. Remember?"

"Oh, we have our feelers out, Roy. Anyway, we're starting for home tomorrow."

That announcement made me feel pretty damn good and I said so. I also said, "Hey, E.M., did you know you finally made some space in *The Sporting News*? Look, it says right here that the 'onct Beleaguered Bowery Bulldogs have been posting wins all over the Northwest' and then it goes on to say something about scouts following the team and all. You being followed, E.M.? Anyone been bothering you?"

E.M. said, "Oh no, they're all very nice."

"Well, unload the team on one of them scout fellers and come on home."

"Roy, it's not that simple."

"Nothing ever is with you, E.M."

"Royal, what's the matter with you?"

"I'm just getting that ol' feeling again. Like there's something you ain't telling me," I said. It was true. I could tell by her voice.

"Oh, it's just that Gus!"

"What's she up to?" I ask, taking a swaller. "She and Sully still sportin'?"

"She is so *heartless*!" E.M. continues.

"E.M.," I said, "Tell me what she's doing!"

"Oh, as soon as we hit Portland she goes out with some other man. Poor Sully. I thought he was going to come all undone. She said it was just a friend, but really, Gus doesn't have just a friend when men are concerned. I'm a little disappointed in her, that's all."

"E.M., you got the railroad schedule there infronta you?" I asked.

"Yes, why?"

"Is there a train out tonight?"

"Well yes, but why?"

"E.M., do you notice anything about my voice?"

"Yes, it's scrabbly. You got a cold?"

"No, E.M.," I said, low and slow. "This is the voice that's supposed to make you know," and here I am sorry to admit, I hollered into the speaking piece, "THAT I WANT YOU ON THAT DAMN TRAIN AND I MEAN NOW!"

There was a silence. I reckoned either E.M. would slither herself through that telephone wire and rip off my ear or else she'd reckon I meant business.

Danged if she didn't round up them Bulldogs and their assorted camaraderie and have 'em all setting on that five o'clock train east. Wisht I coulda been there to see how she did it.

eight

Well, if you thought the Idlehour team send-off was a good one, you shoulda seen how the town of Idlehour put itself out on behalf of our team's return. Sweartagod, there was a sign at the outshirts of town that touted, Welcome to Idlehour, Population 344 and Home of the Idlehour Bulldogs Base-Ball Club! Well, since I hadn't been to town for some time, I thought I'd ride down to the turnaround and see if maybe the Mayor had found hisself the money for our ball grounds. Dang if he didn't! And dang if it wasn't a real nice park, complete with bleachers alongst the sides for spectating, a wire back-stop for wild pitches, and even two of them dug-outs of which E.M. had told me about, so's the teams could be outa ear, tongue, and gun-shot distance.

The sign over the gate said, The Silas T. Burnbaum Memorial Field. I looked skyward and recalled ol' Silas T. and all his banker dealings, and I wondered how he woulda felt about his daughters spending his hard-stole money on such frills-for-all.

So back to town I go, and by then everyone was all turned out and the band was warming up. Reckon E.M. wired ahead somewheres around Cascade Locks so's the folks could all turn out for their team.

Here's another change: the two Pullman cars that pulled into the Idlehour wasn't in any way looking like the same ones that had pulled out. The cars was painted all bright white with red trim and big circus-like lettering alongst the side.

Here Come the Famous
Idlehour Bulldogs!
Best Ball Club in the West!

E.M. always did subscribe to the It Pays To Advertise Theory. She also knew how to soft-soap folks like the Idlehourians. You shoulda heard the uproar when they all saw that! And, I will add, for a team that was fresh offa the road, and traveling all night long, they all looked right impressive. They was in their uniforms, and I guess maybe that was all right, onaccounta they maybe hadn't never had the chance to arrive anywheres so victorious.

There was waving and tootning and a general state of celebration. The Mayor gave another speech fulla decorated words, and even I got caught up in it and whooped and hollered right alongst with everyone else. Besides, E.M. was soon to be in my arms, and the hell with base-ball and the team and the ranch!

Before long, the speeches was over and I finally could wrangle E.M. over to a quiet corner and give her my howdies.

Well, she dang near puffered herself up to my height when she pointed a finger and said, "Don't you *ever* yell at me like that in a telephone, Mr. Royal R-for-R-you-listening-to-me Leckner!"

"Yes, I'm listening," I said, a little chop-fallen. Here I was all ready to get some hugs and alls I got was her finger on the tip of my nose.

Then, just like that, she changed her wind and said, "Now then, why was it so all-fired urgent that we get home?"

I looked around. Didn't need to have anyone but her hear

what I was about to say. I pulled her into the alley and asked her, "Did Gus say who it was she was stepping out with?"

"Yes, an old friend, and why should you care? Really, it's nobody's business except Sully's and Gus's and the friend's, I suppose."

"She didn't mention any names? Like maybe Corky?"

She steps back and announces so loud that it damn near echoed in the alley, "Corky?!? You mean that boneheaded, inferior morning glory? What would make you think of him?"

"I just gotta make sure, E.M., that's all."

Now here she gives me her narrow eyes. "All right, Royal, what do you know that I should?"

So I told her of the Corky-Sully connection. Now, I always trusted E.M. to act cool as Custer when things got tight. So I stood back and waited for her to digest it all.

She just looked at me and said, "No, it wasn't Corky, Royal. She called him Harry. I remember distinctly eaves … overhearing her telephone conversation in Portland."

"You sure?"

"Of course I'm sure. You mean to tell me *that's* why you demanded we all come home? To ask the name of whoever it was she was stepping out with? Hell, you could have asked me that on the phone! Instead, you act like the whole West Coast is going to fall into the Pacific Ocean if we don't lighten it of two Pullman cars and a base-ball team! Well, you can just count on me getting even with you on that account!"

Oh well, she was gonna get even with me on that and *all* accounts no matter what anyhow, so I scooped her into my arms and she fought some, but soon we was kissing and she called me a damn fool and I told her I was glad to have her home.

In the meanwhilst, Sully had gone down to start us up our ol' Bess, which took some doing, being as she was setting all neglected that whole time in Idlehour. E.M. said she had some telegrams to send and so I thought I'd see how Sully was holding up.

I made note that Gus was not on his arm.

"I'm real proud of you, Sully. You and Billy, I reckon, worked a dang miracle with the Bulldogs."

He just said, "Oh, we had some help." That was like Sully, not taking credit. 'Cept there was something else in his voice and I reckoned I knew Sully had been hurt bad by the Old Sweet Tale.

So I said, "Sully, E.M. told me about Gus."

"Oh, I was only fooling myself, Roy. What do I have to offer a woman like Augusta?"

Well, I knew that wasn't the time and the place to set him straight about what he had to offer. So I just said, "Well, now that you're back home, maybe things can get back to normal. Maybe Gus will..."

"No. It's over. Thanks anyway, but it's over."

You know, I can ride through hell on a hatful of water, I can wrestle ol' Gabriel to let a calf live through a winter night, I can even get my wife to come home when I tell her to. But damn if I can say one word of comfort to a man who's been she-bit bad as Sully was.

He started to hum a sad aria and I helped him stoke up the boiler in ol' Bess.

Back home it was good to see and hear and smell women at Four Arrows onct again. We alla us had a ranch holiday and, of course, the bar be que and what was now getting to be our traditional backyard ball game.

Sully had gone right to work catching up on the horseshoeing, mostly correcting all the mistakes I had made in his absence. Dang lucky I didn't lame a horse with my inferior farrier skills.

But it looked to me like Gus was still making flirtigig eyes at Sully, and so I asked E.M. what the hell was happening.

She looked at me like I was crazy and shoulda known better'n to ask a question like that regarding her sister Gus. She gave me the famous 'dance with the one what brung ya' line and added a whole new wing which was, 'just keep two separate dance cards.'

Which we alla us did.

nine

'Course, Sully snapped outa his slough of romantical despond soon as Augusta started to show him some more of her considerable considerations. She always feathered out real spiffy, no matter what was on the agenda for the day, and I made note that she was on his arm every opportunity she could muster. Sure was a pair to draw to: him in his smithy garb and red-roguish beard, and her in her society togs and lace parasol.

It was on a Sunday, latish September, just a coupla days after the Bulldogs had all arrived back at Four Arrows. Not alota work was lined up, so the hands and the Bulldogs was pretty much just scattered around the place ... some went to town, some went for rides, some went Burnbauming, some was playing ball out back. Me and E.M. was just setting on the front porch, reading and enjoying the quiet.

So nobody took much notice when some dust kicks up on the road from town. Visitors was a common thing on a Indian Summer Sunday. E.M. and me just kept reading our papers. E.M. had her nose in *The Sporting News* and I had mine in the society page of the Walla Walla Wash paper. I always liked to keep my eye on who was marrying who, onaccounta I never wanted to give up hope on a Burnbaum.

"Any luck?" E.M. asked me like she had every Sunday we'd been married.

"Not this week," I sighed.

"Oh look, the Spiders lost another pitcher," she informs me. "Glass arm. Too bad. Not that any pitcher could save them this year!"

"You recognize that rig?" I asked, looking at the carriage that had just rounded the corner of our long approach.

E.M. looked up and over her specs and said, "That's the livery rental, isn't it?"

Livery rental meant outa town company and a extra seat at dinner, so we both stood up and wondered who it could be.

It was a city man, I could tell that. Even from far off, you can just tell when someone ain't comfortable behind a horse. Additional, he was dressed real slickery. Funny little hat, stripey suit and all.

He pulled up and we came out to the gate to greet him.

He doffs his hat, exposing some serious balditude, and he said, "Good day, folks. Alfred's the name. Drummond P…"

"How do you do, Mr. Drummond," I said back.

"Mr. Alfred," he corrected, and I knew from then on I was never gonna remember if he was Drummond P. Alfred or Alfred P. Drummond, so I just asked him what I could do for him.

"Well, I know I've been on Four Arrows land for at least an hour…"

"Maybe more," I said, noting the slowness at which he drove his horse.

"And I'm looking for one Leviticus Perrault. Are you by chance he?"

"No, sir, I'm Royal Leckner. This here is my wife. Leviticus is legal owner of Four Arrows but I'm foreman. Anything I can do for you?"

He climbed down from the carriage, but he got his pants cuff stuck in the seat spring and the horse started fidgeting and, if I didn't act fast as I did, that poor Drummond-Alfred feller was gonna be one-footin' it all the way back to Idlehour alongside a runaway rig.

I got the horse settled so's he could get his pants unstuck and invited him up to the porch, where E.M. offered him some lemonade. He sure looked like a fish outa water. City folks are just wonders that way. Makes me wonder what they think of me when I'm treading water in *their* territory.

"Thank you, sir. Actually, I'm not here on ranch business. I understand that Mr. Perrault owns the…" and here he pauses and pats his forehead with his hankie and pulls out a piece of paper. He puts his specs on and reads, "…the Idlehour Bulldogs?"

'Course, he didn't have to go through all that. We coulda told him. But he further goes on to say that he's the (now stay with me here) "Vice-President and Vice-Chairman of Alfred and Lightner Associates, in charge of the Interstate Triparte of Post-Season Exhibition and World-Wide Distribution."

"You are, huh," I said, thinking all them words sounded right impressive, but we still didn't have a iota what the hell the man was.

"My card," he adds, like as though seeing it all in writing was gonna make it easier.

E.M. and me looked at it and I just asked, "So what is it you do, Mr. Drummond?"

"Alfred," he corrected.

"Sure. Call me Royal."

I could tell the heat was taking its toll on him and so we poured him another glassa lemonade.

Then E.M. comes right down to case-cards. "Are you a scout?"

He laughed a little at that. "No, no, madam, I'm an agent."

"Of what?" I asked.

He took a long drink, patted his forehead again, and replied, "Of base-ball. I book exhibition games."

Then E.M. re-looks at his card and says, "Oh, *that* Triparte! Of course! I've heard of your company."

"E.M.," I said, "you and the boys just got off the road. Don't tell me you're thinking about..." — alls I could remember from his title was worldwide — "...going worldwide?"

"We've been watching the Bulldogs very carefully, Mrs. Leckner," he says, ignoring me now he'd found the person in charge a' the Bulldogs.

"Yes, go on," she says.

"And we think you have a..."

Now here E.M. asked if maybe Alfred might want a drink of something more fortifying. Well, I could subscribe to that and so I went in to fetch something. I shoulda known better. By the time I got back out — sweartagod — maybe one minute I was gone — E.M. and him are standing and shaking hands like they've just struck a deal.

Which they had.

We alla us had a jolt of a 'and may the best team win' toast.

For on Saturday, October 22nd, 1898, Idlehour was gonna host what was to be the biggest thing to hit our corner of the world since the Famous Freak Tornado of '78.

It was to be the Bulldogs versus the pennant winners for that 1898 base-ball season.

Well, I had to set down.

"I don't get it, Al," I said. "You mean the winners of *the* pennant, back east? The big boys?"

He sorta laughed at that and smiled and explained that there wasn't gonna be no League Association championship game that year — no series betwixt the two top teams, no nothing.

"But what about that Temple Cup championship I've heard about?" E.M. asked. That's E.M. for you — seal a deal first, ask questions later.

"Well, that was fine'n'dandy for the first four years, but," and here he takes another sip and sounds real wistful, "attendance and enthusiasm among the fans was pretty miserable last year, so they've suspended it. In fact, that nasty little war with Spain hurt attendance everywhere. Which brings me back to why I'm here."

"Well, I got a few 'whys' too. Like why the hell…"

"Royal!" E.M. shushed me. "It's Sunday!"

"Well, why the heck would a team that high'n'mighty wanna come way out here and pick on us?" I asked. "Sure, the Bulldogs has been quite a sensation, but hell, heck, after all is said and done, they're just a scrub farm team." Then I indicated the ruralness surrounding us. Now that I think about it, I reckon we was *the* original farm team.

"Well, of course many of the teams go out on exhibition after the regular season. Preferably the west and the south, for obvious reasons."

I looked at E.M. and she said, "Weather."

"And I have been instructed to book the start of the tour right here, in this lovely part of the world, with your Bulldogs."

I nodded and said, "Well, the weather gets a little iffy around these parts in October. Can't you already feel that nip in the shade? And why Idlehour? I don't think there's even enough extra beds in the whole dang town to set up a base-ball touring team, no matter who they are or what pennants they're touting."

"Oh, don't worry, Mr. Leckner," he goes on. "That's where my company comes in. We'll supervise all the details."

"In just three weeks?" I asked him. "And how you gonna supervise the weather?"

"Royal, you sound like you don't *want* this wonderful opportunity for the Bulldogs," E.M. said.

"Like I said, leave all the details to Alfred and Lightner Associates. Believe me, we'll put Idlehour on the map and we'll make sure every paper in the country knows about your Bulldogs," he said, finishing his drink.

E.M. pours him another one and asks, "Tell me, Mr. Drummond, who do you think it'll be?"

"My money is on the Beaneaters," he allowed.

"I don't know. Those Birds are looking pretty good to me." She held up her copy of *The Sporting News*.

He looked at the date of the paper and noted it was two weeks old. "Oh, that's all old news, Mrs. Leckner. The Reds pulled ahead last week, but the Beaners caught up. Put your money on Boston."

"The hell I will. I'm betting on the Bulldogs!"

"Oh, that brings up another point. We, of course, discourage gambling of any type on the tour."

"Oh, of course. I was speaking figuratively. That goes without saying."

She sure as hell *was* speaking figuratively, as in big round figures, I thought. Then I looked at the contract and thought, I'll be damned. Sometimes the mountain *does* come to Mohammed. 'Course, I knew life, so I wasn't gonna rest on any laurels that I hadn't myownself trimmed.

Them laurels was trimmed, by the way, by Gus. Just then, she rounds the corner of the orchard on Sully's arm and sees the rental carriage, looks on the porch, and calls out, "Drummie? Drummie, is that you?"

She comes a-skirting up through the garden, leaving Sully flat, and I made note he slapped his hat down and kicked it, no doubt thinking his girl had onct again deserted him for another ol' beau. Then he stomped off, and I didn't blame him.

Well, both E.M. and me had a real good idea then of why us, and why the Bulldogs and why Idlehour. Easy. Three little letters spelling one big fe-as-ko:

G - U - S.

ten

Ol' Drummie, as Gus called him, was true to his word. No sooner had the ink dried on the exhibition contract than he had begun his publicity. 'Course, the first thing E.M. did was set up a sorta war-room in the Horse Palace. Numbers went up on the blackboard, and her and Lou taped numbers and names and all sortsa equations and formulas and other such arithmetical horrors on papers scattered hither'n'yon. E.M. ordered up copies of numbers books from that Spaulding feller and some Chatwick man. She was about as busy as a bee in a bucket of tar, and alls she told me was we had to get ready for the game and somehow working on these numbers was gonna be the key.

Naturally, we was alla us watching the papers real close to see which team we was gonna play — and down to the last ten days of play it looked like it was gonna be either the Baltimore Orioles or the Boston Beaneaters. Beaneaters! What a name for a team! How the hell could you take a team serious with a name like that? Only name worse that I can recall was those Brooklyn Bridegrooms. But like you know, it ain't the name that makes the team — it's the publicity.

Like the Idlehour Bulldogs. By the time Drummie was done, you'd a thought we was the greatest conglomeration since Jerusalem Slim and his ten disciples. 'Course, in the Bible it makes no mention if them Holy Boys played base-ball, but if they did, then Drummie coulda sent 'em out on a exhibition tour and alla the Holy-Landers woulda paid big shekels to see 'em.

Now, Idlehour was, of course, beside itself with anticipation, and this I mean in a most literal way. It was like the town had growed in two. Sweartagod, in one week's time there was tents set up for housing for make-shift restaurants, saloons, for every type a convenience that was gonna lure folks in from everywheres. (Yep, even them.)

The townsfolks was making signs offering room and board. Everywhere you went you could hear so much hammering and planning and big expectations being handed back'n'forth, you'd think you was either witnessing the building of Sutter's Mill or the rebuilding of Atlanta. The Silas T. Burnbaum Memorial Field had workers building more and more bleachers, with tents alongst the side for food and drink dispensing. Wasn't anyone in town gonna miss a trick or a tip.

Back at home, we kept strictly to business. Training the team and preparing for winter. E.M. and Lou was busy calculating, calling *The Sporting News* every day for the latest scores. E.M. made the poor phone feller call off the statistics and she jotted 'em down and put 'em up in such a fashion that you'd have to be a mathematical genius to figure out the lines and the abbreviations and such. Naturally, she handed the figures to Lou, whose face would go all grinny as she would more'r'less inhale 'em.

Since we'd begun with a smaller herd, Hardy and me decided to not go to market this year and let the ranks grow over the winter. We sure coulda used the money from the cattle selloff, but just the idea of sending Leviticus to town knowing that them Barnum and Bailey fellers was touring the West Coast made our decision a easy one. Elephants, camels, and clowns would hafta wait for another day.

'Course, the weather had me worried the most. "What if the weather don't cooperate, E.M.?" I asked my wife, following her to the window to look outside at the cold rain that was pounding us that October 14th. "We can't play our series in this weather."

"Series?" E.M. said. "What series? We're playing just one game. Where did you get the idea we were playing a series?"

"You mean to tell me we're alla us, the whole damn territory, doing all this preparation for just one game?" I demanded.

"Yes," she replied simple-like.

"But all along you been doing the best outa five."

"No, Royal, I'm sure I told you it was going to be just one game. That's all the time the schedule has and..."

"One lousy, measly game?"

"Well! Lousy? Measly? Is that what you think?"

"Well, it sure as hell don't seem like anyone's gonna see mucha profit from just one lousy, measly game!" I barked back. I reckon we'd botha us been freezin' for a fight. Pressures was mounting royal. "Just how much we gettin' paid to get whooped by that fancy back east team?"

"*Paid?*" she hollers back. "Nothing. Who said anything about getting *paid?*"

I looked around whilst I thought of the opposite of getting paid. "How much we *paying?*"

"Nothing, Royal. Didn't you read that contract?"

"Not after you sneezed on the dotted line, I didn't!"

Then she pulls it out from the desk and flashes it in front of my face. "There! Right there in black and white!"

I looked at it and she was right. There it was. It said regarding the 'gate' — winner take all.

"Oh, so *now* I see why they wanted to play us. Talk about your guaran-damn-teed pay day!"

Well, E.M. knows when to pat down my hackles. She says, "Roy, have I ever lie … I mean, have I ever steered you wr…?" Maybe the third one was gonna be the charm: "Have I ever let you down?"

Well, no, she hadn't. She'd always done pretty damn much what I expected her to do. She went on to tell me how much the town was gonna make even if we lost. There was lodging, beer, food and oh, the publicity! She ended her spiel in true Elijah-like-prophet fashion:

"No, Idlehour will never be the same after this game, Roy!"

It was then the telephone rang, and dang, I always jumped when it did, especially when I was damn near settin' on it. Close as I was, E.M. leaps up and grabs it first.

"Yes? Yes, I'll accept!" She looked at me and said, "Steve. From *The Sporting News*. Remind me to send him a box of cigars for all he's done."

She starts writing things down and nodding her head, and the language they was communicating to each other sounded like from another place and time. Lotsa numbers and letters of which I soon tired, and so I left the room.

A few minutes later, E.M. comes crashing down the hallway, and if you think it's hard for a woman to run with all them skirts, well you ain't never seen E.M. when she was on a mission.

"Lou! Lou!" she was hollering. "Lou! Boston! It's Boston!"

Lou comes sliding 'round the hallway, fulla papers and books, and they dang near collide with each other. From there they bundle up and go down to the Horse Palace, and they didn't come back till dinner.

When they did, they looked like they had gone through the wash, wringer and all — all wet with rain, hairs askewy, pencils sticking outa hair buns, and Lou even had a ink spot big as a base-ball on her sleeve.

"Well, we've done all we can. All we can do now is wait," E.M. announced to me, rolling her sleeves back down and sounding like a doctor fresh outa the operating room.

'Course, it may not surprise you to know that, in the week following, E.M. *did* have more to do — she didn't just wait like she said she was gonna do. She called her momma. Remember the one on the Mississippi? Yep, I'd met her onct in Portland when she was still talking to Mr. Gallucci. Nice woman, I liked her from the get-go. Held one helluva grudge though, and proved it by taking herself on a gambling junket shortly after Enrico was sent off to prison.

Well, in one phone call E.M. got her momma not only to bet heavy on the Boston Beaneaters, but she'd got her high-rolling gambler associates to join her, and by October 18th — a coupla days before the Boston team was to arrive, they had upped the betting line to damn near 15 to 1. The 15 of course belonging to the Beaneaters and the one belonging to the Bulldogs.

Every paper in the country was reporting it, and I gotta tell you, it's sorta like hog-futures: who knows what hogs will do today, let alone next fall? No one who's ever raised 'em! So who the hell decides these things, anyhow?

It's called odds. And odds are right now you'n'me are gonna have a drink, onaccounta it gets even odder.

PART 5

one

Now, if I had me any luck due, I didn't want to waste it on the Atlantic Variety when I needed it to just plumb stay alive in my Northeast corner of Oregon. Therefore, I ain't no gambler, other'n the regular day-to-day gambles a man takes just wandering down the road of life. Like firinstance waking up in the morning and checking in on your wife's mood; like eating a new kinda omelet set down infronta you, knowing full-well your cook hates snakes; like keeping the sights of thirty men, alla 'em single, on the same goal and not gal. And, of course, like watching close-like 'round that next bend, onaccounta you never know if that's a rifle barrel or a slingshot you see aimed at you. So, you know I was tippy-toein' and looking each direction all at onct.

Now, I've known men that would gamble a month's pay just on whether or not a horse would roll left or right onct the saddle comes off. But not me. Alls I know for sure is the dang horse is gonna roll up. But E.M. was more a risky sort than me, and I reckon it wasn't her fault onct you got to know her family tree and its assorted snapped-off, blowed-off, and sawed-off limbs.

So when that betting line was edging up to the 20 to 1 mark, I made note E.M. was setting right ticklish in the anxious seat.

"Damn!" she grumbled to me. "Damn, I wish I could get my hands on some money. Look at those odds!"

"E.M., you mean to tell me you'd bet money on *our* team? Are you outa your dad-blasted mind?" I hollered. "There's no way our Bulldogs can take a team like the Beaneaters! What the hell you thinkin', woman?"

"Oh, put your hackles down, Roy. First of all, it's illegal for the owner to bet against his team. Even *you* ought to know that. Secondly, who can ignore those odds? Thirdly, did it ever occur to you that the Bulldogs might, just might, have a small chance?"

"Yeah, about the same chance a rabbit has in a hound's mouth, which makes it fourthly, we ain't got any cash money, so both the rabbit *and* the issue is dead."

She flashes the latest betting line on the game under my nose. "But look," she tempts, "from the Mississippi to the Barbary Coast, people are betting the heck out of this game. No one's seen anything like it since Sullivan versus Corbett." She starts eyeballing the silver tea service on the sideboard.

"E.M.," I said, "don't you think you and me have risked enough of the kids' futures already? I say it's a damn good thing you can't get your hands on some bettin' money!"

She looked at me whilst biting her lip, which sent my antennae to twitching. That was her 'should I or shouldn't I tell him' look. But she didn't say anything, so I kept on talking, like as though if I kept talking she was gonna forget her usual she-coonery. "As it is, E.M., I'm just hoping to break even, and that don't count the five thousand we owe your daddy."

It was like mentioning 'Daddy' made E.M. remember the something she'd forgot to tell me. "Oh yes. Daddy. Did I forget to mention I called him?"

"What for?" I turned and gave her my famous slow look.

"Well, you know how Daddy loves a longshot!"

"Yes, but not as much as he loves a sure thing," Gus said, waltzing into the room and into our conversation.

"What?" we both asked, flat and oh-no-like.

"I was just talking to Daddy on the telephone," she said, helping herself to the candy dish on the piano. "He felt *real* bad about his little game over the five thousand. So, when I told him he could maybe make it up to me by placing a little bet for me out of one of his many slush funds..."

"Not in your name, I hope," E.M. said.

"Well, it hardly matters. After all, dear, I'm not the owner. Besides, even when I did own the Bulldogs, I used to bet against them all the time and no one ever knew a thing," she said.

"You'd think she'd be a damn millionaire by now," mutters me to the ceiling.

Then I looked at E.M. looking at her sister. It was like they had one of them telepathy connections betwixt 'em, and I even took a step back not wanting my feeble brain to get caught in the crossfire.

Gus just said, "Well, E.M., after all, I'm responsible for this whole thing getting underway. Without my connections and my influence, your sweet little team of country bumpkins and Bowery pickpockets would be back on the kiddies circuit, losing to the old-folks-at-home teams. Surely you don't think Drummie showing up here was a coincidence, do you? Besides, Daddy owes me. Five thousand, to be exact."

"What's Sully gonna say, you betting against the team?" I asked. "I thought you two was..."

"Oh, we were and we still may," she interrupted. "But I have found out one thing while staying here, under these circumstances: I don't like being poor or dependent. And Sully has nothing to do with the fact that I can make a bundle on this game."

"What's five thousand at 20 to 1, E.M.?" I asked.

"Hardly a bundle," E.M. said. She walked around her sister and said, suspecious-like, "All right, you, there's more. Deliver."

"Well, I would say maybe Royal's wrong about those 20 to 1 odds." She hands E.M. a piece of paper and said, "Here. This is the latest line out of San Francisco. Folks are sure having fun with this one."

"22 to 10?" E.M. asked.

"So, you can see, Daddy and me stand to do a lot better than that. You know, it amazes me the amount of influence he has."

'Course at that point I was expecting E.M. and Gus to finally break into a fisting bee. Instead, E.M. just circles her sister whilst she's thinking. "You know, Gus," she says, "I have underestimated you."

"You *always* do."

"But you do have me to thank for one thing."

"Like what?" Now here Gus wasn't looking so fulla herself. In fact, she was now watching E.M. real close. And so was I.

"Well, for telling Daddy about Sully."

"Sully?"

"Yes, I told him you had finally found the man who could keep you occupied and out of trouble for the rest of your life."

"He can not!" Gus objected. "I mean, where do you get the nerve to tell Daddy anything about me and Sully?"

"Since Sully told me you were the finest woman he had ever ever met, and if he had the money he would sweep you away forever and keep you in the style to which you think you're accustomed. Well, Daddy was elated. Do you know what he said?"

"No," Gus said.

"He said, 'God love her! My little Gussie is happy at last!' No wonder he was so generous to you. Maybe he thinks his money is finally going to a good cause. Like a dowry. I think I even heard his voice crack a little. When do you ever remember Daddy getting teary-eyed, Gus?"

"He called me that? His little Gussie?"

E.M. nodded and said, "He never calls *me* his little anything."

Then Gus sorta shook off this side-track and came back onto the trail. "Well, that still has nothing to do with..." She turns and asks, "Sully really said that?"

Here E.M. crost her heart with one hand, and I had to figure the other hand behind her back was touting a few crost fingers.

"So, this is going to be oddles and oddles of fun," E.M. sums up. "With both Daddy and my mother betting on the Beaneaters, and with *us* (she takes my arm) betting on the Bulldogs, well ... how can I lose? If the Beaneaters win, Daddy and Mother will gladly be generous on the tips I gave them. And if they lose — which they just damn well might — then it's winner take all. 'Take' being the key word here. T-A-K-E, take."

So I reckon she thought she had alla the bases covered, as they say in base-ball. Incept the home plate was wide open, clean-swept, and unprotected.

Gus popped another candy into her mouth, swept over to E.M., and said something which none of us could understand, onaccounta the caramel was proving to be quite a mouthful. And here the lovely Augusta, my sister-half-in-law, takes the caramel outa her mouth so's she could be clear-like understood and restates, "We'll see what the key word is, Elijah Marie. We'll see." And then she pops her candy back into her mouth.

Sweartagod, she floated outa the room like she was so much dandelion fluff on a summer breeze, and who the hell knew just where she was gonna land and take root.

After she left, I said, "Save me the parable and just tell me this, E.M. Are you responsible for them Bulldog odds changing?"

Then E.M. walks to the candy dish, takes a few, hands me one, and answers, "Not with the egg money I put down." She unwraps a candy and says, "Like I said before Gus came in, Daddy *loves* a long shot."

'Course, Gus and her 'we'll sees' put us all on The Big Alert. Just what we needed with the Beaneaters arriving the next day. Now, who really knew what them two Gallucci girls was up to. The last thing I had time for was who was betting what on who. That was all gonna come to light within 48 hours anyhow. So instead I did something I'd wanted to do for about four years. I cut the telephone wire to the house and the one to the barn too.

You may ask why.

Because there'd been entirely too much telephoning of relatives and prisons and book-makers and such. Additional, Gus couldn't telephone anyone now. I knew that if she was planning a coup call to Corky, she'd be the first to make note the line wasn't working.

And that's just what happened. She announces she's going to town and would maybe one of the hands drive her in. Here I saw my second opportunity to box off the canyon. I had Sully drive her. Only I told him she was waiting for him to fire the question and I suggested he take her way off somewheres where they could have the discussion in private. I reminded him how pretty and romantical the country is on the east road toward the Blue Mountains. I did not remind him how the road was real unsure, and I also did not remind him he was a touch behind in his wheel-wrighting. Point is, Sully and Gus needed to botha 'em be far away from Idlehour for the next two days.

"I know why you're doing this, Roy," Sully said.

"You do?" I asked.

"Sure. And I don't blame you."

"You don't?"

"Nope. I'll sure hate to miss that game, but it's the best for everyone. Besides," he added, giving me a shy and boy-like grin, "I think Gus is worth it, don't you?"

Now here I lied. I said, "Sure. You two just have a good time. And Sully? You know women," I said.

"I do?"

"Well, let me remind you. They need lots of pretty talk and such. Oh, Gus will take on some, that's just her fiery nature. But you just stick with it, boy. She'll come around."

I hated telling him that, onaccounta I knew for a fact that Gus had one of them lady pistols. E.M. had told me her Daddy had bought 'em matching ones for their Christmas stockings when they was still unmarrieds. You have to wonder what the hell he was thinking. Maybe it was 'Pistols for two, breakfast for one?'

Well anyhow, now I had even home plate covered.

two

Now, there was a sight'n'sound: Sully and Gus heading down the road toward town and insteada going straight at the west cut off road, he goes east. I could hear Gus hollering way up to the Horse Palace. But Sully kept on driving and I wisht him well.

I went inside and there I found Leviticus setting alone in the middle of the arena. He was tossing a ball up in the air and then catching it. Now it didn't use to be often we'd see Levi without his Lou(ella), so I commenced to worry some when I saw him looking so lonely.

"You okay, Levi?" I asked.

He looked at me and kept throwing his ball. I walked closer and asked him if maybe he wanted to play us some catch. He just shook his head 'no.'

So I set down next to him. Eye to eye is best with Leviticus. "Where's Lou?" I asked.

He just nodded toward the training room and said, "In there with her numbers."

"She been ignoring you?" I asked.

"I hate numbers," he sorta whined.

'Course, I'm thinking uh-oh, can't lose Leviticus now — not to numbers, not to a spat, not to nothing. "She's just working extra hard to make sure alla this turns out good, Levi," says me.

Then he looks at me, and it was times like that, fully growed or not, I wanted to sling my arms round his shoulders. "But I'm scardt, Roy," he said, his eyes filling with tears. "I'm scardt."

Hell, maybe home base wasn't covered after all. "Scardt of what?"

"Of the Beaners."

"Why?"

He just shrugged his shoulders.

"Is it the crowds? You've pitched just fine with folks watching, Levi. Lotsa times. And you did just fine."

"Lou's scardt too," he said. "I know. I can tell."

Levi was just like a critter that way. Picked up real good on the fears of those around him. And I reckon I'd been too busy with my own problems to even think about what Levi was feeling.

"Nah, Lou's just havin' her some fun. You know how she loves her numbers."

"Loves 'em more'n me," he said.

"No such thing, Levi. Look, this is gonna be just like any other game. Only it'll be all your friends and family rootin' and cheerin' for you. Won't that be fun?"

"If I don't pitch good, what'll happen to the Bulldogs?" he asked.

Before I could answer, he asked, "If I do pitch good, what'll happen to the Bulldogs?"

"I reckon no matter what, the Bulldogs will all go on to better things," I said. As the words was coming out, I thought I was getting to the bottom of Levi's concern.

"What about me, Roy?" he asked, looking now at the ball in his hands. "What about me?"

"You like playin' ball?" I asked him. Hell, it never onct occurred to me that maybe Leviticus was destined to not be owner of Four Arrows. Maybe his future was playing ball.

"Do I have to?" he asked.

"Have to what?"

"Pitch?"

"Well, tomorrow you do," I said.

"Forever?"

"After Saturday's game with Boston, you don't ever have to touch a base-ball again, if you don't want," I said.

"But then who's gonna pitch?"

"They'll find another pitcher. Maybe two or three, like the other teams have. They'll do good, Levi."

"But they're *mine*," he said. His voice was fulla despair and agony, sorta like the time he first come to realize that his cattle herds was all gonna become steaks somewheres onct he sold 'em.

"And you want what's best for 'em, don't you?"

"Yes," he said, quiet-like.

"Maybe what's best for 'em is to let 'em move on so's some-one can make 'em into world champions."

"World Champions?"

"Sure. I don't think there's no greater honor you can give your team."

I wasn't sure he understood what I was saying, so I added, "All this base-ball's been fun, ain't it?"

He nodded.

"But them base-ball boys don't belong here. That'd be like making your woollybacks graze in bog-lands. Just wouldn't be fair, would it?"

He shook his head.

"So I reckon you oughta help them Bulldogs get on with their lifes and let us get on with ours. It's hard, ain't it, Levi? Toughest thing in the world's knowin' when to let go."

He then took a deep breath, followed by a big exhale, like he was making the biggest decision of his life, which maybe he was.

"Let go. Gotta know when to let go," he said, standing up and swinging his arm like he was practicing his pitch. Then he hollers, "Suffer Your Age!" He holds the ball to his face like he was talking to it. Then he takes one of his pitch wind-ups and says, "Let go!" And he hurls the ball hard and fast and it goes right through smack-dab the middle of the dangling wheel rim and it WHANG! ricochets offa the wire back-stop.

He looks at me and grins and says, "It's all in the let-go!"

He rubs his shoulder and walks off, saying let-go, let-go to hisself, leaving me now all by my lonesome setting in the middle of the arena, wondering if maybe we'd been talking about two different issues.

Since I'd sent Sully off on a dangerous mission, maybe never to return the same, I knew it was up to me to fire up ol' Bess to run our team into town the morning of the game. Now, I'd done it onct or twice and pretty much knew how to do it, but I didn't have Sully's touch, nor could I imitate his long line of educated adjectives that seemed to get ol' Bess's heart started. But I did my best.

E.M. comes up to the engine and announced the team was all loaded up. She looks around and asked if Sully and Gus had come back yet and maybe she oughta start worrying.

"Now, E.M., I told you. I made sure there was food, water, and lotsa warming in that buckboard Sully took. I think they'll do just fine. Unless compromising your sister's fine reputation is what's got you worried."

She looked at me and issued a big HA!

It was fun, her riding in the engine with me. She helped load firewood into the boiler and I was damn proud of her. She informed me she wasn't in no way gonna risk any of the ball players' staminas or arms by asking 'em to toss firewood before the biggest game of their lifes.

Now, to give you an idea as to the extent of Drummie's expertise, I will describe the outshirts of Idlehour as we chugged through.

There was dozens and dozens of tents set up. Far off in the distance, I'll be damned if there wasn't even a Tee Pee village, which I recognized as the Umatilla tribe. Horses was staked out in rope corrals, dozens of fires was smoking and kids was playing and dogs was barking and I'll bet there hadn't been such a hurry-up gathering of folks anywheres since the opening of the Cherokee Strip.

Closer to town the humankind grew even more. Now the tents and wickey-ups was getting more commercial-like. I made note of the fast-painted signs:

Bank of Idlehour Annex
Beer 5 Cents
Good Food Fast
Best Oregon Whiskey
Aunt Shirley's Homemade Pies
Burnbaum Sisters Health Tonic
Alfred and Lightner Base-Ball Mementoes and Equipment
Outhouse

And so on.

Hell, this was making the Columbian Exposition in Chicago look like a dang county fair. 'Course, by now there was folks all cheering our arrival, walking alongside the train as we came into town. I tooted the horn to warn folks away from the tracks, since scooping a few up in our cowcatcher mighta put a small wet blanket on our big day.

Then we rounded the last bend and come direct into the Idlehour Boom Town.

Have you ever walked into some place and just knew by the leftovers and the dregs of the area what had gone on the night before? Like maybe arriving at a battle scene, or maybe walking in after trusting your sons to set tight to home whilst you left town for a coupla days, or maybe even like New Orleans on the Wednesday after Fat Tuesday? Well, one look at the town of Idlehour and you knew there'd been the biggest celebration there since that *au du Paris can-can* show come to town back in '95. Sweartagod, if a town can be hung over, then Idlehour was damn near a illustration of it in the medical books. Now I ain't saying the town had been shot up or anything, but lotsa the buntings was unstrung from the telephone poles, a few shop signs was down, a small fire in a back alley was still a-smoldering, and if it wasn't for seeing lotsa folks coming to life, hearing ladies' laughters, you woulda thought maybe we'd been raided by them Umatillas on their way to setting up their village.

But the townfolks gathered theirselfs together and hurrahed us as the train snuck in. I tooted the horn and lotsa hands went for heads. Idlehour likes her little celebrations. More'n that, I made note, as the visiting Boston Beaneaters all marched up to greet us, Idlehour just loves to entertain her guests.

And no one coulda been happier'n me.

three

Now, you know me and God. I don't for one minute think He's setting anything up for ol' Royal just to make his life easier … You know, like partying our guests all night so's they might be off their game. I ain't saying that's the case, but the weather was good, I will acknowledge that corn.

Well, we was alla us escorted by the mayor after one of his speeches to the court house where the newly formed Ladies of Idlehour Base-Ball Benefit and Booster League was busy setting up a pancake feed for alla us. 'Course, the Burnbaum girls was all in this league and it was their job to pour the coffee and pass around the juice. Now, I didn't know nothing about their so-called health tonic, but I was willing to bet money that it involved a healthy douse of home brew, and I won't say they was and I won't say they wasn't pouring some into the coffee they was serving the Beaneaters.

'Nuf ced on that account.

There was more speech making and soon it was time to get the ball game underway. 'Course, all this time I'm looking over my shoulder to see if Sully and Gus or maybe just the horses and empty wagon had made their way into town yet. Instead I saw E.M. and Lou(ella) walking ahead with two satchels fulla their hard-wrought numbers, looking like two female lawyers off to argue a case to the Supreme Court boys.

Over the other shoulder, I was looking for that Corky. Instead, I just saw folks on every corner putting money one way or the other on the game. Didn't know we had so many makeshift book-makers in the country, let alone Oregon.

Then, from behind, Billy and Anita come up to me and pull me around.

"Where is he?" Billy demanded, all wrung out.

"Who he?"

"Sully!" both him and Anita answered.

"He's nowhere to be found and how could he run out on us at a time like this?" Billy continued.

"Si!" Anita agreed.

I apologized for not telling him sooner that Sully was maybe gonna be otherwise disposed of that day and, "Hell, Billy, you know the Bulldogs better'n anyone. You don't need Sully now. It's all up to you. Sully will be here when he's here. So go on and do us all proud."

Anita looked at Billy and him at her. I could tell lots more'n the base-ball game was at stakes and he got a big look of re-solve on his face, cocked his glasses, and hell, if he'd a-saluted me I wouldn'ta been at all surprised.

I reckon I was the last living soul in the town of Idlehour and a square radius of I don't know how many miles to arrive at the Silas T. Burnbaum Memorial Field. Which is the way I wanted it.

Insteada going in through the gate and maybe even being suffered to pay a two-dollar charge to get in, I walked around back toward the grandstands, which really wasn't all that grand, but did hold up a goodly number of folks. It was my plan to survey as much as I could, so I snuck around the side.

The Idlehour Band was putting out a brass tune, and by the way they sounded you would think John Philip Sousa hisownself was in the crowd, which didn't matter that he wasn't, onaccounta he wouldn'ta recognized his tunes anyhow.

I looked at the set-up. My heart was pounding, of that you

may be sure. The Beaneaters was set up alongst the left and we was set up alongst the right. There was the umpire man behind home plate and even an official type of man standing on the baseline betwixt second and third bases.

And then I saw this one whole long bench with a table alongst the first base line. There was a banner attached to it, and all it said was 'Press.' Sweartagod, there musta been ten of 'em, newspaper men, even one woman. I reckoned she musta been the one reporting on the ladies' all-spraddled-out fashions that day, but I also reckoned that E.M. would take proper note of her and find out how it was she'd come to be one woman against nine men. E.M. was always real concerned how other uppity women got things done.

Then up above the home plate was a even stranger sight. It was a row of three big megaphone horns and a man was commencing to speak into the middle one. Even from way behind where I was hiding, I could hear him like he was standing next to me. The crowd hushed and he spoke:

"Ladies and Gentleman, Boys and Girls, I would like to welcome you to this beautiful fall day at the (and here he took a pause, I reckon to look at his program to see where it was he was talking from) the Silas T. Baumburn Memorial Field."

Lotsa folks corrected him and then he resaid it right. "Sorry, folks, *Burnbaum* Memorial Field, where today we are going to be treated to the first exhibition game of the finest team in the United States of America today, winner of 102 games this season over Baltimore's 96, the World Champion Boston Beaneaters!"

There was clappning and the announcer man goes on to introduce the "Toast of the Coast, The Idlehour Bulldogs!" Well, I reckon they heard the crowd's roar clear to Boston. Then the man announced each ball player as they walked out onto the field, and I commenced to climb over the fence. Well, a gate man caught me and just held me by my boot and all he said was, "Okay, sonny. Two bucks." He held his hand out and since he didn't know me and I didn't know him, I paid up. Then he let me finish climbing over the fence.

I went around to the Bulldogs' dug-out. The announcer was still announcing names. I have to tell you, when he lastly came around to introducing Leviticus Perrault, I damn near burst with pride watching him walk out — toting nothing more'n a grin, a glove, and a prayer, but a good man from the ground up. He acted a little goosey as he waved to Lou(ella), who, I found out just then, had her one damn good, strong whistle. E.M. musta taught her. The rest of the Bulldogs clapped him on the back as he joined the team, and I got me some jimble jumbles on his behalf. There he stood amongst his teammates. Whoever woulda thought Levi would ever been so welcome, so needed and, best a' all, so liked!

Lou was downright adorable in her uniform and braids, and E.M. was in her most smart-looking wear, and them not even noticing me or anyone else. All they was noticing was Beaneater team names on the player list and comparing 'em to all their books of numbers.

It was time for the game to begin, and since we was the home team, we took the field first. I watched the Boston boys as they came up to bat. Leviticus seemed to lose his grin and he got him a look on his face that I didn't recall anytime ever seeing. His face turns older sorta. Serious-like. Like he was concentrating real hard. He eyes the batter and then looks like he's gonna stare him down, not pitch him down.

Then all of a sudden he stops his stare and looks over to Lou, who gives him a buncha hand signals. Well, he gives her a nod, spits, and then does his pitch.

Strike. Strike. And strike. 1-2-3. Easy as lying. The folks

went crazy and clapped him a good one. Levi looked up at the crowd and took his accolades by doffing his cap.

Well, you know how that looked to the Boston boys and, gotta be honest, that act didn't set well with me, either. So up comes the next man and the crowd hushes.

Now this batter looks to me like he's there to get even for the previous strike out; had him a real mean face and he practice-swings his bat like he was ol' Paul Bunyan making tree stumps.

He finally settled in, and Levi flung him a early Christmas present. Yessir. That Beaneater hit it right on the trademark and you shoulda seen that ball disappear. Reckon some kid's still huntin' for it. Wasn't no use the batter wasting too much air, so he just sorta strolled the bases all 'round. He was welcomed home by his fellow Beaneaters.

The next batter comes up and Levi's watching Lou for her hand signals, which musta said slow the ball down some, onaccounta I didn't know a ball could travel that slow and not be rolling on the ground. The batter swung so mighty it was like he was carving I.O.U.'s in the air. Twice. By the third pitch, he'd figured things out and the Beaneater connected real good with the ball. Hits high to the middle-pasture-man. Musta took a week for the ball to come down and our fielder just kept backing up and backing up till he was up against the fence. Finally the ball re-enters the atmosphere and our man caught it, giving the crowd something to shout about.

Damn, this was gonna be a game! The fourth Beaneater then takes his turn with the bat. Now, sooner or later in all sports betwixt men, things is eventually gonna get personal. After two strikes and two balls, the batter flashes some false ivory toward Jay. Jay takes his usual offense, and they had some nose-to-nose adjectives till the umpire man breaks it up. Now, I don't reckon it's possible for a batter to aim for the pitcher with his hit, but it sure looked like he was doing just that. Levi went down hard as the ball tagged his shoulder, bringing the crowd to their feet. Our short-stopper got even by throwing the ball hard to first base where it arrived the same time the batter did, giving every person there an opinion about which arrived first.

He was judged out, and by then Billy and Jay was out there helping Levi to his feet whilst the players was switching sides. I looked over to Lou and made note E.M. was holding her hand fast. 'Course, I knew that look on Levi's face. He rose, rubbed his left shoulder, and made some eye-to-eye with the batter as he walked past him. Any other man woulda said something smart or maybe even took a swing. But not Levi. He follows the man and grabs his arm. The Beaneater whips around ready to defend hisself. Well, I didn't even have to see Levi's face. I know it was fulla grins. What was fun to watch was the Beaneater's face change from 'oh yeah, you wanna make something outa it' to 'say, I'm sorry 'bout that hit, son.'

But I will mention, there was some real serious looks passing betwixt the other players. It was like the Beaneaters didn't take us serious, and I reckon I couldn't blame 'em. After all, next to them we was nothing more'n a Tim Buck Two League team, long on luck and short on future.

'Course, I had to remind myself I wasn't there to watch base-ball, much as I wanted to. I was there waiting for something other'n base-ball to happen. I took myself to the highest point in the grandstand, where I could see out over the hordes of folks, and I looked hard. More folks was still arriving and they was all taking to the gently slopping hills around the field to get themselves a free view. Sweartagod, there musta been a coupla thousand people in Idlehour that day — about 30 times more'n any other day in history, including the day Teddy Roosevelt layed up there.

'Course, I was looking for the only man who could alter the historical course we was all sailing that day — Corky O'Toole. I'd only spoke with Corky a few times and alls I recalled of him was his big handlebar mustache and that his ego and tongue was well-acquainted. That was a whole year previous, so I wasn't even sure who I was looking for. Additional, if Sully could alter his appearance, then I reckoned so could Corky.

There was a big hollering of the folks and I looked down on the field to see that one of our boys had laced the ball, got past the initial corner, and was safe at the keystone point. It was Jay, and I made note how lickety-cut that boy could run when he wanted to.

I looked down Main Street and saw just a coupla dogs taking advantage of the town's emptiness.

We got us another hit and Jay was now setting on the amen corner — third base, where alota bets and hashes get settled. Hardy was standing close to him, being some kinda coach in Sully's absence. He was a sight. He had him his Bulldogs uniform on, but I made note he still wore his muley-eared boots which came up to his knees. Jay and Hardy exchanged a few words. I didn't ever recall Jay doing anything Hardy told him to at first stroke. So, if Hardy was gonna suggest he run for home or stay put or sprout horns and graze, I just knew Jay was probably gonna stand there and debate the issue.

But Jay didn't. He leant toward home and waited for the next big Bulldog swing. When it came he took off like slick and slid like a duck on ice toward home base and scored us our first run. The crowd goes wild, even me, and whilst everyone was standing and cheering, I took myself back down outa the stands and started to pace by the front gate.

There was a paira binoculars setting unsupervised on a rail. I looked around, but of course everyone there was looking at the field, so I picked 'em up. There was soon a tap on my shoulder and I smiled at the man. It was like everyone there was waiting to make a profit and we finally agreed that ten dollars was a fair price for use of the glasses for the game.

But I wasn't looking at the action on the field. I was looking out over the crowd for signs of Corky who, cut phone lines at Four Arrows or not, could very well mighta been in that crowd. The whole country knew of our big game and hell, looked like halfa the West Coast was there! And you know me, suspect the worst outa your enemy — after all, they're suspecting it outa you.

Sure enough, I made note that not every set of eyeballs or binoculars was on the base-ball players. My look settled on another paira binoculars looking smack dab back at me. We held our gazes for some time, probably eacha us wondering who in hell that was behind the glasses. I don't know if there is such thing as a stare-down acrost a base-ball field or not, but we was doing it. Maybe it was gonna be a matter of whose arms got tired first.

There was a big play on the field and people stood up infronta me, so I lost my field of vision. When things settled back down and I looked again, the man with the binoculars was gone.

From there, I scanned the horizon. My search even included down Main Street. In the distance I saw a horse a-galloping full chisel toward the court house. It was no surprise to me that the man and the woman riding double and bareback, hell west and crooked through town, legs, arms, and hat feathers flying, setting atopt a Four Arrows horse, was none other'n Sully and Gus.

four

'Course, I had to get to Gus and Sully first. I damn near strangled when the owner of the glasses grabbed the strap whilst I started off. I un-slung the strap and started churning my way through the crowds, ignoring the hollering and the cheering and the base running happening all around me. I hopped the turnstile ready to punch the gateman if he tried to get me to pay to get out, and ran through the dozens of tied-up carriages. Horses was getting nervous with me going in and outa 'em, and all's we needed was a stampede, so I hushed and patted noses as I went.

I made a straight coat-tail for the park, down the turnaround, past the cement pond, and stood, gunslinger-like, in the middle of the empty street. No, I wasn't toting Mr. Smith and Wesson, onaccounta E.M. made me leave 'em at home, but I was wishing I had 'em there to back me up.

I saw the horse, still mostly in his harness and all lathered up, drinking outa a trough. Funny how a cowman thinks of his stock over and above all things. I pulled his head outa the trough, led him acrost the street to the shade, and tied him off.

Then I started to look around and poke my head in this place and that. "Gus? Sully?" I called out, gentle-like.

Nothing.

There was a roar from the field and I reckoned I was missing one of the games of the century, or else maybe a Burnbaum was finally getting proposed to. I went acrost the street to the livery, where the door was swinging open. The October sun was low but bright, and you know that half in and half outa the sun effect you get when walking into someplace dark? Sorta blinds you temporary?

"Howdy, Royal," someone said as my eyes was adjusting. I whipped around and saw three people in the shadows. Sully stood to the right and Corky stood to the left and in betwixt 'em both stood Gus.

Gus was toting her one-eyed scribe. It mighta been small, but it spoke volumes.

"Just which one you got the drop on, Gus?" I asked.

"I haven't decided."

"Go ahead, shoot *me*," Sully said, setting down on a bale of hay and crossing his arms like he was in a pucker. "I sweep you away, we have a wonderful time, you cook for me, I show you how to fish, I pop the question, you say yes, we come to town to find a preacher, and then you pull a gun on me. Go ahead and shoot. Put me out of my misery," Sully said.

Clearly, he was confused.

Gus then turns to Corky and, of course, the pistol-point goes there too.

"No, shoot me for tinkin' a skoit like you could pull dis whole thing off widout gettin' involved with anodder man!" Corky said. Then he mimics Gus and says, "Gee whizz, Harry-cakes, wid what you know and my connections, we can make mill-i-ons!" Then he looks at me and asks, "So what's she do? Falls in love with da man what's gonna make us doze mill-i-ons! Shoot *me*, Augusta!"

Then Gus looks downright cluttered with misery and she says, "Oh, I could just shoot *myself!*"

And for a brief second, all three a' us men exchanged glances, like maybe we wasn't gonna talk her outa it.

"Now, Gus," I said, coming a little toward her. "Just give me that pea-shooter and we can all settle this like men."

"No, Royal, not until I have time to figure all this out," she said.

Then Sully rose and said, "Lover, give me the gun and let's do what we came to town to do — find a preacher!"

Then Corky turned and said, "Now, Auggie, give da gun to me and we can still salvage da whole ting. You ain't gonna be happy wid a sap like him. 'Member how you'n'me was gonna run away? You an' me livin' da charmed life? London, Paris, dat place in Rome?"

Well, me being married myownself to a Gallucci woman, I was the one that shoulda known better'n to put three men against a armed woman. But it happened real fast. There was lunging, grasping, screaming, kicking, biting, and a general free-for-all amongst the horses. When the dust was cleared, I had the gun, Sully had Gus, and Corky had vanished.

I fidgeted with the gun and undid the chamber. I slipped out the two bullets, tossed 'em into the street, and handed the weapon back to Gus. She takes the gun and, without a second thought, hikes up her skirt and slips it into its keeping place — a gartered-up holster in the accompaniment of a lacy red leg-bandolero. You know, a belt fulla bullets. What was the world coming to, I remember thinking, forcing my eyes elsewhere.

Whilst she re-slotted the gun, she shakes Sully's hand offa her arm and then shakes the dust and hay outa her skirts, and says, "Well, now you've both done it! At least while *I* had the drop on Harry, he couldn't spill the beans about *you*!" And she points her finger to Sully. Then she looked toward the ball field and said, a small grin of 'oh well' on her face, "Well, at least I bet the right…"

But Sully and me didn't stick around to hear anymore. We

took off pell-mell toward the ball game. By the time we got there, things was all in disarray. Folks had taken theirselfs over the fence into the field, outa the stands and into the sidelines, and there was lotsa shouting. Had all the makings of the birth of a riot.

Be that as it may, the gate man onct again demanded our two dollars admissions. "Cripes, bet you'd charge your own momma," I grumbled, pulling out four bucks for Sully and me.

"And the horse she rode in on," he replied, handing me two more passes. We got inside, and I couldn't make out what the announcer man was saying, what with all the chaos around us. Till we got closer and then I made out a definite way a' speech that was immediately familiar.

"Dat's right, folks! I have here in my pocket proof dat the Bulldogs have been trained by Savvy McTavvy, a banished-for-life player, and I demand da officials stop dis game right now and award da game to the Boston Beaneaters!"

I looked up to the announcer man's place and saw Corky hollering into the megaphone, holding off the announcer at arm's length.

'Course, by then things was pretty free-for-allish 'round us. All the pressmen was climbing over each other to get to Corky. E.M. found me, grabbed my arm, and hollered, "Royal! Do something!"

Ever notice the only time a woman actually wants you to do something about a situation is when it's damn near hopeless? E.M.'s like a unconverted criminal that way: an atheist by day, an agnostic by night, and a damn true believer in the tight spots. Which I reckon we was alla us now in.

Well, I broke through the crowds and made my way to the pitcher's station, where the two official men and Billy and the Beaneater team manager and Drummie was all yelling at each other. Corky quickly joined 'em and was handing out his so-called proof. I grabbed the papers and saw photographs of Sully in his before and after beard status. One from his old days as Savvy McTavvy and some from just that summer, taken whilst the Bulldogs was touring. Glasses was coming outa pockets and they was passing the photos back'n'forth.

'Course, I wasn't gonna lie. The official man asked me, straight out, since I was Levi's mouthpiece, was it true? Was Sully on the payroll?

Now here I could honestly answer, "No."

"This man doesn't work you for?" the other umpire asked.

"I didn't say that. We don't have a payroll. Think of all these men as volunteers."

Well, the two ball teams was standing behind their managers and I thought things might get a little civil warish. I was glad when several police fellers recruited and badged-up special for this occasion was called over to keep folks at bay. The Beaneaters was shown to their benches and the Bulldogs was shown to theirs. We formed a circle around the pitcher's box and there we continued to hash things out.

The announcer man announced, "Now, folks, everyone back to your seats. You folks there in the infield, please go back outside the fence. Maybe the band could play us a nice tune."

So they struck up the Idlehour Brass Band, and I suppose they did the best they could. But to this day, whenever I hear *The Writer's Life Waltz*, I think of the way it sounded being played not by violins and cellos, but by trombones, piccolos and, somehow, a whole new seta notes.

I took note that vendors and such was making good use of the game stoppage. Beer, peanuts, watermelon, tobacco, and such.

Before long, some fellers in fine suits and big beards joined us on the field, and I think about twenty or so folks had their say-sos in the matter, and I didn't blame the umpire man one bit for putting his fingers to his lips and whistling so loud my ears ring to this day.

"Is there a legal opinion in the house?" he called out.

Well, I wisht he hadn't asked that. The last thing we needed was a lawslinger. But, sweartagod, six men come forward.

"Good," the umpire said. "Now, you three stand there and you three stand there, and don't say anything."

Well, you know how I was feeling, sandwiched by three pettifoggers on one side and three snollygosters on the other. Damn near couldn't breathe.

"Now, is there a judge in the house?" the umpire further inquires.

Well, 'course I knew that was gonna be a longshot, at least amongst us gathered on the field. So they ran a man up to the announcer and they asked if there was such a feller setting somewheres in the crowd.

Finally, ol' Judge Blaylock comes down outa the stands. Now, he was not new to me or Four Arrows fe-as-kos, being the circuit judge for ten years until they established him a permanent court in Idlehour, being as he complained he was getting too old for all that trail life.

Well, all the accusations was onct again put out for the judge and the lawyers' benefits, and you can damn well better believe I was thinking fast. How the hell did jack-leg lawyers get into a simple little thing like a ball game, I was wondering. Additional, could maybe I or E.M. get put in jail for knowing about Sully, and would they eventually dedicate a whole wing at the State Pen just for our family?

"Well, as far as I can see," Judge Blaylock said, "there's no proof this man here, this Sully or Savvy or whatever you call him, is in truth the man you say, or furthermore that he had anything to do with this team. You realize, of course, this is not a criminal or a civil matter. After all, gentleman, this is just a friendly little game of base-ball."

I let out a breatha relief.

"Oh, I wouldn't be so sure," one of the lawyers says. "This could be a criminal case. After all, thousands and thousands of dollars are at stake. I think we better get a professional ruling on this."

The other lawyers agreed, in varying degrees, depending on, I reckon, the degree of money each man had riding on the outcome of the game.

"Well," the head umpire said, "I'm afraid this goes far beyond my experience." He glances at the Savvy pictures and looks sorta tooken-away and said, "Great Scott, that Savvy could pitch! You remember him, Howard?"

The other umpire looked at the old photos of Savvy McTavvy. "Yeah, sure do, Kelly. And I always thought he got a foul deal."

"Well, obviously you two men can't decide what to do about this," Judge Blaylock said.

The man next to me was mighty quiet, considering he was up front and center with the resta us and wearing a Boston uniform. I leant into him and said, "Howdy. Name's Royal Leckner. And you are…?

He smiled and offered his hand and said, "Selee. Frank. I'm manager of the Beaneaters. Just how do you figure into all this, Mr. Leckner?"

"Oh, I'm sorta like a guardian to the owner of the Bulldogs, Leviticus Perrault."

"The pitcher? Say, he's got quite an arm."

"Don't he, though! How you reckon all this should oughta go?" I asked him.

He just folded his arms and shrugged his shoulders and said, "I remember McTavish too. Such a waste. So, you tell me, Mr. Leckner. Was he training your boy?"

I mighta aged a year in the few seconds I thought about my response. 'Course, I was thinking maybe sometimes it was better to lie on credit than to tell the truth for cash. But I was rescued from doing either when E.M. comes up behind me, hauls me around, and says, "Royal! I can't find Lou anywhere!"

five

Now, there's never been anything wrong with E.M.'s timing, or her flair for the dramatical side of life. She even onct came close to being an ack-tor, but I took one look at her face and I knew she wasn't saying this to get me outa my lying fix.

"Where you see her last?"

"She was right next to me on the bench. I stood up to see what you were doing out here, and when I turned around she was gone," she said.

Well, I knew little Lou couldn'ta gone far, and in her Bulldogs uniform I was sure someone was gonna notice her. E.M. is explaining to the other men what she looks like and how she don't do good in crowds, everyone's talking all at onct, and finally the umpire man did his big whistle-toot again.

Judge Blaylock glared at the umpire, rubbed his ear, and said, "Gentlemen, I call for a recess."

Then one of the umps said, "There's no recess in base-ball."

"Well there's no judges, lost women, or broken eardrums either! Now, I order a one-hour recess while you two umpires contact whoever you need to to determine if the game is a forfeit in favor of the Beaneaters of if we can get on with it and have us a nice afternoon of base-ball. Now, no one but you and you can leave the field. Everybody else is ordered to stay right here. So you two boys go down to the telegraph office, call your experts, and decide what you want to do. And for God's sake will somebody please shut that band up!" He turned to go, a little red-faced, and added, "I will be in the Burnbaum Beer Garden."

Hell, now what? I was thinking. E.M. had gone back toward the bleachers to look for Lou amongst the crowd. Levi come up to me and he was all wrung out, saying he couldn't find Lou either and what was gonna happen now, Roy?

'Course all the team members wanted to know what the big hold-up was. There was lotsa folks around, remember, so I was thinking maybe Lou'd gone out back to find the necessary, although it sure wasn't like Lou to take herself away when things was so all-fired discombobulated.

E.M. came up to me and said, "I'm worried, Roy. She wouldn't just wander off. Not in a crowd like this."

"Well, you know Lou, E.M. She musta started counting something and got carried away. Think she's counting all these folks?" I looked around for a place where someone could do that.

"No, she already did that. She's been gone fifteen minutes. Ever since they stopped the game. I tell you, she's not here!"

From there we had the announcer man make a call for Mrs. Lou(ella) Perrault. Another ten minutes passed and she was still not anywhere. Levi was damn near frantical by now, and I had E.M. and Jay take him somewheres where he could be settled down.

"Royal," Hardy said, "if this game gets back under way, we *need* Lou."

"I know, I know," I said, looking around. My eyes came to rest on the scoreboard acrost the field. I focused my eyes, then I squinted my eyes. "That say what I think it says?" I asked Hardy.

He didn't even have to follow my blinkers. "We're up by four," he said. "But you know Levi can't pitch a forkfulla hay without Lou's watching. Not to mention her batter-reckoning."

"*We're* winning?" I said, maybe not believing either Hardy or the scoreboard.

"Royal! We need to find Lou!" Hardy hollers at me like I was deef.

I don't know as I'd ever heard Hardy issue a more correct statement.

Then I think — wait a minute! Where the hell is ol' Corky, or Harry-Cakes as Gus called him? I looked around and, come to think, he sure had been quiet onct he got us all roiled up. He had vanished also.

Now things was getting serious. If I was gonna be guilty of knowing about Sully and allowing betting to proceed onaccounta it, if Sully was gonna be guilty of being drummed in disgrace outa the leagues, then dammit, Corky was gonna be guilty of *something!*

I told Hardy to make sure E.M. set tight, and I left. I got out the same way I firstly got in. Over the side fence and, this time, without much notice.

So back into town I go. It wasn't so deserted now. In fact, alla the folks who'd been setting out in the hinterlands was now having theirselfs a little break, and I made note the Glass was open and alota the wickey-up dram-shops was back in business too. That sure made my searching easier — I asked folks everywhere if they'd seen Lou, perhaps in the accompaniment of a nice-looking feller about yea high and blond hair and wearing a pin-stripe suit with one of them round little bowler hats. Folks was pretty much just interested in seeking out their refreshments and no one made note of sucha twosome.

Well, the hour was wearing on, and more'n'more folks was spilling away from the ball field and into town. Everyone was asking everyone else what was going on, what's them two umpire men gonna decide, and do I have time for another beer before they start up again, that sorta talk.

I looked at my pocket watch. The hour was fast approaching being over. I took myself to the telegraph office and looked in. One umpire, the one named Kelly, was pacing, and the other was talking into the telephone. Will, the Western Union brass-pounder, was setting on his desk, munching on a apple.

I stood aside whilst two young boys come running up. Mighta been them two that was playing catch that day a year ago who, if you thought about it, was the ones responsible for this whole dang she-bang. Anyway, they've been running and they throw open the door and one shouts, "They wanna know what the answer is!"

"Quiet down, sonny," Will said. "Can't you see the man's on the phone?"

Then he whispers, "Well, they sent us up here to get the answer so's we can … what'd the judge say, Ricky?"

Then Ricky answered, "Win the mare or lose the halter!"

Yep, thinks me, that sounds like ol' Judge Blaylock.

The other umpire told them that some league committeeman was still mulling over the problem.

"Either of you two boys seen little Lou(ella) Perrault?" I asked. I knew boys see a lot more'n adults do mosta the time.

"Sure, she was at the ball game playing like she's a coach or somethin'," the Ricky one said.

"I mean since then."

They looked at each other like they was gonna have to be in agreement with their answer.

Then the other boy said, "A man paid us a buck not to say anything."

I wasn't gonna waste any more time. I knew them lads was the sort to hold out for more money, so I just started going through my pockets. I pulled out a five-dollar gold piece and, of course, onct they saw that, I knew I wasn't gonna get no change.

"Down there," Ricky said, pointing toward the school house.

Then that Howard-umpire with the telephone sat up straighter and said, "Yes. Yes sir. I'm still here."

Alla us leant toward his conversation.

"I see. Thank you."

Howard hung up the phone and looked kinda all washed out. He scratched his head and muttered, "All he said was, 'it's appalling!'"

Well, Ricky took that information and hollered 'it's appalling!" to their chums down the street and they yelled it further on down the line and so forth, and pretty soon everyone in the streets was shouting and they all started running back toward the ball field.

Well, that was that, I figured. The two umpires got up and paid for the phone call and started back toward the field.

"Too bad, I was really getting a kick out of watching those Bulldogs. Been a long time since I've seen a team like that shoot out of the basement of the cellar like that," Howard said to Kelly.

"Yeah, I agree. After six years of all those money-bagging owners, mean fans, and vain-pomp players, I was having fun too."

Just as I was ready to thank 'em anyway and get off toward the A-B-C-Darium to uncomplicate Lou, some man comes stumbling outa the 'Glass Saloon. He still had a napkin tucked under his chin and he was toting his beer mug and a sandwich.

"Come on, come on! Didn't you fellas hear? It's a ball game!"

And he goes running after the rest of the crowd back toward the field.

Well, the umpires looked at each other. They looked at me and we worked all the consonants around each other — until we ran 'it's appalling!' all the way to 'it's a ball game!'

"Yes," Kelly said, nodding some, "I can see where they might get that impression."

"Yeah, and you know, Howie, my hearing plays tricks on me all the time these days."

"So do your eyes, but what are we waiting for?"

They shook hands, grinned at me, then ran after the resta the crowd toward the field, alla which meant I had to get Lou back to that field and her nose back into those books of numbers, and I had to do it fast!

Onct again alone in the middle of the street, I took the side road toward the school house and careful-like crept up to the front door. It was locked. I then went around to peek through a window and, sure enough, there was folks inside.

I saw Lou working her a long series of numbers on the chalk board and I saw Gus setting on the corner stool, the dunce hat on the floor beside her.

"Why don't ya come in an' join us?" Corky said from around the corner, behind Gus's pearl-handled gun. "School's just startin'."

six

I put my hands up, ladies' Christmas pistol with pretty pearl handles or not. As we went into the school house, I made note Gus's bullet garter was now holding up Corky's coat sleeve. Looked better on Gus.

All the tables and benches had been stacked up against the wall, and there was just sleeping cots all around. I reckoned even the school marm wanted a little profit from all the visitors.

I nodded to Gus in the corner and went to Lou to make sure she was all right. Well, anytime there's mathematical equations on the chalk board she was happy, and I knew the teacher was gonna be real surprised come Monday morning to see someone had not only solved all the problems she put up on Friday, but had added some real long ones of her own. Living proof that God warms the shorn lamb.

"Have a seat," Corky said. I took a cot. Then with a nod toward Lou he added, "So, dey're gonna play da game anyhow. Good ting I had me dis little ace up my sleeve. See, widdout your liddle gen-i-us here, I don't tink dis'll take long. Dem Beaneaters oughta put your boys away in no time. Ain't dat right, Auggie?"

I looked at Gus. "So, I see you made up your mind. Too bad, Gus. You sure as hell picked the wrong feller."

"Oh shut up!" she snapped, hopping down from the stool and turning around, showing me her hands was tied behind her back. "Does this look like I chose him? I'll get you for this, Harry! You just wait and see!"

"Ah, pipe down!" he said, "Or I'll make you wear dat dunce hat."

"You musta bet alota money on Boston," I said, "if you're willin' to face a kidnap charge."

"I didn't bet nuttin'. Auggie did, but she's gonna pay me real good, ain't ya, Auggie ol' girl?"

"No! Not a dime!"

"Oh yes you will. Just like we planned. Den I'm outa your life, and yous and your Savvy can hitch up at long last. Once he gets outa jail, of course."

"Jail? He's not going to jail! You are! And you want to know what else?"

"What?" Corky asked.

"You're a rotten kisser!"

"Dat does it!" He went over to her, picked her up, plopped her down on the stool, whirled her around to face the corner, and put the dunce hat on her.

We heard a big cheer from the field. Corky said, "Sounds like one of your boys got a lucky hit."

I was watching Lou, wondering if hearing that cheering might remind her of something else she oughta be doing besides proving Godknowswhat theories of physics.

And it did. She announced, "I got to go now." She handed the chalk to Corky and thanked him for the nice time. He stood infronta her. She walked around him. He kept blocking her until she said, frowning big, "Roy, he won't lemme go!"

I got Lou pulled down and told her we was gonna hafta wait a bit until Corky got hisself together. She looked up at me and said, "Levi."

"He'll be fine, Lou," I said.

"Hard to believe dat liddle ting knows anyting 'bout base-ball," Corky said. "When Auggie foist told me 'bout her, I said ha ha, tell me anudder one."

Gus kicked the wall infronta her.

"Den I saw her call every batter, and I'll be damned, she knows her stuff," Corky went on, setting hisself down on a cot.

We heard another cheer. Lou stood up and I pulled her back down.

Now I wasn't sure, but I think I saw something outa the corner of my eyeball. Something sorta reddish just under the window ledge. I looked at the next window down and, sure enough, I saw Sully peering through the window.

"So, Corky, where do you go from here? Folks said you was a good ball player onct. What're you gonna do with all your winnings? Maybe buy you a team?"

"He's *not* getting any winnings!" Gus said from her corner.

"Oh yes I am and you know why?"

"Why?" Gus asked, slowly peering around outa her corner. Even under that dunce hate she was a looker.

"Because you're gonna want me outa your life, dat's why, and da only way you can do dat is to buy me off. Odderwise, I'm blabbin' all sortsa tings I know about you. An' your sweet Savvy McTavvy ain't gonna like soma dem!"

From where I set on the cot, I could see the shadow of the back door opening wider, and I reckoned Sully was making his move. I sure hope he was remembering about the gun, hoping maybe he had one of his own. I stood up, and that made Corky turn toward me.

"Just stretching my legs. Pardon me, Gus, limbs."

I looked at Corky and now saw Sully creeping in behind. His weapon was, I might as well tell you, a base-ball. He held it like he was feeling its weight and I was wondering where I could toss Lou to if bullets was gonna fly.

Now if this wasn't like Sully I'd like to know what was: he announces his presence so's he could look at Corky straight on.

"Hey, Cork-Head!" he calls out.

Cork-head reels around and Sully hurls the ball at him and KONK! beans him on the head so hard that the gun goes galley-west flying and Corky goes down like his feet had been lassoed out from under him.

Just then we heard another crowd cheer, and I thought that was sorta nice. Like alla Idlehour was rooting for us there in the school house.

Sully goes to Gus, I go to Lou. And Corky was out for extra innings. I picked up the gun and wondered what I should do with it. Now I'm a range man and guns don't bother me none, but I gotta tell you there's something downright scary about a gun that is made to look nice whilst it carries out its dirty work.

Sully said, "Quick, Roy! Get Lou back down to the field. Levi is falling apart without her there! Gus and I will stay here and make sure he stays right where he is."

I handed him the pistol and he added, "Roy, I'm sorry I've caused you all this. Maybe you should have let me run off last year after all."

I smiled at him, glanced at my sister-half-in-law, and said, "Hell, Sully, and miss all this?"

I then grabbed Lou by the hand and we ran off toward the ball field.

You will be interested to know that the gate man charged me for the third time as I entered the field, plus another buck for Lou onaccounta she was either a kid or a lady. But hell, with a winner-take-all gate, there still mighta been a chance that I would get my nine dollars back, onaccounta when I glanced up at the scoreboard I saw that it was Bulldogs 10, Boston 9, with Boston having just retired our side.

I don't know if it was the tension of the close score in the ninth inning or what, but the crowd looked to me like it had doubled. Folks was now standing in the outfield with the cops-for-a-day holding 'em back best they could. Folks in the bleachers was sorta leaning in closer and lots was lining the fence line that kept 'em offa the field.

E.M. saw us and hauled us through the gate to the field and over to the Bulldogs' dug-out. "Thank God! Lou, where have you been?"

"School," she answered, plain-like.

E.M. signals to Leviticus as he was taking the pitcher's box.

Levi comes running in to scoop up his wife, and folks cheered, thinking maybe she was his little good luck charm come to help usher us a win. E.M. shooed him back to the pitcher's box and put a book under Lou's nose. E.M. had been keeping tabs on the Boston boys' hits and brought Lou up to snuff on the percentages.

Them two: I'll always have the picture in my mind of my wife and Lou(ella) setting there, heads together, noses in books, papers scattered all about 'em. I reckon there ain't been a team like 'em since in any sport, since or ever will be.

Maybe that's a good thing. Hard to say.

The announcer man announced the Boston batter, and the crowd hushed as Leviticus did his windup. Lou looked up and they contacted their eyes, she did some hand talking, and Levi grinned big and hurled him a fast one. The batter fanned the air and almost corkscrewed hisself into the ground.

But the next two was balls. Levi kept rubbing his shoulder and I commenced to worry. I made note the Beaneaters had 'em three pitchers on their roster and alls we had was Levi, with Jay as a back-up.

He pitched two more balls, so Boston now had a man on base.

"You reckon he can hold up?" I asked E.M. "He's looking like he's hurtin'."

"He's pitched full games a hundred times, Roy," E.M. answered. "I think when Lou wasn't here he just fell apart and threw anything just to throw. That'll kill your shoulder." Then she calls out to him, "Come on, Levi! Over the slab! Over the slab!"

Lou was busy inspecting the Boston boys' lineup on their bench, calculating odds and probably dividing by hair color. When the next man comes up to bat, Lou stands up and signals Levi.

I reckon her signal meant change the pace for this man and that's just what Levi did. Sweartagod, he pitched such a puzzler I'll bet the batter coulda counted all two hundred and sixteen stitches in it as it a-sauntered by. And whilst he did, he struck at it and made quite a swosh.

"Strike!"

The next one looked even slower, and one look at the batter and you could tell he was mad. It's one thing not to make contact with a fast ball, but something of a humiliation to miss one that's just wandering on by slow as freight delivery.

"Strike!"

The third pitch he hit and it went ballooning straight up. Jay throws off his mask and places hisself under the ball and it falls — plunk — into his mitten.

One away.

The next batter drew a walk, and now two men was holding down bases. Billy went out to talk to Levi and check on his shoulder. Now I know lots was resting on this game, but I didn't think the wasting of a shoulder for the resta a man's life — a life that was gonna need lotsa shoulder work, by the way — was maybe worth it all.

But I could tell by Levi's stubborn-as-a-fact stance that he was gonna pitch this game out or lay him down and die right there on the spot. God knows, I'd seen that sure-footed look about a million times before. I'd come to both love it and hate it, but mosta all admire it.

He got the next man out in three strikes and only one ball.

Two away.

The next got a short line-drive single, and the coach didn't want to risk sending in the man on second. Now all the bases was occupied.

The next man comes up, and I could tell E.M. and Lou was struggling to figure out who he was. See, they didn't have any names or numbers on uniforms back in those days, so if a man was taken out or pinched out, then you sometimes needed the announcer to let you know who was who.

And that's just what this man was, a pinch hitter. His name finally gets announced and that sent Lou and E.M. flying through their books and papers. A breeze sent one piece of paper flying and Lou ran to retrieve it. Billy was stalling the game by going out and onct again talking to Levi. But Levi wasn't looking at Billy, he was looking around for Lou.

She'd done it again. Disappeared. Only this time she'd edged herself under the stands to collect her paper.

The umpire called for the batter to take his place. Billy ran off the field and Levi did his wind-up without Lou watching.

So it was high and wide.

"Roy!" E.M. hollers at me from down the bench. "Get Lou!"

I looked under the bleachers and I saw the problem. She was trying to reach for the paper and in so doing, got a braid tangled in the steel under-rigging.

I was wondering how the hell I was gonna get her unstuck. She was saying ow! and I was reaching in and trying to pull it loose.

"Stay there! Don't move!" I called, and I went back to E.M..

Levi had now pitched him three balls and two strikes making one of them full counts on which fames and fortunes and memorized poems sometimes rest.

I told E.M. to go help Lou and leave Leviticus to me.

Billy was ready to go out one more time. I told him this time let me.

Now, I will not say I was exactly a local celebrity, but I will mention that lotsa folks recognized me when I went out on the field, and I liked their cheering. Well, there was a few boos too.

I went out and howdied Levi, then whispered something in his ear. I put my hand on his shoulder, then came back in to watch the last pitch of the inning, maybe of the game, maybe of Levi's entire base-ball career.

He did his stare over his shoulder at the batter man. His sweet face is more like stone, his eyes is now as cold and calculating as a regular man's. He looks to third base and then goes into his wind-up. The ball lets go and the crowd is still as death.

It was a perfect, right acrost the smack-dab center of the slab fling, and the umpire called it right and true.

"Steeeeee-riiiiiike!"

The Idlehour Bulldogs had beat the Boston Beaneater Champions of the World, 10 to 9.

The crowd was everywhere. E.M. had come out from under the bleachers with Lou, holding a paira scissors and a cut-off braid. We all hugged each other and Levi was being carried off the field by his teammates. The Beaneaters was all amazed and the umpires was even looking happier'n impartial judges maybe shoulda been.

So, what did I tell Levi that brought his concentration all back together for that last pitch? Alls I said was there was a whole lotta sheeps counting on him.

final summary

So there you have it — base-ball and me and the story of how Jack of the beanstalk fame came outa nowhere, worked hard, and took a win over the giant, even though to this day you might hear some sour-graping Eastern folks mention that the Boston aggregation toted one helluva hangover, which mighta added to the toppling of the giant. But that's nothing more'n pure speculation.

Oh yes, I knew you'd want a summary. Well, let's start with the fiduciary factors. First off, the team did real good in the 'winner-take-all' category, including nine dollars outa my own pocket.

The town of Idlehour, of course, made out right equitable with alla their peddling stands and such. The Umatillas did one of their tribal celebrations that night and charged folks to come and watch, and so they too made out fine.

The Burnbaums did just fine as well, what with their various concession stands of staggered soup and all. Yep, and since four of 'em finally got married to four of our Bulldogs, they retired their debts of sponsorships. So no matter what the outcome of anything else, leastwise four heretofore hopeless spinsters got reprieves, proving onct again that steady wins the race and the last suitor wins the mare. I mean, maid.

The team known as the Idlehour Bulldogs? Well, the team broke up, being as the majority of the boys realized there wasn't any way they could ever make any real money at it. So no, we never did sell the team to make back our investment. Well, I ain't naming names, onaccounta we alla us signed a pact to keep our mouths shut about certain elements of the year of 1898. But of the four who sold their spikes to get married, two became some of the Four Arrows' best hands, one became a banker in Idlehour, and the other ended up becoming a damn famous circuit preacher, but we all liked him anyhows. Three Bulldogs went on to Big League Professional careers — and even if you ain't familiar with their own records, I'll lay you two to ten that you'd sure as hell know their offsprings, one of which is heading the National League right this very minute in home runs.

Yep, Gus and Sully got hitched, and I am glad to report, although it was a rocky ride, the marriage lasted. 'Course, I'll never forget Gus that day back at Four Arrows when we was alla us planning the resta our lifes.

Sully got down on his knee to offer Gus an official, infrontawitnesses proposal on the front porch. Well, I don't think Gus had ever gotten the one-knee treatment by her previous husbands and she said Yes! before he'd even finished his spiel.

"Of course, I have little to offer you in the way of material things," Sully added, sad-like.

Well, we was watching Gus, and her mouth did go sorta twitchy at that prospect. E.M. of course knows when to fill in a gap in the conversation, even if it was another woman's marriage proposal.

"Well, you never know, Sully. Maybe that family of yours will send you an all-is-forgiven letter."

"All is forgiven?" Gus asked, a little light of hope coming to her face.

"Oh yes, surely Sully has told you, Gus," E.M. says. "He comes from one of Rhode Island's richest families."

"You have *money*?" she asked down to him.

"No, I'm disinherited," he admitted.

At that she pulls him up offa his knee and slips her arm around his and says, "Well, we won't let a little legality like that interfere, will we? Once your father meets me, I'm sure…"

Well, I didn't hear the rest onaccounta she was leading him down the steps and into her future plans. Well, like I always said, Gus had her quite a beauty and I reckon a beauty like hers can undo all sortsa entanglements, including undoing disinher-itments and even restoring base-ball reputations.

They was married a few days later and I gave Sully a new Hinckley Special for his wedding present. I'd used the money from the No Juice Jar, onaccounta it was mostly my investment in there anyhows. E.M. gave Gus a Weee Geee board, a box of caramels, and guess what else. Yep, the broach Gus had hocked, I had bought, and E.M. had got the Christmas previous. That told me two things: One, there was more love than love-lost betwixt 'em, and Two, somehow I was gonna end up owing my wife another broach.

Ol' Elijah Marie and Augusta — what a paira Gallucci girls to draw to. Hell, they out-cahooted each other their whole lifes. But each time it was only 'daggers at 80 paces' — lotsa false challenge and out-doing the other until the family chips was low and the decks was stacked against 'em. Then it was 'Everyone outa my way! My sister's in trouble!'

Damn, it was always an impressive sight watching 'em together … as long as you was smart enough to stay in the bleachers and just enjoy the game, maybe pass a Cuban to your father-in-law, then Hot Cha!, everyone had a real boss time!

'Course, now that I think about it, E.M. always did insinuate herself betwixt me and ol' Gus ever after. Don't know who she was protecting — me, Gus, or her own interests.

Well, turns out it was a double wedding, onaccounta Billy Rohrs and our cook Anita hitched up too. Billy took her back east, where he'd been offered a fine job as assistant manager to the Cleveland Spiders, and even though that next year was maybe the worst season for the worst team ever in base-ball history, he was working the Big Leagues at last. He did have to move around some, but he ended up in Chicago. He and Anita had nine kids, opened a restaurant, and was about as happy as a coupla kids on a lifelong hooky spree. It's good to know folks you care about end up happy. Yep, even though he was a touch on the short side, Billy Rohrs finally lived up to his name, and he's always stood ace high with me.

Now about us at Four Arrows. Well, we did just fine. And I reckon we owed that status to none other'n Enrico Gallucci. After the game, we got us one of them telegrams I always dreaded. The telegram rider came up, and E.M. for about the hundredth time reminds me to rehook up our cut telephone lines so's we might be spared telegrams.

It was issued to me, but E.M. allowed me to read it over her shoulder.

"It's from Daddy!" she said.

> Dear Children;
>
> I hope you know that a good accountant can not ignore odds. Stop. Nor can a good gambler. Stop. Bet it all on the Bulldogs. Stop. Have wired the amount of 12,446.11 into Four Arrows account in Idlehour this date. Stop. I withheld the 5,000.00 you borrowed, E.M. Stop. New family tradition. Stop. Your mother will be visiting soon. Stop. She bet Boston and lost her shirt. Stop. Oh yes, the parole board is meeting next week and I hear they all followed my betting advice. Stop. Be home soon.
>
> Your loving father.

So, even setting in prison ol' Enrico had his ways of getting even, getting paid, getting out, and even getting to E.M. and his wife, late of the Mississippi gambling circuit.

Now, whilst you're scribbling up this fe-as-ko, better leave room for a few more things.

The ranch had its investment back and I had E.M. back and Levi had, onct again, his herda sheeps back. Hardy had his old job back of second in command. And Jay? Well, he coulda had him a base-ball career onaccounta he made a remarkable mask'n'mitten man. Additional, he sure could maul the marble, having damn good wood on the ball. But when it come time for him to sign on the dotted line with that Frank Selee feller of the Boston team, well ol' Jay looked around the place. His horse, Levi, me, and E.M. Even Lou(ella), who usually drove him plumb loco. Well, I reckon he wasn't ready to leave his family just yet.

But the Beaneaters didn't leave empty-handed. Turns out they admired the two Pullman cars, and E.M. made out real mean with her $400 investment, and Frank's boys had them real comfy transportation for the resta their West Coast tour.

So everyone was pretty much all the richer after that world-famous game. Me included. Around Thanksgiving, after the dust had settled, the team had broke up, and winter had settled in, E.M. calls me down to the Horse Palace using the rewired telephones. I said I was up to my nosehairs in saddle soap, but she insisted, and so I threw on my slicker and walked down there.

Now I described to you the sight of that new barn all crackling new and warm and all, and I described that place with all the Christmas decorations too. Even described to you the place when it was fulla training base-ball boys. Well, now's time to describe the place when it was fulla what it was meant to be fulla.

I walked in, and the gushing winds seemed to help me through the door. I knocked the rain offa my hat and focused my eyes. I heard a snort and it wasn't coming from E.M., who was standing next to the arena gate holding a lariat.

"Come here, Roy," she said, "there's someone I want you to meet."

She hands me the lariat and steps aside to show me six of the most gorgeous quarter-horse fillies I think I ever did see in one remuda. They was snorting and prancing and making show-offy spectacles of theirselfs to a stud, who was kicking up his heels whilst galloping up the middle.

I was lacking for speech. My mouth went all watery and I had a hard time swallering. The sight of good horseflesh does that to me. Alls I remember doing was whispering, "Well, Suffer Your Age."

Then E.M. whistles and I'll be damned if that stud didn't stop short and come galloping right on over. She holds out her hand, taunting a carrot, he nuzzles it, and she says, "Well, he practically *followed* me home."

"Then I reckon we oughta keep him," I said, stepping into the arena and meeting my new passions. The fillies then get curious and come trotting over, and not only was they pedigree-pure and bred for racing, they was also friendly as a whore's hello, and I loved each one of 'em from the get-go.

And Leviticus? Well, like you know he coulda had him a career as a pitcher, and even though he got a few offers, he and Lou said life on the road was too mean and, besides, who was gonna tend their sheeps if they was off somewheres getting famous?

I wasn't the only one got a gift that fall. Lou gave Levi a gift late that year. Yep, she and him musta finally followed that book of theirs all the way to the epilogue, onaccounta Lou come up pregnant.

So that's about it. Everything from A to Izzard about 1898, which was a good year, all in all. We'd had us runs, errors, hits, and more foul balls and bad calls than maybe your average team oughta get. But Hot Cha! we also ended up with more'n we lost, and none of us was none the worst for wear.

Incept maybe Hawaii. In case you forgot, 1898 was the year ol' Uncle Sam took under his wing the Hawaiian Islands. Well, E.M.'s nose picked that opportunity right up when she was setting in the Howell, Powell and Gallucci offices in Portland.

Well, I ain't saying we did and I ain't saying we didn't, but you know that big huge cattle ranch over there? Well, I promised some folks — mostly dead politicians now — I'd never tell the true story of that fe-as-ko, so I reckon for now that's…

…'nuf ced.

THE END

Randall Beth Platt is the author of seven novels, including three *Fe-As-Kos*; one coming-of-age novel, *The Cornerstone*; one environment animal fable, *Out of a Forest Clearing*; and two novels for young adults, *The Likes of Me* and *Honor Bright*. *The Four Arrows Fe-As-Ko* was made into the film *Promise the Moon,* although the resemblance is hard to see.

Ms. Platt lives in Gig Harbor, Washington, and plays handball anywhere.

The jacket illustration was done by **Paul Hoffman**, an artist in Greenfield, Massachusetts. The book was set in Adobe Garamond and printed by Quebecor Worldwide in Fairfield, Pennsylvania. The jacket was printed by Strine Printing of York, Pennsylvania.

Catbird Press was founded in 1987. Its specialties include American and British fiction, Czech literature in translation, and quality humor. For a copy of our catalog, call us at 800-360-2391, fax us at 203-230-8029, e-mail us at catbird@pipeline.com, or write us at 16 Windsor Road, North Haven, CT 06473-3015. Or visit our website for even more information, including first chapters of our books: www.catbirdpress.com.